THE WEE SMALL HOURS

Rosa Temple

Book Cover by Rima Salloum

Author's Note

Each chapter in *The Wee Small Hours* is named after a jazz standard—songs that kept me company during my own sleepless nights. Like Annie, I've spent more than a few wee small hours wide awake, and jazz has always been my lullaby, my comfort, and my muse.

Love, Rosa x

The Wee Small Hours

Rosa Temple

1

In the Wee Small Hours of the Morning

I walk along the dark high street in the middle of town. My nose is frozen and so are my fingertips, though I'm wearing gloves and have my fisted hands deep inside my coat pockets. The shops don't open for a few hours, so the only footsteps I can hear are my own. Across the street, the entrance to the shopping mall is a cave of shadows where nothing moves, except Phoenix. He sits to attention when I pass, his ears pricking up as he sniffs the cold air. He doesn't bark the way he usually does when he sees me. Dez has him trained not to yelp in the early hours of the morning while he sleeps. Tonight Dez's bed is in the doorway of the print shop, holding onto Phoenix's lead. Dez is curled up in his ageing, red sleeping bag on top of an open cardboard box, so I won't go over to disturb him. Phoenix's tongue lolls down the side of his jaw, and he snaps it shut in one slobbering motion before crouching beside Dez and settling down. His droopy eyes follow me until I'm out of view and heading uphill towards the market place.

The wide stone shoulders of the Market House emerge in the darkness, the clock tower faintly illuminated. The Market House sits on top of tall stone pillars that form arches over the cobbled ground beneath it. Upstairs in the house, the art gallery closed hours ago and glints of

1

moonlight reflect off the blackness of the small windows. I can feel them staring down at me with pity as I draw closer, searching the underbelly of the tall structure for anything or anyone who shouldn't be out in the town on a bitter Halloween night. Then something moves on the large stone steps at the entrance to the Market House. I slow my pace, knowing that if I change direction, it'll take longer for me to get home. Dez and Phoenix are the only ones who sleep under the stars in this town and I know it isn't them. The figure moves again, swaying and rising like a black phantom who will spot me at any second. My heart thuds and the dark figure stands upright when a sound from somewhere behind me draws its attention. Phoenix's whimper calls to me, so I cross the road and run back to him and Dez. There's safety in numbers.

My boots scuff the smooth tiles in the mall. Dez sits up and releases his hold on the lead so that Phoenix bounds towards me, raising his front paws up to my waist.

'Down boy. Good boy,' says Dez. Phoenix springs round to his master and back to me in a dizzy circle, barking so that the sound echoes throughout the mall.

'Annie Get Your Guns!' Dez always plays with my name, always has a big smile for me and always reprimands me when he sees me out on my own in the dark. I kneel on his cardboard box, and Phoenix sniffs into the corners and the shop entrances as if checking that the coast is clear. I start to calm down.

'What you doing, Annie? Out here in the freezing cold.'

I turn my head towards the mall entrance and squint at nothing.

'I thought someone was there.'

'Okay, come on.' Dez scrapes his things together. 'Let's get you home. You know you shouldn't be out here.'

Dez has said this to me a thousand times. Or at least for the last few years since the insomnia started. I couldn't sleep, that's why I'm here. Again. I'd woken at midnight, about an hour after I'd fallen asleep. My sleep patterns are such that I remain awake for two to four hours in the middle of the night with about two hours on either side of restless sleep, but those are the good nights. On bad nights, I can't get back to sleep after 2 a.m. and I stay awake until it's time to get up for work. Tonight is a bad night. As usual, I felt compelled to stretch my legs, get some air, though it's frigid and bites at my face.

Mum would be upset to know I'm out here, walking on my own in the dark market town, a padded coat over my pyjamas, snow boots over my bed socks and a fur-rimmed hat pulled down low over my big hair. When I lived in the studio flat, she used to ask me to call her if I couldn't sleep, no matter the time, and she'd sing to me or tell me a story so that I could settle, as if I were a toddler and not her grown-up, twenty-nine-year-old daughter. I did call Mum, sometimes, when we were living in the same town; now that there's a time difference of about eleven hours, it's difficult to catch her in. God, I miss her. She used to sing *In the Wee Small Hours of the Morning* to me. She has all the jazz versions of that song in her many albums and compilations. She loves jazz, she loves to sing. But she hates that my insomnia is such a big part of my life and that I give in to rambling thoughts when the rest of the town is fast asleep.

'Ready?' Dez clicks his fingers and Phoenix reports back. I take the dog's lead and we head to the market square, Dez throwing the sleeping bag over his shoulder but leaving a plastic bag and the cardboard box where they are. We must look just as sinister as the figure I thought I saw and is now nowhere to be seen as we pass the Market House. The large steps are vacant and the main door is bolted shut.

'Annie, Annie, Annie.' Dez shakes his head as we walk. We take my usual route home, through the graveyard and along the side of the church. 'What are we going to do with you?'

'I know and I'm not telling Mum about this.' She always hates me walking past the graves.

Naturally she worries about me, but I've never stopped worrying about Mum now that she is on the other side of the world. I'm thankful she lives close to my sister, Cat, but I wish Mum was in walking distance so I could keep an eye on her, look out for her, the way I used to.

Just on the outskirts of town, Dez stops and I hand him the lead.

'Thanks, Dez. You didn't have to do this.' I look down the quiet road of four houses and no streetlights.

'Go on, Annie. You're safe now.'

It's useless asking Dez in because he doesn't do roofs and doors, he says. No solid walls around him, that's what he prefers. I pet Phoenix before they leave and I walk the few metres to my door.

The house creaks a welcome but frowns at my decision to go out walking instead of staying safe indoors, counting sheep. I've tried most of the sleep-inducing remedies and routines on the planet. Warm milk, I tell the cracks in the hall ceiling, I've had so much it came out of my ears. I've tried chamomile tea, hot baths, warm baths, steamy showers, yoga, meditation, over-the-counter medication, music, reading, not reading, I insist to the creaky, old floorboards.

4

All devices are off by 10 p.m. No blue light here. And even though I set the temperature of my bedroom to between 16° and 18° Celsius, just as they say to do, I'm still an insomniac.

I switch the light on in the kitchen. At the sink, I stare out of the window into the inky expanse while filling the kettle. The sky isn't close to brightening. The pipes bang and clang, but I'm not likely to wake anyone as the next house, Fee Milligan's cottage, is a way off. Our vast gardens back onto large green fields that neither of us own and are separated by a row of coniferous trees. When the sun rises, my view from the sink is of the fields and a distant forest that lines the hills. It's the perfect setting; it's just a shame that the house, with all its creaks and cracks and noisy pipes, is falling to pieces around me. Our well-worn, rickety family house, with its history of music, laughter, love and drama, is all mine now to live in on my own, and I can't get used to that.

I sip my tea in the cold kitchen – which feels like being on the upper deck of an Arctic trawler in a T-shirt – staring up at the invitation on the fridge door. It's been there months, both tempting and torturing me because of who it's from. I should RSVP in the negative, but a spark of hope that I'll find the courage to attend on my own isn't completely gone.

Soon the sky is white with a pink dye rippling through it. I shower, disguise my dark circles so as not to frighten my first patient and drain a mug of black coffee. I leave an empty bowl of muesli on the kitchen table before returning the milk to the fridge. I pat the swirly writing on the invite, leave the house and walk back into town.

2

Someone to Watch Over Me

I wave goodbye to Bob as he heads in the opposite direction to me. We both work for the Ross Physiotherapy Centre, above the estate agent's on Gloucester Road. In complete contrast to Bob, Amira, who only comes in part-time, loves a good laugh. When she's at work, the day goes by quickly. We steal moments in the kitchen between patients as she regales me with stories of her husband and two teenage boys, about how she is the only one of them who seems to know where things are in the house. Sometimes she deliberately hides socks, phone chargers, remote controls and that stripy tie, the one with the thin stripes not thick, and sits with her feet up watching as they hunt for their missing items.

Bob covers his balding head with a grey, knitted hat, pulled down so far I hope he can see where he's going, and disappears around the corner while I head uphill towards Rhiannon's Eatery.

Rhiannon closes early on a Monday, the only weekday that she does. By the time she and her assistant, Tyler, have cleaned up and tidied everything away, the Monday Afternoon Knitters arrive for a session of knitting, revelry, banter and serious stitching into the early evening.

Before Mum changed time zones, she not only handed ownership of the house to me, she also left me lifetime membership to the Monday Afternoon Knitters Circle. I reluctantly accepted the latter, too, especially as the three remaining members were over seventy-five and I had no idea how to knit. But the Monday Afternoon Knitters came into Mum's life at a time when she needed them and they'd entered mine in the exact same way.

I would never have inherited the house or the knitting circle if things had been different for Mum and if my sister Cat hadn't left home and found love. All three of us have abandonment issues for various reasons. Mum was born in Australia but was left an orphan as a teenager and grew up with an aunt just streets away from where she'd lived with her parents. She'd married an Englishman and moved to Ross, but they divorced and he left her to raise my sister, Cat, on her own. Her second husband, my father, died before I really got to know him. The three of us have always been close, except if you count the time Cat took off to find her estranged father, telling Mum she'd rather live with him. But that was because she was a hormonal teenager who'd had enough of looking after Mum when she was going through one of her "quiet" phases. Cat, being four years older than me, had lived through a lot more of those than I had. I don't remember how often in my lifetime Mum became a shadow of her real self, sitting quietly in the kitchen, not able to cook, take us to school or do much more than drink tea and wipe tears from her eyes. I try to block out the silences, the times in my life when Mum slipped into a world that Cat and I didn't have access to, only to return to us at some indeterminate time as though nothing had happened. I prefer to remember the times of Mum being present, insisting on playing loud jazz in the kitchen, singing and cooking casseroles and stews to fill the freezer with.

Just after university, Cat left town to travel. She met, fell in love with and married a brilliant lawyer from Mum's native Adelaide when she was twenty-four years old and set up a new home in Australia with him. A few years later, Cat had her first child. It was when Mum took a trip on her own to Adelaide to help Cat cope with postnatal depression after her second child that her longing to return began. After having been made redundant from her job at the library, she made the decision to return to Australia for good, and I encouraged her. It seems a lifetime ago since Cat left for Adelaide and Mum has been gone for over three years. The two people I love the most are on the opposite side of the world, and now I've become part of the knitting family Mum left behind.

Mum was torn when she made the decision to go back. She said it was like *Sophie's Choice,* but I insisted I'd be absolutely fine and there was always Google Meet. I knew I wouldn't be fine, but I could tell that the prospect of Mum returning to Adelaide for good brought on a change in her. There was a brightness in her eyes and an aura around her I'd never experienced. She was more of her happy self, even happier than when she'd sung along to Ella Fitzgerald at full belt. Mum needed to leave Ross, and she didn't need me whining about missing her and holding her back.

Not long after Mum left, the pandemic came and my work as a physiotherapist dried up. I had more time on my hands than was advisable. I spent my days re-reading old books, sketching and painting in the back room which I'd turned into my studio. I had no one to talk to apart from odd conversations over the phone with Amira. I was missing Mum and Cat so much, and the fact that I couldn't fly out to see them made the heartache and loneliness ten times worse.

When I arrive at Rhiannon's Eatery, the trio of lively seventy-somethings are luxuriating in the cosy chairs by the front window. Their coats are hung up on the stand by the door, their works in progress already out. Left sides of cardigans and sleeves of jumpers blossom from the knitting needles, and wool spirals out like charmed snakes from the bags at their feet as they sit around the low coffee table. Mum always asks how my knitting is going and what everyone is up to. I know she's checking to make sure the women are looking after me, as charged. She has told them to make sure I'm getting out and seeing people other than my patients and not hiding myself away in the studio, painting and drawing as if the rest of society no longer exists. I do get lost in my illustrations and paintings. I've always loved to draw but I didn't go on to an Art A level, despite Mum's encouragement. I couldn't handle the attention my artwork garnered from other people. I was always too shy.

'Come in, my lovely, you're letting in the cold.'

'I'm sorry,' I say to Rhiannon as she guides me inside. She helps me off with my coat and the unravelling of my long scarf which makes me look as if I've been sucked into a multicoloured well of wool, my head bobbing on the surface. She takes my bag away from me and ushers me to the last easy chair by the window. I can do all of this for myself but Rhiannon loves to assist people. Especially me.

'There you go, my love. I'll pour you a tea just now. That Rooibos you like. And I saved you some carrot cake.' She disappears behind the counter and begins to rattle crockery. 'Have you spoken to your doctor about lack of sleep? You look as pale as a vampire, and I hope you're not out walking in the dead of night as though you are one. Anyone could be

9

out there, and I told your mum I'd make sure you'd stay safe at home.' I don't need to answer because this is the routine with Rhiannon. She lovingly swaddles me in concern and I awkwardly try to sidestep because I think the only remedy to my sleep deprived state would be hypnotherapy or hard drugs. I don't fancy the former and don't know how to get hold of the latter.

Rhiannon comes back to the coffee table with a small tray of goodies for me. Her cakes are famous in the whole of Ross-On-Wye and the queues for them on the weekends trail down the hill, the length of three shop fronts. She is like a caricature of a farmer's wife, though she doesn't live on a farm. Never has. She came to Ross from a town on the north coast of Wales. Her husband retired from an electricity company and she convinced him of moving to Ross because their son had moved here with his then fiancée, now wife. Rhiannon has two darling grandchildren. She had longed to open her own café for quite some time and leapt at the chance to take over this one, in a prime spot near the market square, as soon as it was advertised.

Rhiannon is cuddly. Everything about her is round and soft. Her cheeks, her tummy, the curls of her white hair. She is a mumsy, sweet grandma wrapped into one, and she called me almost every day to make sure I was coping when Mum left for Australia.

'You're late today,' Bea says, not looking up from her knitting. Her fingers are swollen at the knuckles from arthritis and her nail gels are painted frosty pink to match the fluffy sweater she has on. As usual, Bea is in full make-up. Her eyebrows were tattooed on years ago but she makes them thicker with a touch of brown brow powder. Her platinum blonde hair is spiky on the top and cropped close at the back and sides. Her eyeliner is heavy and navy blue today and makes her grey eyes sparkle intensely, the laughter lines deep and well-defined. She isn't wearing her varifocals and she squints at her fast-working knitting needles, clicking a merry rhythm as the left side of the Christmas cardigan she is knitting for her current boyfriend lengthens. Bea is into younger men at the moment. Her "main squeeze", as she calls him, is sixty-seven but she'll ditch him, unashamedly, if he can't come up with anything more inventive than a tea dance by their date next week. As with the majority of jumpers, socks, cardigans and millions of scarves they knit, the cardigan she is working on will go to a charity if the "va-va-voom" in Bea's love life is not restored.

'Have you finished those socks you've been working on?' Judith asks, looking over the top of her reading glasses at me. Bea says that Judith's default expression is one of a person who has just sucked the sharpest lemon ever grown. The thing about Judith, although she tries not to show it, is that she's a good-natured softy. I know that because of the heartfelt way she sympathised over cups of tea, cocoa and the occasional glasses of sweet sherry from her cupboard during our chats and well-appreciated pep talks when Mum left. Her hard exterior is convincing though. She is thin and straight-backed and was a headmistress at an all-girls private school before she retired. Her hair is grey, hints of her dark tresses still appearing within her stiff bob, parted to the side and tucked behind her ears. She wears the same pearl earrings every day and is rarely ever seen without one of a multitude of cardigans buttoned to the neck. A slight waddle caresses the neckline of her collection of floral blouses worn under her cardigans and also buttoned up to the top. Judith has a selection of brooches and always wears one on her cardigan. Something small and delicate like the wedding band on her ring finger. She is a widow now. She married just once, like Rhiannon, though Bea has had four husbands. But, as Bea says, she started young.

'I got stuck,' I say, pulling my project from the plastic bag inside my shoulder bag. I pop my coral-coloured sock onto my lap and cover it with my hands. 'I needed help with the circular needles so I abandoned it until today.'

'You won't make much progress if you dally.' Judith sucks on that lemon before placing the baby dress she is knitting into her knitting basket, offering me the flat of her palm.

I reluctantly hand my sad almost-sock to Judith. She frowns when she sees I've only got as far as the cuff of one, about an inch and a half of brow-creasing, knit one, purl one stitching. I see Bea's mouth ease into a smile, not because of my poor attempt at knitting with circular needles for the first time, but because Judith's nostrils are flared and her lemon is about to be drained of juice.

'It's complicated,' I say in my defence. 'Plus it's so cold in my house I can hardly close a fist let alone knit something so intricate.'

'Have some tea, my lovely.' Rhiannon tops up my cup. I tuck into a large mouthful of carrot cake and wash it down with Rooibos.

Bea and Rhiannon live a short drive from my house. Judith is just around the corner from me. Every time the women pop over for a visit, they comment on the repairs needed to the house and quiz me constantly about what I'm planning to do with it. I didn't have the energy to do anything with it, first with Mum leaving and then with a pandemic starting just months after; all I had the energy for was to order art

12

materials until it looked like I could start my own shop. In the year and a half we lost in lockdown, I was more or less in solitary confinement, spending all my time huddled in the studio with a canvas facing the window as I painted the changing view of the seasons. Sometimes I took pictures of the town so I could go back to the studio and create a painting from the images. Or I was outside in the garden, my sketchpad on my knee, drawing pictures of Rosie, Fee Milligan's tabby cat from next door, who hates me for some reason. She winds through the trees and plops her fat body into the centre of my garden and lies there for most of the day during the spring and summer months, hissing and arching her back if I approach. Or I painted the hills and countryside views. It was a wonderful distraction from the chaos outside my front door and the paint flaking off the walls inside. I do have my energy back now and I could make plans to renovate, I suppose. Besides, I don't want to freeze my extremities off for another year now that the cold weather has well and truly set in.

'I'm going to sort out the heating,' I say, and the women respond with 'at lasts' and 'about times'. 'And I'm going to get started fixing up the house. Soon as. Tomorrow in fact.'

For the past couple of years, I've been in a bit of a fog. The thing that helped me emerge was that damned invitation on the fridge door. It reminded me that people were getting back to normal, socialising again and that I'd been invited to take part in real life, not the virtual one we'd all been used to. The invitation was an opportunity to do something other than fixing other people's bodies, knitting badly and illustrating my life away in the back room every evening and weekend.

'I know a top builder.' Bea sits up and places the Christmas cardigan back into her knitting bag after securing a marker and pushing her knitting needles into the soft spool of swirling blues. 'Well, he's a painter and decorator and does general building work. He'd have your place whipped into shape in no time. He's such a nice guy, and if I were ten years younger, I would have grabbed him when he was replacing the garden shed last summer.'

Bea has the dirtiest laugh I've ever heard. It starts in her Pilates-flat tummy and rumbles up to her throat in a low, gravelly wheeze that blasts from her mouth several pitches higher and is relentless. I get Bea's sense of humour. She can always make me laugh. I love that in social situations Bea repeats a joke to anyone not laughing as if they couldn't have heard her the first time.

'Great,' I say. 'I'll take the number from you.'

'On it,' she says and sends a generous wink to the other women as if she is hatching a devious plan. This makes me nervous. Bea takes out her phone and sends the builder's number to me. I hear it arrive at my phone and turn to see Judith unravelling every last stitch of my sock and busily wrapping it back around the acrylic mix ball of wool.

'I think,' says Judith, looking over her glasses at me, 'that since you've made such little progress, you might be wiser to start a different project, using straight needles this time. Something more appropriate to your skill set.'

I slump forward in my chair, then take a mouthful of carrot cake. Judith is right. I was aiming high. Circular needles. Who was I kidding? I've been knitting with these three for years, beginning when Mum left before lockdown three years ago, then virtually during lockdown and now weekly on a Monday since the easing of restrictions. I thought I had advanced beyond square-shaped knits with no increases or decreases. I thought that after my beginners jumper I could take on a pair of socks or at least one sock, especially now that I understand what knitting patterns mean when they say Tog or Yo or SL. But the truth is that I'm still a beginner and my jumper would only have fit if I was eight months pregnant, had one arm longer than the other and I had the neck of a heavyweight lifter. Judith had wanted me to unravel that one, too. In the end I had agreed it wasn't a very good fit. She told me she would add it to the others she was sending to charity. Bea had rumbled with laughter at the very idea that anything I knitted would be good enough until Rhiannon threw a tape measure at her. I knew full well that Judith was going to shove my jumper in her wheelie bin when she got home.

'Never mind, pet,' Rhiannon says as Judith finishes winding my wool back onto the original ball. 'I'll help you start a beanie for winter.' She sees my glistening eyes as Judith pushes the ball of wool into my plastic bag to keep it safely hidden from me. 'Have you decided what you're wearing to that party, Annie?'

Oh God. The invitation. I wish I'd never mentioned it. The large, silver envelope, the only post I'd received in ages that wasn't a bill or a bank statement, had arrived two months ago. I'd thought it was a wedding invitation at first because it came on expensive-looking card with silver, glittery writing. One of my best friends from school, Becs Sprigg, got engaged during lockdown, and while she'd waited for restrictions to be lifted and for parties to be allowed again, I learnt from Instagram that the guest list just grew and grew. Eventually she had decided to come home to Ross and throw a massive party in one of the country house venues – as if it were a wedding. I'd seen pictures of the ring on social media. I had Liked both her Facebook and Instagram posts but never imagined Becs would invite me to her engagement party. Perhaps she felt bad about leaving me behind when she and my other "best friend", Zarina Cooke, took off to London after university and didn't invite me. I didn't hear from them for ages until they both Friended me on my lonely Facebook page, which I'd set up to see pictures of Cat's house and children in Australia. In the years that followed, I saw their social media pages swell with posts about their new flat in Primrose Hill, their new jobs, new boyfriends, Zarina's wedding in the Maldives four years ago, every meal they'd ever had, including snacks, and every party they'd gone to – together.

I Liked and Loved all their posts, and one day, after she got married, I summoned up the courage to DM Zarina to ask why they'd never mentioned their exodus from Herefordshire to me before they'd left. *Darling*, Zarina had said a week later, *we never thought for one moment you'd leave your mum*. In many ways they'd been right but it would have been nice to be asked. They had no idea that in the end Mum was the one to leave me. I look around at my default group of friends. Of course I'd told them about the engagement party, who else was I going to tell? I'd told Mum over Skype and she'd only said, 'Oh dear. You don't have to go if it will make you miserable, darling.'

Becs and Zarina, before they'd befriended me, used to tease me about my glasses, corduroy dungarees and handknitted jumpers when we were ten years old. They called me Charity Shop Girl. They looked down their noses at me and made my life hell. After telling Mum about them, she asked the girls' mothers if they could come over to the house to play after school. She laid out a beef stroganoff, two pasta bakes and two large pizzas along with a litre of lemonade for the three of us. While we ate pizza and burped our way through glasses of lemonade, Mum sang all the swing jazz standards she knew to us. They stared from me to Mum and left two hours later when Mum was quite hoarse. They said they looked forward to seeing me at school. The next day, Becs and Zarina became my best friends.

'I suppose they love Mum's singing as much as we do,' I told Cat later.

'You idiot, Annie,' she'd said. 'They feel sorry for you because Mum is a nutter. That's why they want to be your friend.'

The GP who used to visit Mum told Cat not to say 'nutter.' She gave us reading material on mental illness and I began to search the library for more information. When I'd asked Cat if I might become like Mum, she'd laughed at me.

'You think it's hereditary?' she'd said. 'What Mum has?'

I had nodded, earnestly, scared of what she might say because nothing in the leaflets mentioned anything about that side of things.

'Look, Annie, just live your life. Go out there, be friendly, be kind and help people.' Then she'd gone back to flicking through a magazine. To this day I remember what Cat said, but to this day I'm always looking for symptoms.

'I've decided not to go to the party,' I say. I run my finger over the icing from the carrot cake left on my side plate and lick my finger. Rhiannon shoots up out of her chair.

'That was the last of the carrot cake but I've got something even better.'

I don't try to stop her fetching me seconds because Rhiannon feels it is her duty to keep food in my mouth and my stomach full.

'I'm really going to get stuck into fixing the house up,' I say. 'I won't have time for parties and things.'

'It's one evening, Annie.' Bea rolls her eyes. 'There'll be single men in smart suits there who have had a wash. Lots to choose from. You really should go. I could come with you.'

'Don't be ridiculous,' Judith sniffs. 'How would it look if she took her grandmother along?'

'Aunt!' shouts Bea. 'I could pass for her aunt. The trendy aunt who knows how to have a good time and shows the youngsters how it's done.' She holds her elbows up and begins gyrating in her chair. She starts rapping Salt-N-Pepa's *Push It!* but doesn't know all the words so is mainly singing "Ooh, baby, baby," over and over, much to Judith's dismay.

'Stop it, Beatrice,' Judith says through clenched teeth. 'You'll put your back out again.'

Bea purses her lips and picks up her knitting.

'If you don't want to go,' says Rhiannon in her lullaby voice, 'you don't have to. But wouldn't it be nice to get all dressed up and have somewhere glamorous to go for once?'

I look down at the coffee table and at the whopping chunk of chocolate cake on the shocking pink side plate she has placed in front of me. It's tilted to one side, thick icing glistening, chips of chocolate embedded into the soft cream filling, dark cocoa dusting the pink ceramic glaze. I pick it up and the sponge sinks deep into my open mouth, crumbs scatter on the waiting side plate and the women look at me, amazed that I can comfortably eat two helpings of cream cake in a row. I begin to chew with my eyes closed and consider the invitation again. All that damned thing has ever done is made me want to eat cake.

'I won't come in,' says Bea when I finally open my eyes and start wiping vigorously at my mouth with the napkin Rhiannon has just handed me. 'I'll drop you to the door. I can wait for you outside.'

I shake my head.

'Or you could just stay home and not stress about it,' says Judith.

'Or she could pluck up some courage and go out for a change.' Bea glares at Judith. Judith stares her down.

'Okay, okay. I won't rule it out completely,' I say quickly because the two of them have been in bickering matches before and it usually turns ugly. There is something, a resentment of some kind, that is deep-seated in their history, and I wonder sometimes how the two of them remain friends. Something is keeping the two of them together, something I don't know about and obviously can't understand. I wish so much that I could ask them what it is but I don't want to stir up bad feelings. Still, I'm curious. Not even Mum understands what this dynamic is all about. I think Rhiannon is the glue that bonds them or the referee that sends them back to their corners. Somehow they always come back to each other and carry on as if the last argument didn't happen.

Rhiannon stays quiet as she and I watch Judith and Bea in a glowering competition that neither will win.

'Okay. Maybe I will go to the party,' I say. I gather my things together and put my plastic bag away, the rustling splintering the silence. 'I'll think about it a bit longer.'

'You're not off already, my pet?' Rhiannon pleads as if she doesn't want to be left in the middle of what is now a "who is going to blink first" contest. I clumsily angle my way through the gap between Bea and Judith just so I can break the eye contact between them, and it works.

'Oh, don't go because I'm being a moody, old cow,' says Bea. 'I'll be nice.' Another thing I notice is that Bea is always the first to wave the olive branch, always ready to take the blame for whatever disagreement she has with Judith, even if she isn't the one at fault. Judith sucks on her lemon and Bea smiles, eyes twinkling as she completely changes the subject of their disagreement and has us all smiling again.

'I'm meeting Ian later,' she says. 'We're going to the cinema. I hope he has a nap first so he doesn't fall asleep again. I'd better remind him.'

Bea sends a text to Ian as I put on my coat and start wrapping my scarf around my neck, several times.

'Here,' says Rhiannon, coming at me with a cake box. 'Take the rest with you and text when you get home.'

'Will do,' I say, giving the women a hearty thumbs up at the door. Rhiannon is busy tucking my curls into my hat and pulling it down further. 'See you next Monday.'

'Call that builder,' Bea shouts over her shoulder.

'And find a simple knitting pattern,' calls Judith. 'See you.'

I leave the knitting circle not having knitted a single stitch. As always, I take one step forward and two back with my knitting projects. I'll find a simple pattern. I'm sure I can.

I hurry. It's another bitter evening and I can hear Mum humming *Baby, It's Cold Outside* as she does the washing up. I should be home in fifteen minutes or so, and I can be tucked up in my cold living room, nestling within a blanket on the sofa, eating cake and watching *Money Heist*.

Tomorrow I'll call the heating engineers, then I'll call that builder.

3

Stardust

The heating engineer grunts and wheezes and talks to himself as he works. It'll take a while for the warmth to circulate around the house, the stonework being so thick it can feel chilly in spring. Everything is so cold: the glassware and anything metal feels icy. I've been wearing gloves indoors since October started. I see that Becs' invitation has slipped down the fridge door and that I have to turn my head sideways to read the details on it, even though I have them memorised. I'm still not sure I'll go. I'm used to hearing about their exciting lives on Facebook where I can at least roll my eyes and tut at the ridiculousness of posting pictures of your husband's new goatee. Zarina loved her husband's facial hair so much there was a second picture of her kissing his cheek, eyes slanting towards the camera, and I wondered how many times they froze in that position until the picture was just right.

I let the heating engineer out of the house and I hurry to work. I always finish early on a Monday so that I can be at the knitting circle for 4.30 p.m. I have only one appointment at the practice today. A new patient with a frozen shoulder, a past injury that still troubles him, which happened during a football match.

I tap the invitation as I leave and it turns upside down.

The door beside the estate agent's creaks open and I jog up the stairs to the practice. Amira is leaving just as I arrive, tucked up in a white coat and white woollen hat, her hair like black silk against her collar. Her gloves are also white and she waves them in my face as though she urgently needs my attention but isn't allowed to speak. Her eyes are bulging as she grins, a hint of mania in her expression.

'What?' I ask her and look down the corridor she keeps nodding towards.

We don't have a receptionist, just a waiting area behind a partition whose top half is frosted glass. Behind it are comfy chairs, a desk and a bell for patients to announce their arrival. There is a notice that says *Please Ring and Take a Seat*, but it's obscured by Amira's yucca which thinks it's a beanstalk and really needs to be moved elsewhere.

'What?' I say again when Amira mouths something and points to the waiting area. There isn't a waiting room door so she obviously doesn't want to be heard by whoever is waiting, so the game of charades continues.

I have no idea what Amira is trying to say, but I suspect it has something to do with my patient whose outline I can just about make out through the frosted glass. He's not on his own, there's someone sitting next to him who is on the phone and who keeps saying, 'Yes, yes. Sweet. Okay. We can do that. Done.' Did my patient bring his dad? Boyfriend?

'You'll see,' Amira says, exasperated. She leaves, shaking her head and giving me a gloved wave.

I pop my head around the partition wall and smile. I'm greeted by a set of brilliant white teeth, the ones famous actors have and the ones that gleam from Becs and Zarina's faces on their social media posts. I might have followed them to London if they'd asked me but I would never have bleached my teeth.

'Are you my three thirty?' I ask the teeth. They are positioned within a wide mouth that looks smooth and glossed with balm. His skin is tanned, flawless. His hair is dirty blonde and pulled into a man bun. He wears a chunky, knitted sweater, one that would have ended up as an aubergine tent had I tried to knit it for him. He rises from his seat and extends a large white hand that is silky to touch, and I can't help noticing that his fingernails are manicured to the expensively well-groomed standard the rest of him appears to be. He smells like the whole perfume counter of a department store, the counter where they stock the expensive colognes and aftershaves for rich men who want to seduce unsuspecting physiotherapists.

'Reef Mayer,' he says with a deep, regionally accented voice.

'Er,' I say, tongue-tied, my neck craning upwards so I can meet his eye. 'Just–just give me a second and I'll be right with you.'

'It's okay. I was early so…' I blush furiously so I need to get out of here.

'I'll … er…' I ungracefully turn towards the doorway and jam my arm into it so that the whole plasterboard partition shudders for several seconds.

'You all right?' he asks. I can't quite place his accent. Birmingham? Definitely Midlands.

'Yes, yes. With you in two ticks.' I turn my reddened cheeks from view and speed down the hallway to my treatment room.

Shit. Shit. Shit. Shit. So not cool. I unravel my scarf, whip off my coat and gloves. I wash my freezing hands thoroughly with piping hot water that turns them red. I put on my white tunic without fully drying my hands, so I wash them again and rub them so dry they are even redder than before. I take a deep breath, open the door and casually glide back down the corridor to the waiting area.

'Reef Mayer?' I inwardly kick myself hard in the shin. He's already told me his name.

He follows me to the treatment room, and his partner, now off the phone, stands. Reef signals that he has this and I know now that this must be his boyfriend. The care and attention he has for Reef is palpable. My shoulders droop as I acknowledge this, but at least I can conduct his treatment with calm professionalism. He's not going to be interested in me.

Reef takes his top off behind the screen. He's so tall I get a good view of his lateral and deltoid muscles bulging around his neck. He comes from behind the screen holding his gown rather than wearing it and I quickly divert my attention from his chest to the gown. He puts it on. We swallow at the same time and both say sorry. I'm sorry that I'm not making a good enough attempt to disguise the fact that I think he is gorgeous. I'm not sure I can continue to treat him and remain professional, and maybe I should refer him to Amira who, as a married woman, might have some self control. That said, her eyes were extremely wide when she left, not at all professional on her part either. I remind myself he is gay. Or probably gay because he might just have a very concerned friend with him. I remind myself that I *am* professional and that I should act accordingly so as not to lose him as a patient.

'Please take a seat.' I nod to the one beside my desk and begin the routine questions regarding his injury and his

25

general health. Is he on any medication? Can I take his blood pressure? What is his profession?

'I'm retired.' He's smirking and looks at me as if he knows what my next question will be.

'Oh, wow,' I say. 'And you're how old?' I look back at my notes. 'Retired at thirty-six. That must be the dream, right?'

'Right.' He falters and starts to look at me questioningly but I have no idea what he wants to ask.

'And what did you retire from?' I suspect he must have made a killing selling an online business or made millions floating stocks and shares.

'I was in sport,' he says but it sounds like a question.

'Oh, right.' Now I understand why he has the body he has.

'You know you're really good,' he says, shaking his head. 'Funny.' He smiles his ultra-white teeth at me and sniffs out a laugh. I'm even more confused. How am I funny? I casually glance down at myself and surreptitiously touch my hair in case something is caught in it. A twig, bits of muesli. It wouldn't be the first time. My hair is thick with oversized waves, curls and frizz; things get stuck in it all the time. I once had an earring in my hair for two days.

'Okay, have a seat up here.' I pat the bed and stand on the other side so that his broad back faces me. His muscles are tough and thick and I have to dig in hard to manipulate his body. I ask him questions like, *Does it hurt when I do this? Can you feel that? How about if I do this?* Then I reel off physio talk and the medical names for muscles. As I start to treat him, I say things like, *I'm just going to … Just sit up straight while I … Yes, that's it, just relax for me as I …*

Next I ask him to lie on his back while I dig my thumbs into his lats. I lean in very close and my hair falls onto his tanned skin. I'd forgotten to tie it all back as I normally do when I see patients, only Reef Mayer isn't like any other patient I've treated in either the practice or during my training.

'Oh, sorry,' I say, pulling a yellow scrunchy with childish black dots on it out of my pocket. I rake my curls up to the nape of my neck and try to bundle it through a scrunchy that has lost most of its elasticity. Reef rolls onto his side and smiles up at me. Not with teeth this time but with his eyes, and there is a look in them that I can read perfectly well.

'Your hair is beautiful.' His tone of voice has dropped. It isn't light and breezy, but decidedly sultry and legato.

'Thanks,' I say coming back to the table and gesturing for him to roll onto his evenly spaced and well-defined abdominal muscles, but he doesn't move. He looks straight at me and my reddened face, his eyes sparkling under the examination lights.

'Your friend will be wondering where you are.' I nod my head towards the door.

'Jack? Jack's not a friend as such. He's my agent. Someone who tells me what I can or can't do.'

'Oh?' I prod him onto his stomach. 'You have an agent but you're retired.'

Reef turns his head towards me, a short laugh leaves his lips and he shakes his head.

'You really don't know who I am, do you?' he says. His hands are propped under his chin, elbows out to the side, shoulders wider than my exam bed.

'I know your name,' I say.

'No, I mean, you don't know *who* I am.' He sits up again, his legs at the side of the table are now astride me.

'No more than you've told me.' Now I look nervously at the door because this is sounding all too much like the build

27

up to the part where the handsome man on my bed is about to reveal his deadly intentions. I have sharp objects in the room, he can overwhelm me at any time. And his so-called agent, well, he could be an accomplice. There is a sharp rap on the door and I jump.

'I've called the car round.' His agent's voice barks from the corridor. 'Two minutes.'

'I have to be somewhere,' Reef says and slides down in front of me. I look up into hazel eyes. They are alive with glints of desire behind a boyish charm.

'But we haven't finished,' I half stammer.

'I'm sorry. Jack has a tendency to double and triple book me sometimes. But…' He steps towards me and I step back. He moves around me and heads to the screen. Of course, he was just going to get dressed – not lunge at me.

'Is there any chance you and I might go for a drink some time?' His voice is muffled by the chunky sweater as he pulls it back on.

I don't answer the question and he comes from behind the screen.

'If it's a patient-doctor thing, I'll find another physiotherapist.' He's quick to make this point and takes my hand.

'Reef! Mr Mayer. What are you…?'

'I'm sorry to do this but I know I won't be back here for a few days and I really would like to take you out.'

His agent barks his name and Reef tuts.

'He makes these appointments with not enough time to get from one to the other. Like I have a jetpack or something. Mad.'

Reef shakes his head; his man bun has been disturbed by the disrobing and sweater replacing and he tucks a long strand behind his ear.

'But seriously, I would love to see you again.' He's at the door, a look of pleading in his eyes.

'Your next appointment?' I raise my shoulders to my ears.

'I'll get Jack to arrange it,' he whispers and then leaves.

I pull my scrunchy off with a furrowed brow and try to play back the conversation. I'm still going over it as I leave the practice and head off to Rhiannon's for our Monday afternoon knit-in. I can't wait to tell them what happened, mostly so that I can make sense of it all.

All three women stare at me in wonderment after my story. Bea is the first to speak.

'Reef *Mayer*? Reef Mayer is your patient? Honestly?'

'You know him?'

Rhiannon has supplied me with a pot of Rooibos tea and a superbly stacked chocolate and raspberry cake with fresh cream. It's honestly no wonder I can't learn to knit when there are snacks like this around.

'Of course I do.' Bea starts knitting again. 'But you obviously don't. He is, or was, a world class footballer. Used to play for Aston Villa. Don't know how many caps he has for England.' This means absolutely nothing. 'He received a sports person of the year award a few years ago. Had to retire through injury. You really haven't heard of him? He married a famous model. Natalia De Veras.'

'Oh I know her,' I say. 'She's always in my Instagram feed advertising plant-based multivitamins. She's gorgeous. So he's married?'

'Divorced.' Judith sighs as if she doesn't want to admit she knows something of celebrity gossip. 'Honestly, Annie, this is popular culture. Why don't you know these things?'

'I don't follow football,' I say licking cream off my bottom lip. 'So he's a real big deal then.'

Bea shoves her iPhone under my nose. There's a picture of Reef walking through a crowd of people. His hair is longer and he wears a tight, single-breasted suit. The legs of his trousers are narrow at the ankles and he takes a long stride as he smiles off to the side at someone. It's a news item about the local boy coming back to his roots.

Reef Mayer is now a local of his childhood town and buys a six-bedroomed country manor on eight acres of land in the Forest Of Dean. He continues to work for his charity, Children First, but needed to take a break from his London life. Mayer has won a long custody battle with former model Natalia De Veras whose six-year-old son he adopted when the couple married five years ago. She had denied the footballer access to their son, but the court ruled that Mayer should have part-time custody on arranged weekends and occasional holidays. 'I just need to slow down and learn how to breath again. I can't wait to spend time with my boy. He's everything to me.'

I look up from the phone.

'With all this going on, I'm surprised he asked me out.'

'He asked you out?'

I love the harmony they make when the women exclaim simultaneously. They stare at me.

'Well, this is what I was trying to say. It was a weird conversation. I'm sure he thought I was weird. Now I get why he kept asking me if I knew him.'

'And you are going to go out with him, aren't you?' Rhiannon looks at me as if this is a done deal.

'Well, he'll come back for an appointment at least. I'm not so sure I should go out with him. It seems like he has a lot going on in his life. Complications.'

Bea stands up. She puts her hands on her slim hips. Today she wears a black mohair sweater over her skinny animal print trousers. I could never get away with those but Bea can pull off everything she sets her mind on wearing.

'Weren't you the one who wasn't going to this engagement bash because you were afraid to go on your own? Imagine what those fancy London girls will think when you turn up with a celebrity on your arm.' She flops back in her seat as if the statement has taken it out of her. 'Did I tell you about the time I dated Tom Selleck?' Judith sucks her lemon and her needles clack at double speed. 'I ended it because of the moustache but I was the talk of the town for while. The glamour, the elegance. You can't beat a celebrity boyfriend, Annie. You know you have to take him to that party.'

I'm just finishing my cake, and though I'm very tempted to lick the plate, I put it down and wipe my mouth.

'More cake, my lovely?' Rhiannon is on her feet, grabbing my plate.

'No, she won't have more cake, Rhi,' Bea pipes up. 'I'll be taking her dress shopping for the party so that she can measure up to Reef Mayer. His suits are probably hand-stitched silk. Annie needs to dress to impress and it's better to do that in a size twelve rather than a sixteen.'

I open my mouth to protest. I'm a size fourteen. But Bea starts telling us about the minor royal she nearly became engaged to, so I pick up my knitting needles and ask

Rhiannon to show me – again – how to cast on stitches for my new beanie hat.

4

In the Still of the Night

I decide not to walk too far tonight. Not as far as town because the quickest way back home is through the graveyard and the film I was watching late into the evening, as contrived and ridiculous as it was, has me worried that a very tall man with a hooded, oversized coat is going to follow me.

I pass Judith's house. The gate to her upward sloping drive is closed and all the lights are out making it look tall and sinister. Her double-fronted house with its light blue door and silver door knocker is very welcoming in the day time with the branches of the weeping birch in her front garden dipping towards the pavement like a courteous bow. Behind the double glazed bay window to the right is a sizeable through lounge. The furniture is large, the sofas deep. The sideboards and shelves are chestnut, the soft furnishings are muted lilac and pink. Not an ornament is out of place and dust, if it were to float into the house, doesn't linger. Judith has a yellow duster and a canister of Mr Sheen at the ready and she isn't afraid to use it. Behind the smaller window to the left is Judith's study. It's a snug room with packed bookshelves and framed pictures of birds on the wall. Her late husband was a birdwatcher, and she has lots of bird pictures in the hallway and along the wall to the kitchen and dining room. Judith and her husband never had children and, therefore, none of the turbo-charged grandchildren that Rhiannon has which makes it easier for her house to remain immaculately clean and orderly.

She has an open-door policy. For me, anyway. After Mum flew back to Australia, Judith filled my gloom with photos from her collection of albums and the tales attached to each photograph. Judith, a good-looking woman in her seventies, was once a stunningly attractive young woman. When she married at age thirty-two, she looked like a glamorous film actress from the 1950s. Her hair was jet black and shiny. It was thick and full of life, so were her eyes which are hooded now and never seem to sparkle the way they did in her wedding photo album. Her lips were fuller then, painted red so that her teeth gleamed in the close-up shot of her and her late husband, Richard.

I had been surprised to see that Bea, considering she and Judith had been best friends since their late teens, was only in one or two of the wedding photographs. Back then, Bea had her signature trim waist and wore a peach dress that looked a little like a wedding dress with its silk waistband and dramatic bodice, and she carried a small bouquet. I'd asked if Bea had been the matron of honour.

'No,' Judith had said without expression. 'She almost didn't make it to the wedding. She came back a week before and I had to at least make her a bridesmaid when I hadn't intended to have any.'

I'd gone on to ask another question. I wanted to comment on how amazing they both looked. To ask who Bea was married to at the time or whether she was between husbands, but Judith slammed the album shut, got up and started fussing over a pot of tea, admonishing herself for being such a terrible hostess. She'd promptly turned the topic of conversation back to Mum, asking after her health when we had already spoken about her on my arrival. She'd become so flustered talking about Bea disappearing before her wedding that I don't think she remembered our previous conversation.

I walk aimlessly past Judith's house knowing that she is fast asleep. Her cat, Phoebe, will be curled up, purring away on the window seat cushion behind the bedroom curtain. I turn the corner at the top of the road, my thoughts still on Judith. I really want to ask her about the wedding and why she and her best friend were not in any pictures together and why, though Judith looked elegant, her smiles seemed forced, apart from the one of her and Richard outside the church.

I think about Bea now. How she bundles and blusters through my life on a very regular basis these days. She's always shut me down when I've asked why, if she and Judith are such best friends, it sometimes seems as though they can't stand each other. She waves a small hand at me and says nonsense before going on to tell me about a dance they went to as teenagers.

'The men loved Judith but were always too afraid to talk to her. They looked on her as if she were royalty and very often came to me to ask if they should dare ask her to dance, as if I were the lady's maid.'

Bea never tells these stories with any ill feeling towards her friend and I genuinely believe they love each other. Theirs is a love-hate relationship and I'll never understand the nuances of it. Both Judith and Bea are adept at subject changing and offering refreshments so that I won't be able to ask. Perhaps my best bet is to question Rhiannon but I suspect she will be loyal to them, and there is a chance she is as clueless as I am. She hasn't known them since childhood, just for the ten years she has owned the café. Rhiannon had discovered that she shared an interest in knitting with Judith. Both were hardcore knitters, and together they coerced Bea into sitting still for five minutes to join them in a knitting circle.

I've walked around in a circle, and back at the front door, I'm feeling more awake than I did at 2.30 a.m. I wish I could sleep for a few hours but I'm feeling wired and full of curiosity, once again, about my friends. Presumably Bea has done something wrong and Judith is tolerating her because she doesn't want to lose her as a friend.

In the kitchen, I start to make some tea. By now, my body must be programmed to wake up in the middle of the night expecting to go for a walk and come back for a cup of tea. Maybe it's time to consider that I myself have ruined my circadian rhythm after years of getting out of bed, flinging clothes on over my pyjamas and taking to the streets. Maybe there is no turning back for me and I'll never have a good night's sleep again.

My hands shake with the prospect that I might have to change my whole life. Sleep in the day and do a job that takes place at night. I consider the idea of the first ever midnight physiotherapist as the kettle boils. This week it's all about ashwagandah tea to help relax me for sleep. Hops, valerian, lavender, chamomile – all of my sleep teas are lined up in what I call my sleep cupboard. It contains every herbal sleep tablet on the market, most of which I order from Amazon at three in the morning after I've turned off my sleep app. I have so much information on how to fall asleep, I could invent my own sleep app. I know all about sleep, sleep patterns, what process your body is going through during each sleep cycle. I know what happens to your body if one doesn't get enough sleep, and I've read all the scientific reports on how much sleep a person at various stages of their life requires and the things that could go wrong if one doesn't get their quota. As it stands, I will be dead by seventy-eight, either from heart disease or respiratory weakness, provided, of course, I haven't died from early onset dementia.

My life expectancy arranged, I snuggle down on the sofa with some ashwagandah tea and call Mum. I sit with one small lamp on in the corner of the room. It's four o'clock in the afternoon in Adelaide.

'You're lucky to catch me in,' she says with a laugh behind her voice. 'I had planned to go to a yoga class but I got involved in the afternoon matinee. How are you, darling?'

In a couple of hours, I wake to find that I've dropped off to sleep after my chat with Mum while the song *Misty* in the style of Sarah Vaughan replays in my mind. Mum sang that as well as others before my eyelids grew heavy. That was my sleep app idea right there. A repertoire of dreamy jazz standards on repeat. It's no longer dark and I have to get ready for work.

5

You Go to My Head

I call the number Bea has given me for the general builder. He answers quite quickly but seems distracted.

'So, basically,' I conclude as I ramble on about the state of my dwelling to someone who doesn't appear to be listening, 'do you think you could come and take a look? Give an estimate for repairs?'

Wherever he is, his voice echoes as if he's in a bathroom and I make an *eugh* face and try not to imagine the toilet roll on the wall beside him and his jeans bunched at his ankles. Then it dawns on me that he might have picked up the call while mending something in someone else's bathroom. Bea had sworn by him. 'Good builders are hard to find,' she's told me every day since she's given me the number as well as to call the builder before he gets too booked up. His name is Anton which doesn't sound like a builder at all, more like a hairdresser or a chef or something.

'Yes, of course, but I won't be able to come until...' It goes quiet at his end. He's going to tell me he can't come for months, and Bea will be cross because I've dragged my feet and now he's booked up. 'Actually, how are you fixed for Monday morning? Something got cancelled. Ten o'clock?'

'That's great,' I say. 'Brilliant. I'll text the address and my name is Annie. Annie Lambert.'

'No problem, Annie Lambert. It's in my diary now so I'll see you then.'

His baritone voice is slow and warm, and I picture a man in his forties with a pot belly, long hair and a ponytail. He sounds casual and laid back, and in for a big shock when he sees the place.

The streets are cold and unusually quiet by the time I get to Gloucester Road. No large vans loading or people waiting at the pedestrian crossing. Pot plants and flowers are out on the pavement in front of the florist but no one is there to stop and look at them. The sign at the barber's shop sways in the easterly breeze but I don't see any takers for a trim or a shave in any of the seats. The woman in the estate agent's downstairs from the practice looks up at me hopefully but looks back at her computer as I pass. No one is buying houses today.

Up the stairs, Amira is showing a patient out. She's wearing a thick polo neck sweater under her white tunic and blows into her hands. She pulls me inside and closes the door quickly.

'Time for a tea before your next appointment?' she asks while pulling me down the corridor into the tiny kitchen at the end of it. Amira pays me no attention as she fills the kettle and lets two Ross Physiotherapy Centre mugs bang clumsily onto the narrow counter. She pulls out a packet of Earl Grey and plops a tea bag into each mug.

'So?' she says over her shoulder, and before I can ask, *so what?* she goes on to say that her youngest son wants his autograph.

'Whose autograph?' I'm taking my coat off and unravelling my never-ending scarf. Amira swings around.

39

'Oh, so your diary is so full of celebrity clients you don't even know which one of them I'm talking about?' Her black hair obscures half of her face. She hands one of the steamy mugs of tea to me. It burns my frozen fingers. 'Mr Famous Footballer, silly. I told the boys Reef Mayer is your patient. It is the only thing I've said to them in six months that's even caused a raised eyebrow, let alone a full on turn around on the gaming chair. Zain actually stopped playing his game. For a whole minute he stared at me. I was so thankful to Reef Mayer for that. It was getting to a point where those boys were in serious danger of not recognising me anymore. Their dad could have moved a random Pakistani woman into the house and they wouldn't know it wasn't me.'

I giggle at her earnest expression. 'To be honest, I had no idea who he was until Bea and the others told me. I googled him when I got home. He's my first famous client.'

'Around here, he'll probably be the only one, so you better make the most of it.'

'How do you mean?'

'I mean get him on the company Instagram so we get more calls.'

'You seriously think we'll attract more clients because I treat Reef Mayer?'

'It'll put us on the map.'

'I didn't even treat him fully. He says he'll come back.'

Amira's eyes do that bugling thing, which is quite disturbing, seeing as she has large eyes to start with. Just then, my work mobile rings.

'Annie Lambert speaking.'

Now my eyes bulge when I hear a friendly, male voice. Reef Mayer is on the line and I walk his call to my office while Amira shouts out, 'Get a selfie. Get a few. I want to be in one. My sons will love me again. They'll respect me.' I run to my room and hope Reef can't hear her.

'Bad time to call?' Reef asks.

'No, no.' I grab a pen. 'You want to reschedule your unfinished appointment?'

'Actually, I was calling to ask about that drink. Or dinner?'

'You mean…?'

'I mean like you and me, a table for two. What do you think?'

'I think I might just have won the respect of Amira's sons.'

'You what?'

'It's okay. But a drink? I mean, that would be nice.' As I draw out my answer, I catch the image of my lower tummy in the mirror and suck it in. Reef couldn't have noticed it or my blotchy skin when he came for his appointment or he wouldn't be asking me out now. After googling him, I know full well I don't look like any of the women he's dated. Not one of the women on his Instagram look any shorter than six feet tall. They are all high heels and leggy beauty, and if Reef Mayer thinks I can squeeze into any of the designer clothes those women had on, he has another think coming. I don't do heels. I don't do glamour, and I'm beginning to wonder if this is a joke, a dare or a publicity stunt cooked up by his agent. That must be it.

'Um, Reef, are you sure you want to go for a drink with me?'

'Of course he does,' Amira hisses from the doorway. I shoo her with my hand.

'Why would you ask that?' Reef sounds somewhat dejected. 'I get it. You found out who I am and you don't like football? Is it because I have a son?'

'No. It's nothing like that. It's just that. I'm not sure I–'

'You're going out with someone. Damn, you have a boyfriend. I didn't even ask. Are you married?'

'I'm not dating. I'm not married. I just wouldn't have thought I was your type.'

'I don't have a type. I just like you. Didn't I make it obvious enough?'

The only thing obvious to me had been that I'd felt like jelly around him. I was a lustful woman who saw a handsome man and realised it had been years since I'd kissed a man, handsome or not, let alone one who was half naked in a room with a bed.

'Okay,' I say and it blurts out on a loud sigh because I've been holding my breath.

'Well, don't do me any favours.' He laughs aloud, and I picture his smile and the crinkles at the sides of his eyes. 'How about Saturday?'

'I thought you weren't sure when you'd be here again?'

'I won't be, not for a couple of weeks, but I can't wait to see you. I'm in Birmingham filming a documentary. It should wrap up by the weekend and then I'm in London recording a football programme.'

'You are busy.'

'Well, got to make the most of the attention. It won't be on me forever. Some other football celebrity will be in the spotlight and I'll have more time for Noé again.'

'Your son?' The cute little boy in the pictures online.

'Yes, he's mostly with nannies at the moment. His mum is in yet another reality show, away on some farm in Norway. God knows.' He sighs heavily and takes a few moments to consider his next sentence. Amira is mouthing something to me but I bat her away again. She lets the door slam behind her.

'Sorry, where was I?' asks Reef. 'Yes, so, I can send a car for you. What if they collected you about six, six thirty? There's a restaurant at the hotel but we can go anywhere you like. You decide.'

'I don't actually know Birmingham.'

'It's fine. I'll choose something and next time you can choose.'

Next time? This is all moving a bit fast for me. Usually, if I like someone and they like me, it generally takes weeks of skirting around, finding ingenious ways of crossing paths and rereading *One Day* before anything actually happens. But here is this breath of cool air, whipping life into my lungs and reddening my cheeks. The gust of Reef Mayer leaves me tongue-tied and my pulse thrumming though my arteries.

'Okay,' I say, so loudly I shock myself. 'I can be ready for six and I'll see you at your hotel. Can't wait.' I sound like a robot because Amira, whose head is round the door, is feeding me the lines to say to Reef.

'Brilliant, I'll see you Saturday, then.'

I need time, I think to myself as soon as I hang up. Time to think about what I've just said yes to. *Who* I've just said yes to. Reef is a celebrity for goodness' sake. While Amira is quizzing me about what I'm going to wear and what the hell I'm going to do with all that hair – she knows a brave hairdresser – the buzzer in the waiting room sounds and my next appointment has arrived.

6

The Good Life

Bea has come to help me prepare for my date with Reef. She's more of a hindrance than a help. For every outfit she pulls from my wardrobe and asks, 'What about this?' she tries it on herself. Before giving me the opportunity to choose anything at all, she looks herself up and down in the mirror and says, 'No, this won't do.' Bea is a foot shorter than me and about two sizes smaller, so my clothes swim around her and look absurd. She cinches everything she tries on around the waist with something from my accessories hanger, my small collection of belts and scarves.

'Don't forget, Bea, I'm the one going on the date and they might look better on me being as they're my clothes.'

I sit on the pillows on my bed, leaning on the headboard, my knees crossed, cradling a cup of peppermint tea. We've been at this for an hour, and in my head, I've already chosen what I'm going to wear. It's the only thing I have that's less than a year old and should still fit me. It's a dark blue silk dress I'd bought to cheer myself up with from the Next website one night when I'd been awake for hours and didn't know what to do with myself. It fitted well, and though I'd thought the colour might have been sombre, it looked classy and I'd convinced myself of keeping it in case of emergencies. Bea had tossed it over her shoulder towards the bed, unconvinced. It had sailed up in my general direction,

44

but being so light, it had fluttered like a leaf down the small gap between the side table and bed, a sleeve holding onto the quilt for dear life. I have it lying neatly on the bed by the pillows.

'This will be fine,' I say looking at the thin belt around the waistline and the slight pleats around the skirt. The neckline is deep and v-shaped, and while I consider a necklace or chain, Bea wriggles out of my dungarees.

'Are you sure?' she asks with a frown. 'Won't it make you look frumpy?'

'I hope not,' I say, re-arranging it on the bed as if someone were wearing it. I had thought it made me look sophisticated, yet sexy, in an expensive sort of way. It had also occurred to me that I needed silk lingerie to go with it but hadn't gone as far as making a purchase. Something I am regretting now that I discover Bea's underwear is sexier than mine and she's more than twice my age.

'Well, I suppose it will have to do.' Bea busily pulls on her own clothes and shoes. 'What about make-up? Can I trust you to get that right?'

I nod.

'Good, because I need to get going. I have a booty call.'

'A what?'

'You heard. This old friend of mine, haven't seen him in yonks and he's up for a wild evening, so I'd better get ready and go over there.'

I look at the time on my phone. 'Bea, it's five in the afternoon. I thought booty calls were late at night.' I hold my dress up in front of me and look in the mirror.

'I know,' she says, 'but by the time I shower, do my make-up and things, it could be almost seven. And you know what these old codgers are like. In bed by nine with a cup of

Horlicks. I need to get in there before rigor mortis sets in or he forgets he suggested a get-together in the first place. Old people forget things, that's why I don't date them.' She touches my cheek. 'You have a bloody good time, my darling, and make sure he spends a fortune.'

I give a weak smile. I'm just happy to be on a date.

'And make sure you mention that engagement party. Get him to escort you. You'll be the talk of the town when they hear who you're on a date with tonight.'

Like a rushing wave, Bea leaves the house and I know full well that no one in this town or anywhere is going to be talking about me. One dinner with Reef Mayer is hardly newsworthy stuff and I wouldn't dare mention the engagement party. It'll make me sound as if I haven't had a date in ages and Reef doesn't need to know that.

At six fifteen the taxi arrives. It's over an hour to Birmingham city centre and over sixty miles of creases being etched into my new silk dress. I try to sit sideways on one hip for a lot of the way, swapping from hip to hip when the numbness gets to me as we zip along the M5. I undo my coat and begin to smooth along the seat of my dress, hoping I won't have that 'seated' look people get in their clothes by the end of an evening out.

At least I'd worked out what to do with my hair. I'd blow-dried the whole mass of it that morning. It had taken well over an hour and my arms ached. Now my buttocks ache from sitting awkwardly for so long. My abdominal muscles have undergone an intense workout because, in the end, I've decided to hover above my seat to prevent more wrinkles in my dress.

I get a text from Reef to ask how far away I am, and I tell him I've just seen a sign for Birmingham O2 Academy so I must be close.

'Great,' he says. 'I'll look out for you.'

When the driver pulls up outside the hotel, Reef is standing outside in a raw silk suit of peacock blue. It started raining minutes ago and a fine sheen of water droplets covers his hair which he wears loose and collar length tonight. He is backlit by the hotel foyer, and though his face is in shadow, his teeth still shine through. He steps up to the car door and pulls it open with a flourish before offering me his hand to take. It's large and smooth, a thick ring with a green stone circles his little finger. I step out and adjust the strap of my handbag. Reef runs a hand through his hair and smells expensive. The rain begins to pelt down from the starless sky. He crooks his arm and rushes me to the glass doors of the hotel which open automatically.

'I had them set up a room in the suite for dinner.' He turns to me. 'Are you okay with that?'

Reef has a suite, not just a room. I've never stayed in a suite. All of a sudden I am aware of how I must look in my coat which is far too thin for this weather but is the dressiest I have. It's French Connection, which isn't bad but still very High Street compared to my date.

'Er, yes, that's fine.' I'm starving, and the fewer people who see Reef Mayer out with a woman in a crumpled dress, the better.

He places a warm hand into the small of my back and glides me to the row of lifts beyond reception. As we ascend, I glance at his smiling eyes briefly before focusing my attention on the floor numbers blinking their way skywards. I have no idea how many floors we have or will be travelling

47

through; my mind has already shifted to the scene in *Funny Girl* in which Omar Sharif invites Barbara Streisand to dine in his hotel suite. Because it's a musical, she proceeds to sing her way through a decision-making process of whether she will sleep with him or not. Without singing a note, I have already decided I'm not staying overnight. I won't be sleeping with Reef until I'm sure this isn't some kind of social experiment and that I'm not part of a candid camera reality show. I must wake up in my own bed, in my house, in Ross-on-Wye, no matter how tempting the prospect of spending the night in a luxury hotel with this man is.

It is with a nervous shiver through my arms that I tentatively take off my coat to reveal my wardrobe faux pas. Reef takes in the deep V in the front of my dress, rather than the creases, as he helps me off with the French Connection offering. I rush over to the sofa and flop down quickly. This will incur further creasing but I need to steer his hopeful attention away from my cleavage. I'm not going to stay the night. I'm not.

'I've got some champagne on ice.' Reef gestures to the set table by the window that looks onto a rainy city night with yellow lights from distant buildings visible from miles away. Two high-backed chairs are tucked underneath, their seats covered by the crisp table linen draping onto the deep pile carpet. There's an ice bucket stand beside the table. I don't recognise the label on the champagne bottle but the expense surrounding me knows no bounds.

'Champagne?' I say in a small voice I hardly recognise. 'Shouldn't that be for special occasions?'

Reef bounds over to the bottle and begins to open it.

'It's special for me,' he says as a loud pop makes me jump. He pours some champagne and brings over two frothy glasses. Handing one to me, he sits beside me on the sofa so that our knees brush. 'Cheers.'

Our glasses touch softly together, and Reef sips his champagne with Omar Sharif eyes that never leave mine and I down my champagne with gusto and no attempt to savour it. I hold the near empty glass and begin smoothing the skirt of my dress down my thighs in a way I hope isn't suggestive.

'You can't go wrong with champagne,' says Reef. 'I didn't know what you drank, so I thought we could start with this.' He lifts his glass again. I giggle because I don't know what else to say or do. I feel the reality of not having dated in forever in my vocal cords. A physical force renders them inactive, and though my mind cycles a list of topics we could discuss, no voice comes out, not even the action of moving my lips to allow for sound. All I can do is drink. I drain the last of my champagne and Reef leaps off the sofa.

'More?' He already has the bottle in his hand and I've already angled my glass towards him knowing that ending up drunk is the worst thing I can do, especially as I intend to leave straight after the meal.

'I've got menus.' Reef hands one to me and I happily put my champagne glass onto the side table.

'This all looks tasty,' I say. 'What's the food like here?'

'Pretty good.'

It's difficult to concentrate on the list of starters and main courses with Reef regarding me so closely. I can't imagine how many times he must have wined and dined a woman in his hotel suite before.

'I haven't been out with anyone for a while,' Reef says and rests his menu on his knee. 'If truth be told, I'm a bit nervous. I ordered champagne to break the ice a bit and I thought dinner in the room might seem romantic.'

A nervous guffaw gushes from my lips into his face and he blushes.

'Sorry. No,' I say, 'it's very romantic. I love it, I do, but I'm shaking like a leaf. I got myself so worked up about tonight, and on the way here, my dress got creased. I mean, seriously, I didn't know it was possible to suspend yourself above the seat in the back of a taxi for that long. I didn't think my abs would hold out but they did. For a good ten miles. And I don't want to stay the night and I wish I could stop talking so fast and embarrassing myself in front of Reef Mayer. And I'm really sorry I didn't know who you were. I just don't follow football. I'm sorry.'

Reef's eyes have been bright with a smile during my monologue. He takes the menu out of my hand.

'There's a Pizza Express around the corner. Fancy it?'

'Love to,' I say, puffing my cheeks as I exhale.

The rain comes down more heavily as we leave the hotel. There are a couple of photographers at the door, two tired-looking, middle-aged men. Somebody from the hotel must have informed them that Reef was here on a date. I hear one or two clicks of the camera and I turn to see the men vanish into the rain-splashed night. Reef completely ignores them and has his arm around my shoulder as he guides me down a side street of closed shops and open restaurants. Their lights reflect onto the wet ground making the puddles dance with flecks of pale yellow. Water splashes my ankles, it settles in my hair and Reef pulls me towards the door of Pizza Express.

'Table for two?' he asks a moon-faced boy who stares at Reef with his mouth agape. The boy nods, pulls two menus from the glass pocket by the door and wordlessly leads us to a table that is slap bang in the middle of the restaurant. His lips move like a goldfish in a bowl blowing bubbles as he points out a table for two hemmed in by two rather boisterous ones. The rowdy diners are alarmed when they see Reef. They hold up their phones and begin a series of one-sided conversations. 'Is that him?' 'You're joking, right?' 'Low key, that's Reef Mayer.'

'If you've got something a bit quieter...' Reef says.

'Um,' says the boy and takes us to a small table by the window which faces a narrow street of expensive apartment buildings.

'This is great, thanks.' The boy puts the menus on the table, mutters something about a waitress and leaves us to it. Reef offers me a chair and I sit in my wet coat before peeling it off at the shoulders and pulling it out from under me, one buttock at a time. Reef gets up, grabs my coat and looks for a coat stand, as do I, but there is none in sight, so he eases the coat onto the back of my chair.

'Right,' I say, looking at familiar pizza names.

'Is this okay?' Reef leans forward.

'Perfect,' I say as a short girl bobs up to the table.

'Any drinks?' She hasn't acknowledged me, only Reef, who nods towards me and asks what I'd like.

'We could share a bottle of red. The house wine looks nice.'

'And some still water,' Reef says.

I ask Reef how the documentary is going and he begins to tell me all about it. The subject is a footballer I've never heard of and Reef is following the course of his intriguing life: the journey starts in his boyhood home in Selly Oak to the playing field where he first scored a goal for the school and on to Birmingham City FC where he scored his first goal against Wolverhampton Wanderers.

This is the waitress's third trip to the table. The first was to deliver the drinks and ask if Reef was ready to order. He'd smiled at her and asked for more time. He was enjoying telling me about filming and what it was like memorising his lines for the "docu". Apparently, there is media speculation about Reef becoming the new manager at Birmingham City FC where they have had a caretaker manager in place since the last one was sacked, but no decisions have been made. He tells me this with his eyes on the small pink flowers in the white vase between us.

'So, what are we having?' The waitress looks at Reef who in turn looks at me, and as the waitress's eyes reluctantly land in my general direction, she gasps and looks at the area slightly above my head. I immediately want to touch my hair but resist the urge. There can only be one reason a person would be alarmed if they saw me with blow-dried hair. It would be because I'd been caught in the rain and the once smooth lines of my blow out are no longer smooth but frizzed up and wiry and weirdly misshapen. How could I have forgotten the fundamentals of straightened hair and precipitation? I lower my eyes and feel the heat travel up my neck, into my face, past my temples and onto my already clammy forehead. I pray that my hair is hiding most of the redness and shame. I ask for a Margherita pizza when I actually always want a La Reine. Reef orders a Sloppy Giuseppe and hands our menus back to the waitress.

'More drinks?'

Reef and I both say no at the same time and I can't bring myself to look up. Just when I thought the evening was picking up and I was finally able to relax. I desperately want to get to a mirror or to find a hat shop but I know everywhere will be closed. The napkin could act as a bandanna but I dare not move a muscle.

'You've gone quiet,' Reef says.

'I'm just... That is...' I look at the pink flowers. 'How bad does my hair look?'

'Oh that! Not too bad, really.'

'If someone says that, it means it is bad. Shit. Sorry. I wanted to look nice. I know I'm no match for–'

'Who? Look, Annie, I'm not looking for a replacement for Noé's mother. I know what they've been saying in the magazines and everything. I saw that thing on TikTok with all the similarities between my exes.'

I'd seen an article myself. A parade of women who all looked like Natalia De Veras: Moroccan mother, Spanish father, her honey-coloured skin and thick black hair, eyes large, her feline charm. I have the whitest skin, I'm shapeless and even my attempts to do something with my hair hasn't come close to Natalia's or any of the other women Reef has been pictured with. The paparazzi had papped us for a total of two seconds when they saw who Reef was with outside the hotel earlier. I wasn't pappable.

Reef leans forward and I still haven't looked up from the vase.

'What about me?' he says. 'Do I need to feel insecure because you've never dated an ex-professional footballer?'

'Who says I haven't?' My eyes slant towards his face and finally I smile at him.

'As long as he didn't play for Man United, that's okay.' He takes both my hands and I sit up fully. Looking around, I catch the reflection of myself in the window beside me. The upper half of my hair is a fuzzy ball and pretty much like a used pan scourer. The rest lies limply down my back and, just like popcorn, each massive wave and curl is getting ready to explode back to its true nature. Wild and crinkly and too big to tuck into my coat on the way out. I make a mental note to myself that rain brings out the Mr Hyde in my hair and to check the weather before attempting a blow-dry.

The waitress places two large plates in front of us and offers Reef some additional black pepper and a grating of Parmesan cheese. He accepts and I say no thank you, although the offer wasn't exactly extended to me. She asks Reef, personally, if there is anything else we need. He looks at me and I say no but she says to Reef, 'Just let me know if you need anything else, okay?' And I say, 'Thank you very much,' and she leaves our table.

Half a tiramisu and a *coppa gelato* later, we're walking aimlessly through puddles and I've forgotten about my hair, my dress and the rude waitress who denied my existence even when I thanked her for her hospitality. She'd asked Reef for an autograph but he said he had a no autograph policy for restaurants as it can get out of hand. He'd winked at me as he paid the bill. I was so glad he'd noticed how she'd tried to freeze me out.

'What would you like to do next?' Reef asks. I picture the king-sized bed I'd spied through the open door of the lounge in Reef's hotel suite.

'It's a long way home for me,' I say. 'I'd better call the taxi company.'

'Really? I thought we could do something. Go for a coffee at least. Do you need to be anywhere tomorrow? It is Sunday.'

'I know but I have masses to do in the house to get ready for the builder.' Among the many things we'd talked about over dinner, I'd told Reef about my plans to do up the house. I'd told him about the fun times Cat and I had had there as young girls. I didn't go into any of Mum's mental health issues, but I did talk about her jazz collection and how I knew the head of hundreds of jazz standards. Reef can't stand jazz.

'I'd better make a start before they come and give me a quote.'

'Ah yes, the big renovation,' Reef says. 'I know a great interior designer who could give you a great price.'

'I think *great* is the operative word. I can't afford the kinds of people you hire, and besides, my house is so small, I'm sure your designer has never had to work on a shoe box before.'

'You're funny.'

'And economical.'

He laughs and then takes my hand.

'Of course, I'll call the taxi for you, we can wait in reception for it, but you have to promise I can see you again.'

'You know where I am, and I'll have to start treatment on your shoulder because I can see it's causing you pain. You really need to watch your posture.'

Reef has disregarded everything I've said and pulls me close so that he can kiss me. He hesitates just before he does and I move my lips towards his so that he will kiss me and stop me rambling on about his shoulder. It's a nice kiss, soft, with lots of film-worthy sighing coming from Reef. When we break away, he looks so happy and I smile back, just as cheerily, and allow him to lead me by the hand, back to the hotel. Reef orders two black coffees from reception as we wait for my car.

On the drive home, I can fully relax into the seat. My appearance no longer matters. I let out a prolonged sigh and settle in for the long journey home.

The traffic in the city has thinned down considerably. I rub condensation from the glass to look out onto tall buildings and shiny black roads as the driver speeds merrily along to the sound of Nat King Cole on the radio.

'Don't mind, do yer?' he says to his mirror.

'Love this song,' I say.

We listen as Nat King Cole sings *Unforgettable*, one of Mum's favourite shower songs. I can't wait to tell her about my date: she'll be happy I've met someone and that he wants to take me out again.

7

Softly, As in a Morning Sunrise

I arrive home by midnight and fall asleep quickly, only to wake up just as quickly so that I can toss and turn and reminisce about my evening with Reef. Of course, I'd love to see him soon, but he has to go to London for work and I probably won't see him until his agent books his next appointment at the practice. I get out of bed and pull on a sweat top. I contemplate the idea of a walk around the block to calm my mind, but the rain from last night still pours down. I watch the shimmering patterns of raindrops down the window pane and remember my shape-shifter hair from the date. Instead, I opt for a cup of hawthorn and chamomile tea.

Sitting on the sofa, I wonder how long Reef and I can maintain a relationship, should one develop. We are polar opposites and so far I've not had a long-term relationship with a man, let alone a long-lasting friendship with anyone. My tea tastes disgusting, but I sip it anyway as I wonder why it is that I can't keep hold of anyone in my life. Is it me? My personality? My appearance? Mum dressed me like a miniature bag lady when I was a child. Baggy clothing with lots of layers as if my body was a travelling wardrobe. I'm pretty sure Mum was trying to bulk me up because I was thin and unhealthy looking back then. She probably thought I'd get bullied at school if they thought I was a wimpy pushover. Most of my clothes were baggy because I had to wear Cat's hand-me-downs. She had been a taller, fuller child than me. She was certainly healthier and more sporty, so I often wore tracksuit bottoms which Mum used to roll up above my T-bar shoes and supermarket trainers. Cat had never once been my exact size. I endured a good ten years of ill-fitting clothes, usually ones that had been mended because Cat was the boisterous type. She had her own gang of boys and climbed and fought on a regular basis. I did a lot to improve my appearance once I had full control of it, but that never made me popular enough for kids to want to stay friends with me. For all I know, Reef could be rethinking the idea of another date. I looked like crap tonight.

At eleven in the morning I wake up in bed and can't remember going up the stairs. I'm woken by the sound of a WhatsApp message which is quickly followed by rapid pounding of the front door. I try to hold on to the diminishing pieces of a dream of me and Reef in a large, all-glass shower unit, warm water rippling down our naked bodies. I reach for my phone and check the message. It's from Bea who is outside with Judith and Rhiannon and they have brought brunch. They'll want to hear all about my date with Reef.

I roll my face into the pillow and can't move but Bea starts calling my name through the letterbox.

As I plod downstairs, zipping a big red fleece up to my neck, I hear Bea saying to the others, 'She is in and she looks terrible.' I open the door as she continues. 'Must have been a good night.'

Their exultant greetings flutter through the corridor as the women make their way to the kitchen. Something in Rhiannon's basket smells heavenly and I thank goodness that she never shows up at my house empty-handed. Bea is buzzing around by the sink with the kettle as I enter the kitchen, asking if I'm going to put the heating on or what, and Judith is washing the kitchen table.

'I'll get some plates,' Rhiannon says, opening the cupboard and knowing exactly where to find what she needs. Which of course is the case, being as she has reorganised my kitchen three times until she was happy with where everything is now kept. 'The bagels will need heating up and what can I serve the juice in?' A rhetorical question, really, as she is already filling a jug with apple juice, a jug she bought for me because she said I needed a jug.

Judith dries the wooden table with paper towels from the roll she arrived with. Then she takes out the pink, paisley tablecloth she also arrived with, flicks it towards the light fixture above the table and lets it flutter onto it before smoothing it flat and tugging at the corners to make sure it absolutely is flat. Bea and Rhiannon immediately begin to cover the tablecloth with a carafe of coffee, a platter of cold meats and sliced cheese, a bowl of fruit, a basket of croissant and pastries, warm bagels, cold butter, a jar of blackcurrant jam, a jar of marmalade and more accoutrements than I've encountered in all my years of dining.

'Wow,' I say. All three are smiling and waiting for me to sit down. I signal to the door with my thumb. 'I just need to…'

'Bum!' Bea exclaims. 'Is he here? I never thought to check.'

'I just–'

'By all means grab some of this and take it upstairs and use it as foreplay,' Bea continues. 'There's nothing quite like morning sex.'

'With morning breath?' asks Rhiannon pulling a face.

'Don't tell me you're a lights out only kind of girl.' Bea rolls her eyes. 'A cup of Listerine by the night stand. Gargle, spit and off you go, if you have to be so prissy.'

'Yes, but–' I say.

'Or you could ask him to join us,' says Bea. 'We really should vet this young man. It's what your mum would want us to do.'

'No, Bea, I just need–'

'Condoms?'

'For goodness' sake,' hisses Judith. 'Will you let her speak?'

'Er, thanks Judith.' I use my small voice. 'No one's here. I'm on my own. I just need the loo.'

Bea tuts and rolls her eyes and signals for me to get a move on. Judith sits with a deep sigh. Rhiannon sits and starts putting bagels onto side plates.

When I return to the kitchen, the room is cosy with warmth from the toaster, the grill, the beginnings of the heating coming to life and the chatter from the table. Someone has put the radio on. It's still set at Mum's favourite station, Smooth FM. I take a seat in front of a plate of two croissants and a bagel. Rhiannon hands me the butter without breaking from her commentary about her daughter-in-law who doesn't know how to cook and orders from Just Eat every other day.

'What do they eat on alternate days?' Judith asks.

'Domino's,' says Rhiannon. 'Except when I've done some cooking for them and taken over a tray of something they can warm up. As well as some broccoli that she can microwave.'

Bea chuckles as she dabs her lips with a serviette. She sits up, puts her elbows on the table, incurring a tut from Judith, and tucks her fists under her chin.

'Right,' she says. 'All the juicy details and don't miss a beat. Start from what you wore in the end.'

'In the end, I wore the silk dress,' I say as I pour myself a coffee. 'Big mistake. *Big* mistake.'

I tell them the story of last night, from creased dresses to haystack hair, from hotel room seduction to plain old pizza. The sparse trees blow wildly in the wind outside and rain beats onto the kitchen window. I eat, more than everyone else even though I'm doing most of the talking, and hours go by as I listen to first date stories from all three women. Rhiannon's first date ended up being her husband. They hadn't rushed down the aisle and it hadn't been love at first sight. No, she'd test-driven a couple of the local lads.

'The grass is always greener when we're young,' she says. 'But in the end, it was always William. Married at nineteen and I haven't regretted my decision, not one bit.' Her round cheeks swell with a blush of pink, blue eyes sparkling while she blinks rapidly a few times.

Bea's first date was when she was fourteen and pretended to the unsuspecting nineteen-year-old that she was sixteen, but Judith interrupts her and I don't get to hear the full story. Judith's first date was a twenty-year-old whose father owned land and hunted foxes. He was also an ex-boyfriend of Bea's.

Bea is desperate to hear about the sexual chemistry on my date and whether Reef kissed me.

'We did kiss,' I say, and just as Bea pulls her chair closer to the table, there is a knock on the door. We all look at each other in bafflement because everyone at the table knows that

61

my only visitors, apart from tradesmen and next door's cat, are all already here.

'I'd better go and see who that is.'

I'd taken my fleece off during brunch so I've only got on my 'Keep Calm and Drink Beer' T-shirt over a pair of saggy leggings. I open the door and immediately go to close it again when I see Reef standing there with a bright look on his face. I use the door as a shield. Last night's wardrobe and hair fiasco was shameful enough but moth-eaten leggings and no make-up is a bridge I'm just not ready to cross. Why isn't he running away? Why isn't he pretending he got the wrong house? Instead, Reef beams at me.

'Sorry, but I can explain,' he says. More beaming. I can't breathe.

In one hand he holds a large, exotic bouquet and in the other, the hand of a small child. I recognise the full black curls, the cute round, sand-coloured face. It's his adoptive son, Noé, smiling up one side of his face with a worried look in his eyes.

8

God Bless the Child

'Noé, this is Annie, and Annie, I'd like you to meet Noé.'

Noé looks up at me with the same almond eyes his mother has, only his are larger, jet black and his eyelashes curl upwards and remind me of the chocolate shavings on a fudge sundae. Reef tries to angle him through the door I'm holding open but still hiding behind. Noé won't budge because he spies the knitters huddled in the kitchen doorway. Reef would have told him he was coming for a visit, I don't suppose he was expecting three women wedged through a door, one of whom is holding half a croissant. Rhiannon steps up.

'Hey, my lovely.' She leans towards Noé. 'Any chance you'd like to help me with some chocolate covered cookies sitting on the table in the kitchen? I don't think we can manage any more and we don't want them to go stale, do we now?'

Noé looks at his dad who gives him an encouraging nod. He releases Reef's hand and moves tentatively through the narrow corridor to join the women in the kitchen.

'Any allergies we need to know about?' Judith says, putting up a hand, stopping the boy in his tracks.

'He can eat or drink anything,' Reef says. 'And he does.'

I close the front door slowly and look down at the bouquet.

'Your knitting group?' Although I'd told Reef about The Monday Afternoon Knitting Circle, I hadn't let on that the women were my only friendship group. I didn't think it did much in the way of impressing him, and Bea had told me that I should be aiming to impress him. I nod and quickly change the subject.

'I thought you were on your way to London this week and you wouldn't be seeing Noé until next weekend.'

'That was the plan.' Reef looks upset now. So far I've only experienced the friendly, happy, sexy Reef, but a shadow has clouded his face and he shakes the bouquet which I'm not sure I should take as he hasn't actually said it's for me.

'Eight o'clock this morning, Natalia turns up at the hotel with Noé and these flowers. The poor kid looked exhausted.' He lowers his voice. 'I don't suppose you know this but she got voted off *I'm A Celebrity Farmer* and her agent quickly landed her a spot in *Dancing On Ice Down Under – Celebrity Special*, so she wants to take off to Paris with her trainer for a month of intense body sculpting before the show is recorded.'

'Oh,' I say, pulling my T-shirt down to my hips, hoping to hide the resulting bulge of a huge brunch. I've not heard of the shows Reef mentions but it doesn't mean they don't exist, no matter how ridiculous they sound.

Natalia was a top model in her twenties. She married an actor I *had* heard of and her career went into decline because she lived constantly in his shadow. I read that she was always being hounded by the press who talked non-stop about her weight gain, hair loss and their subsequent divorce. She'd appeared in an episode of *Oprah* in which she bared all to the eponymous host about how terrible it is to give up your career and ambition for love. She became sick and tired of seeing unappealing shots of herself in national press, and one day she raged at a group of photographers who had not allowed her any space to breathe. 'Honestly,' she had told Oprah. 'What right do they have to judge me when all I do is eat three meals a day, just like everyone else?' Since then, Natalia has written an autobiography, lost two stone in weight and continued to date celebrities, which in itself gave her all the celebrity she needed to start her own diet and nutrition range and to write a cookery book.

Noé was the result of the affair she'd had with the French celebrity dance choreographer, originally from Martinique, a good ten years younger than her. He'd been an absent father which had led to a very public falling out with Natalia whom he'd accused of trying to burn his New York apartment to the ground. She claimed she'd forgotten to take a vegetarian lasagne out of the oven. Reef had adopted Noé after meeting and falling in love with him and Natalia. She declared to the world, well to *Hello* magazine, that at last she had found the love of her life. She appeared at most of his international matches, was approached to be the face for a cosmetic range and reportedly snubbed Victoria Beckham.

Reef won't know I know this. Since not recognising him, I haven't revealed that I'd spent a whole weekend ploughing through all their posts on social media and all the footage I could find on YouTube. It had been the longest, most revelatory weekend of my life.

'So now she's more than happy for me to have full time custody of Noé. She didn't even pack a bag for him, just handed me these flowers, said I was her hero and walked away. I have no idea when she'll be back for him, and when she does, she'll moan non-stop about something I've done wrong and that I don't know how to look after him properly.

Anyway, I called my agent, Jack, as soon as she left. He got me out of next week's recording and they found someone to take my place. Rio Ferdinand is always up for some TV work, especially as he's got a book coming out for Christmas. So … we were driving home and all I'm thinking about is you since last night. I had your address from booking the taxi, so I hope it's all right that we just showed up here. Is it okay? I mean, please don't be angry. I thought you might like to meet the kid.'

Finally, he hands the bouquet to me. I can't help but contemplate the implications of this. Was Reef so taken with me that he decided to introduce his son to me after just one date? I'm not sure I'm ready to be stepmother. I've never even babysat for anyone, not a real child anyway. Only the class gerbil for a week in half term, and that was hard work because gerbils move fast and are deft at breaking out of cages. Reef stands and waits for my answer with a large knot in his handsome brow. How can I tell him that it would have been more sensible to wait until he had got to know me better himself? What if I was a dangerous criminal? I look down at my attire and decide that's the least of his concerns.

'Are you sure you want me to meet him?' I whisper and look down the corridor. There's laughter coming from behind the closed door of the kitchen. 'I mean, so early in our relationship. That is, assuming we're there yet. You know? Are you saying we're at relationship status?'

'I know it's early days but I didn't tell him we were together or anything, just that you were a friend. Besides, if we keep seeing each other, you'd have to meet him at some stage. Don't worry, he's a sweet kid. Down to earth and really, really smart.'

'Oh.'

'Look, I'm sorry to just spring it on you but I know what I want. I want you, Annie, and if you want me, you have to know that I come as part of a package with that gorgeous little boy in there. For all I know, Natalia might decide to give him over to me full time one day.' He tuts and lowers his voice even more. 'She's never there for him. He's with nannies on the weeks she has custody, and who knows, she might run off with an ex-ice skating pro from down under and never come back. Maybe it's time I stop making the shaving gel ads. Stop all the rest of it and just be his dad. Noé needs security. And anyway, you're the closest I've got to normal so you could be a good influence on him.'

I'm normal to him. Just normal. Nothing more than that.

Reef makes his way to the kitchen where Rhiannon has Noé standing on a chair by the sink, holding his chocolate covered fingers under running water while Judith is rubbing his smudged face with a damp, paisley napkin.

Bea is clearing the table but perks up immediately as Reef and I walk through the door.

'So, has Annie mentioned the party, Reef?' she asks and winks heartily at me. I widen my eyes at her from behind Reef and dare her to say another word.

'Party?' Reef turns around to me and I do a quick expression change. I shrug as if Bea is someone I hardly know and has probably lost her mind. I know not of what party she speaks.

'Yes,' Bea pipes up. 'Her best friend is having an engagement party.' Becs Sprigg is not my best friend any more. 'It's in a stately home that does catered events. It's actually not too far from the grounds of your mansion.'

'It's hardly a mansion.' Reef shakes his head.

'Don't be so modest. I googled it when I heard you were moving here. It's huge. How many bedrooms?'

'Just six and then there's the master suite.'

Bea pulls a face not unlike a bawdy madam from a *Carry On* film and I turn crimson with shame. Luckily for me, Judith reaches out a hand to Reef and stops Bea from saying something I will later regret.

'I'm Judith, this is Bea and that is Rhiannon. We're about to leave now. Aren't we, Bea?'

'Oh yes,' Rhiannon chips in. 'Time to go. I'll pop by another time for these bit and bobs.'

Bea is all set to quiz Reef but Judith and Rhiannon take an arm each and, with gentle determination, persuade her to leave the house without another word.

I'm left alone with Reef and his good-looking son who stopped smiling the second the women left the kitchen. I can tell he has doubts about me, so I quickly think to ask if he wants to help me find a vase for the flowers. Presumably, at some stage, he would have seen Reef with other women and his mother has had three other boyfriends since splitting up with Reef. I can't blame him for being wary. I wish to goodness Reef hadn't sprung this on me and I wish even more that I can find a vase, now that I've suggested some flower arranging.

'There,' says Noé, pointing to the large ceramic vase on the top of a shelving unit.

'Oh yes,' I say. 'It's not very pretty but it'll at least be big enough.'

Reef gets the vase down and helps himself to some coffee which he warms up in the microwave. Noé and I set about clearing a space on the table and laying the colourful tropical flowers out. Then I fill the vase with water and Noé follows me back and forth from the sink to the table, looking up at me with soft, friendly eyes. How Natalia managed to find such exotic flowers in early November I have no idea, but she must have planned to buy them in advance of her surprise visit to Reef's hotel. A pity she didn't remember to pack anything for her son. His leather flight jacket is hardly a winter coat and expensive trainers won't do him much good in all this rain and countryside mud.

I help Noé up to a chair so that he can reach the table. He leans against it and lays a small hand on mine as I cut the stems down significantly to fit the vase. He keeps his hand on mine as I carefully arrange each flower.

'You do one yourself, Noé. You don't have to leave it all to me. You look like you could do a much better job.'

He shrugs and continues to allow me to lead the way. Reef grins broadly but leaves us to it. He walks around the kitchen, taking in its flaws. I hope he can look beyond them and I wish I'd employed a builder sooner. None of this is fair. I'm here wearing unflattering nightwear, my hair is all over the place and my house is a wreck. I have a small child closely regarding my every move and looking suspiciously from his father and back to me, as if we're up to something and he is about to be dumped here with me.

As Reef walks by the fridge, he stops to look at the invitation. He reads it with his head at a slant because it has now slipped further down the door and has a jam fingerprint on it.

'Is this the engagement party your friend was talking about?'

'Don't pay any attention to Bea. She loves to stir trouble and I don't think I'm going.'

'Then why did you keep it?' Reef has the invitation in his hand and Noé's eyes bore into the skin on my face.

'I don't know.'

Flowers are entering the vase at a greater rate than before and Noé has given up helping the stems into what is an already full vase.

'It's in three weeks,' Reef says, as if I didn't already have this information. The third of December, the third of December. The date has taunted me. *You don't have anything nice to wear, you don't have a date, you shouldn't bother.* 'I make a very good plus one. I'm always polite and I'll only speak if I'm spoken to.'

We're smirking at each other across the small divide of my kitchen-diner. I can't help but picture the looks I'll get from Zarina and Becs if I arrive with Reef Mayer. It pains me to admit that I'm more intrigued by what people would say about my plus one than I am the party. I'd need a new dress, shoes, accessories, everything. The idea of new clothes and finally having someone I can ask to come with me sparks anticipation in my tummy. So it was worth holding onto that damned invite after all. And now I'm so excited about going to the party, I don't notice that water is seeping from the vase and onto the pink paisley tablecloth.

'Spills,' says Noé and looks at the line of water on his tiny designer jeans where he's been leaning against the table.

'Oops,' I say and lift him down. 'Good thing I've got you here to stop me making such a mess of things.'

He grins up at me with tenderness as I set him down on dry land and an unexplained feeling expands my chest. All I want to do is swoop down and hug the little boy I've only just met. He looked so sad and scared when he arrived, and now I feel as if I've known him forever and I no longer feel awkward about trying to communicate with a small child. How Natalia could live without him for a whole month I have no idea.

'Well, think about it,' says Reef. I'd forgotten he was there. 'If you do decide to go, I'm free that evening. But for now, me and this little guy here' – he stoops to both cuddle and tickle his son – 'we should go and let you have your afternoon back. We've got shopping to do. I'm not organised enough at the house. We need clothes, toys, a football and net in the garden. Don't we, Noé?'

He shouts, 'Yay,' and holds Reef's hand again as they walk towards the front door. I bend down to give Noé a hug and he squeezes my neck very tight.

'This is amazing,' says Reef at the open door. 'Noé never reacts to new people like this. He must really like you but it's easy to see why. You're very likeable, Annie Lambert.'

He leaves a gentle kiss on my cheek before they both depart. I hear a crash in the kitchen and return to find the vase on its side and exotic flowers all over the floor.

9

Bewitched, Bothered and Bewildered

I look out at the garden as I wait for my coffee to brew. I'd spent a sleepless Sunday night, after their visit yesterday, thinking about Reef but in particular, Noé. I imagine if he comes here again, he could kick a ball around out on the grass. It would hardly compare to the acres of land Reef has at his house, but Cat and I had hours of fun, going wild among the tall grass, running, falling, grazing our knees. We climbed trees, planted radishes and all kinds of fruit that grew in irregular shapes and colours. A loud knock on the door shakes me from my reverie.

Anton the builder has arrived to give me a quote for the repair work. He's wearing a thick cable sweater under white, paint-splashed dungarees which has one shoulder strap undone and hanging down. He places a hand on his chest as if he is about to announce himself, the dark brown of his hand contrasting with the white bib of his dungarees. There is a pencil behind his ear, and for a moment, I wonder if he is a real builder or a tall and very good-looking male model posing as a builder. He is nothing like I pictured him. I expected someone older, not as handsome and not as happy to be at my dilapidated door as he apparently is.

'I've come to do an estimate for your repairs?'

I haven't said anything; I might be smiling. I hope I am. Anton's face radiates goodness and a large dose of joy. Is that for his work or is he just being a good salesman? That said, it strikes me that he is unaware of just how sexy he actually is and probably takes his height, build and the contours and features of what can only be described as the perfect face for granted. I'm still staring as he looks up at the front door, probably checking he has the right address.

'Oh, yes, yes. Yes, that's me. I called you. I mean you're expected. I was expecting you.' For some reason, I find myself bowing multiple times as I back up from the door and allow him in. He is trying not to laugh out loud at my unconventional form of greeting. He grins slightly and nods his head just once.

'So, what was it you're looking to do?' His voice is rich and dark, like his skin tone. His sentences are constructed with slow, measured syllables, the sort of voice I could listen to all day. It takes me a while to get my brain in gear before answering. I want to lose myself in his words. His is the deep and positive voice I look for when I'm searching for guided meditation videos on YouTube. Or the sleep meditation guide I love to listen to on relaxation apps.

'Um,' I say, my eyes sweeping the hallway. 'I don't know where we should start.' My gaze leads me to the kitchen door where the smell of coffee gently filters through. 'The kitchen, I suppose.'

I lead the way. Anton follows and pulls a notebook out of the back pocket of his dungarees. He could be an artist the way he is dressed, a painter of watercolours rather than a painter and decorator of houses. Or a sculptor. His hands look masterful, large with long fingers that delicately caress the HB pencil from behind his ear. Not that I'm diminishing his trade or skills, it's just that I think he has talents that lie deeper than his GoDaddy website implies. Yes, I did google him, too.

'Coffee?' I ask.

'Love one, thanks.'

I sit at the table with my hands around my coffee mug, watching Anton pull, poke and examine the door frames, the old kitchen units, the paintwork and the cracked floor tiles. I don't even have to point out what needs fixing. Everything screams decay and I can't help marvelling at how restrained and calm Anton is being. I'd half expected him to see the first room and demand the place be razed to the ground, a monument built in its place with a plaque saying, *It was good while it lasted*.

'Right.' Anton says the word as if it were a measure of melted chocolate dripping from a spoon. 'I'd have to sub-contract out some of the work. I could repair the doors, fix the floor, do the painting. But you'd need a kitchen fitted. Which I could do but I'd suggest a proper fitter.'

'Oh,' I say, taking a look around the kitchen and then down at Anton's coffee on the table which will grow cold before he gets to it. He takes his coffee black with one sugar. That's easy enough to remember. 'Can you look at the rest?'

The cost is going up into the thousands but still within my budget. The rest of the house is in good repair apart from the ceiling in the bathroom and the grotty kitchen which, I suppose, hasn't had any attention since the seventies, long before we ever lived there. Other than that, I'm looking at paint jobs just to freshen and brighten the place up. I'm liking the idea of making the house my own. In some bizarre parallel universe, I hoped Mum would come back and so would Cat, along with her husband and two young children, and we'd all live together happily ever after in our old house. But that is a ridiculous notion because I have to grow up and stop living in the past. I can't slide down the bannister with Cat anymore. We can't have scrabble tournaments at the kitchen table or at the rickety garden table as we did when the weather was nice. Cat and I can't put on plays in the garden or try to grow strawberries and tomatoes that never grow red and juicy like the ones in the supermarket. The three of us will never dance around in the brown and cream living room, listening to Mum's jazz songs or lying on the sofa browsing books and magazines while Mum sits silently in her armchair or entertains us with a scat and encouraging us to dance to bebop music.

The house is all mine and I need to put my own stamp on it and I need Anton to help me with this. Of all the people who could help me transform this old but fine piece of stonework, according to him, it should be Anton.

I remember as we walk into the last room, the one that has been a spare room, a dining room, a junk room, a dance studio (when Cat was in her musical theatre stage) and now my art studio, the look that Bea gave to the knitters as she put Anton's number into my phone. Did she know then that Anton would be the perfect builder for me or did she have other motives? Like trying to matchmake me and Anton. He'd be a great catch for a single girl but I'm not single now. There's Reef. It's clear to me that Reef wants us to be involved. He knows what he wants and goes for it. He wants me and I like that he does. Romantically, that's more than I could have hoped for in this small town. I wonder if Anton is single and try to check for a wedding ring. Then images of Reef and the wonderful Noé come to mind. Anton's marital status no longer matters and I stop trying to fathom out his love life.

'Wow,' Anton says as he walks into the studio. On my easel is one of many sketches of Noé. I'd started them not long after meeting him, and the one still up is the one that holds the most promise. I look at it now and see what I need to do to capture the joyful soul Noé's bright eyes exude. 'You saved the best room until last.'

Anton walks around and looks at the paintings and drawings I have on the floor leaning against shelves, the walls and on an old table. Many are out of sight, covered with dust sheets. These days no one comes into this room apart from me. Bea, Judith and Rhiannon all know not to enter anymore because I'm too shy about my artwork and they are well and truly bored with my self doubt and lack of confidence when it comes to showing my paintings and sketches.

Light beams in through the large window in my studio, which looks onto the back garden. The back of the house has always been the sunniest, whereas the front of the house needs artificial lighting to bring it to life. I suppose that's why Mum, Cat and I spent so much time in the sunny kitchen rather than the rest of the house. Even more reason for the kitchen to look so old compared to everything else – we wore it out. It was our place to huddle, to do homework, to sit and read while Mum cooked up stews and soups for the freezer, supplies for me and Cat when Mum wasn't capable of cooking. I used to draw at the kitchen table. Cat learnt to tap dance on the kitchen tiles and to spin around uncontrollably when she claimed she was practising contemporary ballet wearing a swimsuit and a sarong tied around her tummy. I used to say she looked ridiculous, secretly wishing I had boobs like hers. But she was thirteen and my chest was still as flat as an ironing board.

Mum always said the studio brought her peace and serenity. When I left home, I kept my art materials there and all my old still life drawings, scenic paintings and my experiments with chalks and charcoal. Mum used to bring her tea in here and plug in a CD player so she could sit and listen to jazz standards and dream of touring as a singer with Count Basie and Duke Ellington. I once painted Mum with a lily in her hair, like Lady Day. She has the picture in her living room back in Adelaide.

'Is this you? Did you paint all these?' Anton asks.

I'd forgotten myself, hadn't I? Forgotten that an estimate to repair the house meant all the rooms, my studio included, and that the builder would find themselves having to compliment me on my art or make a comment that would have me sinking into my shell and becoming tongue-tied.

Anton and I had walked around the rest of the house. I'd led him from the kitchen and he'd taken a cursory glance at the dark wood panels and outdated wallpaper in the hallway and marched straight on up the stairs. He had commented on the spokes in the bannister which would all have to go and I'd flashed back to the times Cat and I had played firemen, sliding down to the engine waiting at the foot of the stairs on our way to put out a fire. We'd saved a lot of lives but the banister had obviously taken the brunt of our rescue missions. We were the whirring sirens, we were the firefighters as we slid down in red pyjamas and red jumpers with a black belt strapped around our waists. Cat made us helmets out of card, stapled together with pictures of clouds on the sides for some reason. Maybe they were supposed to be smoke. Then I'd shown Anton the bathroom and bedrooms and he'd made notes I couldn't read upside down. We'd checked out the dour living room which I was considering painting yellow and now we find ourselves in the back room. My studio with all the artwork I'm too embarrassed to let anyone see.

'Guilty,' I say and sigh a weak laugh.

'They're amazing. Wait, should I have heard of you? Are you a famous artist or something?'

'Absolutely not.' An uncontrolled snort leaves my throat and I cough to cover it up. 'It's just a hobby. Completely for my own personal pleasure and no one really gets to see these.'

'I don't get it. I mean you're so talented. If it were me, I'd show them off.'

Here Anton begins to pull apart the stacked up canvasses. He may as well be undressing me because I'm full of shame and want to apologise for not having made more of my naked body. But mainly I feel like a fraud. I only pretend to know what I'm doing when I'm in here. I returned to my passion as an adult. I'd stopped painting in school and decided not to pursue an Art A Level, even though Mum and my art teacher said I could get somewhere. But Becs and Zarina thought art was lame and I'd trusted them since they'd coaxed me out of the bag lady chic and introduced me to fashion, tweezers and Year 13 boys. And while none of those boys particularly cared for my new look, I wasn't lame anymore and I continued to steer clear of mixing watercolours, ceramic paint and anything resembling a paint brush. Doodling on scraps of paper throughout my Physiotherapy BSc at university was all I allowed myself to do. Not once did I glance at an easel. I stuck to keeping up with fashion and it paid off. I had boyfriends at uni, I made new friends. That said, for the whole of my university life, I hadn't managed to find a proper best friend and I hadn't had a romance that lasted longer than eight months. Which is why I eventually returned to art. At least it was something I loved and I knew where I stood with it.

I want Anton to stop looking at my work, but there is something quite sensual about the way he carefully pulls one canvas apart from the pile, holds each with care and attention and looks them over. His brow softens and his eyes hover for several long seconds over each piece. Suddenly, he looks up at me and my cheeks are ablaze with colour. I'm hot and flustered and I wish he'd turn away.

'Annie, I'm not an expert but I love them. All of them. Has anyone looked at these? I mean an art critic or someone?'

I can't stop an outburst of laughter and I simultaneously pull his hands away from the paintings.

'No. Not all. You're right, you're not an expert. So just stick to what you're good at. Give me a quote for fixing up this room.'

He looks abashed but I hadn't meant for this. I just wanted to take the spotlight off me. I don't know how to deal with this kind of praise. I really only paint for my pleasure, I don't search for compliments and it's obvious I really haven't learnt how to take them.

'But wait,' says Anton. 'What are these over here?'

He stomps over to my nighttime scenes of Ross-On-Wye. I've painted these all from memory and started to imagine them as far back as when my insomnia began.

'Oh, don't look at those.' I put my hands to my cheeks.

'Er, too late. I'm sorry. I'll stop. It's just that the images you create are so compelling.'

'Now you sound like an art critic and you're not one, so please just stick to your job.' God, there I go again. I'm telling the builder off as if he is a naughty boy in my classroom when all he wants to do is compliment me. Now he does stop but he looks annoyed. He retrieves his notepad from his back pocket, but this time he says nothing as he continues to assess the small room without looking at any of the artwork. He writes something down, goes to speak but stops for a brief second when he catches the unfinished sketch of Noé again.

'Okay, Annie,' he says without looking at me. Since he arrived, he's made eye contact whenever he says anything at all. I find myself missing his attention. I wish I could be like normal people and just bloody well say thank you when someone offers me praise. 'I'll write you up a quote and have it to you in a few days. That okay?'

'That would be fabulous. Thanks, Anton.'

He's already in the corridor when he announces he'd better get going. He opens the front door and puts the pencil behind his ear. As he turns, he looks directly into my eyes and says absolutely nothing. It isn't a good job to piss off the person working on your house, your car, cooking your food or performing a life-saving operation on you, so I dread to think what Anton's full quote will be.

'Look forward to hearing from you,' I say, smiling so hard to make up for being a twit that I can't straighten my face. 'Perhaps next time you'll get to finish your coffee.'

At last, warmth returns to his face and he shrugs playfully. I know nothing is broken between us. My house will be in safe hands. I've already decided to hire him because of how attentive he seems, not only to me but in the way he has described how he intends to carry out the repairs. There is something comforting about the old, dented, blue van he walks towards. It suits him: unassuming, hard-working and lasting.

10

Ain't Misbehaving

My phone pings with a message, so I roll over, throwing my arm towards my phone on the side table hoping it's a cancellation, only to hit my elbow on the corner edge of the table. Then I remember my phone isn't on the table, it's underneath it. I shoved it there to stop myself watching a stream of related videos after I promised myself to only watch one.

I rub my eyes and roll my upper body towards the floor to retrieve my phone. My hair strokes the carpet and I create a crack between eyelids so that I can read a text message. It's from Anton.

Hey Annie, the numbers for doing up your place, by room, are below. Have a look and tell me what you think. They're as close to accurate as I can be. Never know what can come up once you remove a cupboard or strip a wall. Had a job in Hereford cancelled so can be available as early as next week if you want to go ahead.

If you want this as an email, let me know.

With blurry eyes, I scan the figures he has quoted and they don't seem too outlandish and I don't have to get everything done at once. I reply to say, drop me an email to confirm the quote and please can he start next week.

As soon as I click send, my heart begins to thump against my chest and the image of stubble on Anton's chin wrestles with the image of how strong his shoulders look beneath his cable sweater and I realise I'm squirming under the bedclothes. I finally crawl out of bed to take a shower. It's late.

Between clients, and I had a full list today, Bea sent messages about her impending date and wanted to borrow a few things from me. I was flattered yet bemused. We're talking about a seventy-five-year-old woman of outstanding wealth, having inherited family money and property, not to mention the odd divorce settlement that weighed heavily in her favour. She has a walk-in wardrobe the size of a small museum and I kept texting back asking if there'd been a fire and she'd lost everything. She sent laughing emojis and insisted that my wardrobe suited the occasion, that she was looking for something solemn and no one had as solemn a wardrobe as me.

Not feeling as flattered as I did at the start of our text conversation, I arrive at Bea's house with a holdall of her requests.

'Ah, there you are. Fabulous.' Bea answers the door in a black kimono with a red collar. The intricate outline of a cherry tree with frail branches and dusky pink blossoms are embroidered on the back by someone with a delicate hand and limitless patience. I've seen Bea wearing this before and often wished I could get away with something so elegant and tasteful. The kimono sweeps behind Bea as she makes her way through an airy hall towards the kitchen. Three of the walls are all glass and look out onto a beautifully manicured garden. Bea's house is set back from the road and sits within a generous plot of land. The lawn is vast and immaculate with rambling rose bushes and a fountain and a few concrete sculptures of ballet dancers pirouetting and posing on platforms of stone. It's bare of flowers now and the trees are naked, but it is beautiful all the same. Plants and hedges are cut back and pathways swept clear of fallen leaves.

Bea's kitchen smells of pine, an indication that she had the cleaner in today. In this large kitchen, the most lavish of catered dinner parties have been prepared, with uniformed staff darting between it and the high-ceilinged dining room carrying trays and platters of expensive food. It's been a while since she's entertained so lavishly.

'I've got a pot of tea on the go, if you'd like to join?' Bea's kimono swoops around her body as she turns to look at me. 'Put the bag down, Annie, my darling.' She points towards a cupboard door where I rest the holdall.

'Tea sounds great,' I say and plop onto a stool by the island of the super white kitchen. So white I feel as if I'm in heaven or I'm about to be the subject of a clinical experiment. Bea serves tea in white china and I'm reminded of the wealth she has always been surrounded by. She has a part-time housekeeper, a gardener, a cook and a cleaner. As a child through to the time she left home, Bea's family had live-in staff. I've seen photographs of Bea as a young woman. Like Judith, she's no stranger to the photo album, though hers go way back to when she was a little girl. She has an amazing photograph I'd love to paint of her sitting on the beach with her father. He is sitting in a deck chair on Brighton Beach and she stands holding a leaky, pink bucket in a puffy, candy-striped swimsuit. Her mother took the photographs of a five-year-old Beatrice posing in various angles. Some with hands on hips, some with a finger pointing to the sky, some with head back, arms stretched out behind her as though she could take off and fly. In a later photograph, she stands with school friends holding their thin-framed pushbikes. Bea's hair was mahogany, worn in two thick braids just like the other girls, only Bea sported flame red ribbons on the ends of hers as if she'd just auditioned for *The Wizard Of Oz*. Bea's classic good looks shone through in her photographs, many with each of the four husbands she'd had in her lifetime. Flicking through the pages of Bea's photo albums was like looking through a gallery of fashion and glamour through the years. She was certainly photogenic and as beautiful as a young Elizabeth Taylor. She'd admitted to me once that she would have loved to have become a film actress, but her father, an affluent banker from the city whom she rarely saw growing up, strongly advised against it. Bea grew up in a large house in Surrey but became bored with the countryside and craved a life of parties and friends in London. When she was seventeen, her mother invited the new neighbours for lunch as a welcome to the village. The son, twenty years old and full of life, drove a yellow sports car and wore a cravat. Bea fell in love with him and they eloped to London. A year later, after she'd discovered he was a bore, she returned home to her parents who had moved to a country village near the town of Ross-on-Wye. Her parents packed her off to a secretarial college seconds after her decree nisi arrived in the post: they'd tried in earnest to marry her off to a suitable boy.

Bea always dressed in the latest clothes and posed in every photograph as though she was on a film set. The colourful life she led is evident in her albums. I did notice, however, that Bea hadn't any photographs of Judith's wedding. I'd been secretly wanting to ask Bea about the wedding ever since seeing Judith's photo album, but without a precursor to the subject, I'd always chickened out. I've decided that Bea must have done something terrible to Judith and that Judith won't let it rest, no matter how hard Bea tries to make it up to her. Was it over a man? They had shared at least one boyfriend that I knew of. Perhaps Bea stole one of Judith's suitors away – had an affair. But I'm spiralling again and it isn't any of my business really.

'So, Bea, now can you tell me why you want my solemn clothes and how on earth you think they're going to fit? I can't imagine why you of all people want solemn clothes for a date.'

She laughs until she is drained of sound.

'Oh, bless you.' She leans over to touch my cheek once she has regained control. 'It is a date but the date is at a funeral.'

'What?' I splutter tea onto my chin and mop it with the back of my wrist. 'Firstly, are you trying to tell me my wardrobe is only fit for funerals? And secondly, a funeral isn't a date.'

'Well, it is. Sort of. You remember my really old friend, Bertie? Well, the other week I ran into him coming out of the theatre and we got talking. I keep managing to bump into him lately. He's over from Gibraltar. Spends half the year there, as you know, so he can see his grandkiddies. But he's staying here for Christmas this year, trying to sell off one of his properties. At a loss, I might add, but he can't be doing with the pressure of the upkeep and renting it out.'

I'd met Bertie Lowell-Hughes while out for a meal with Bea. He's retired, ex-air force, very chatty, eyes that sparkle mischievously, a real, old-fashioned gentleman who kissed the back of my hand on first meeting and forgot to release it for a good second or three.

'I can't believe you were asked out on a date to a funeral.'

'Haven't you heard, darling? Funerals are the new hot date.'

'Really?'

'Well, once you get past eighty, the only way you get to go out is because one of your doddery old friends popped their clogs.'

'I can't see it somehow. Not with you. You're too full of life. Besides, you and Bertie are still in your seventies.'

'I don't need reminding. It's his sister who died. The poor girl was only eighty-five and I wanted to pay my respects.'

'So, not a date then.'

Bea picks up our cups and takes them to the counter so that the cleaner can wash them up. She turns with a cheeky smirk and leans across the island like a teenager would.

'I'm trying to make it a date,' she says. 'I've been growing quite fond of Bertie.'

'Isn't he a little on the old side for you?'

'A year and a half older than me but there's life in the old boy yet.' She winks and I picture Bea and the silver-haired Bertie at a rave. I blink the idea away as I try not to giggle.

'But he's only here half the year and what about the guy you were seeing? Christmas jumper guy.'

'I've never been to Gibraltar and I've kicked Mr Passionless to the kerb.'

'Too boring?'

'Too boring, Annie.' She puts her hand on mine. 'He showed such promise at the start.' After having had four husbands, Bea has always maintained that she's not a bad wife, her exes were always to blame, giving one of two reasons for why the marriages ended. Either they were too boring or they were a bully.

Bea claps her hands together. 'Well, come on, honey, let's see what you've brought me.'

Up in Bea's bedroom, she shows me the dress she has chosen for the funeral. It's a heavy, black, crepe wrap dress with long sleeves and a modest opening at the neck. She will pair it with the fine-knit, black shawl I'm lending her and my block-heeled shoes that are a size too big, but she'll wear thick tights and will stuff the toes. Bea exclaims that she never buys "clompy" shoes like mine but that they'll make her look more sympathetic at the funeral. All of her formal shoes have a minimum of a four-inch heel. She's like the seventy-something Carrie Bradshaw of Ross-on-Wye. Rarely seen without heels and never partaking in anything that doesn't require them. Funerals excepted.

Now that Bea has the right outfit to seduce Bertie at the funeral, she sits me on the chaise longue in her bedroom and tells me about the fling she and Bertie had just before he married his fiancée about forty years ago. She inches closer and places a hand on mine.

'What is it, darling? You're either bored or distracted. I doubt it's the former because my and Bertie's fling needed a Parental Advisory Explicit Content sticker slapped onto it, perhaps two. So if you're distracted, can I take it you were thinking about that handsome footballer? He is a catch, isn't he?'

'He is. But don't you think he's a little … I don't know… out of my league?'

Bea leaps up and almost turns an ankle in my shoes.

'Let me get these ridiculous things off.' She sits again and unbuckles the clasp. 'No offence.'

'None taken.' A lie. I really like those shoes.

Bea replaces her hand on mine and gives it a squeeze.

'Now, listen to me,' she says, leaning in close so that I can't look down or away. 'You are a very attractive girl. I'd go so far as to say beautiful. Not only outside but inside, too.' She points a false nail at my heart. It's painted red. 'You're a wonderful and warm person and any man would be lucky to have you.'

'But could you ever see it going anywhere?'

'Who cares, so long as you're having fun?'

I pull my lips into my mouth and break eye contact for a split second.

'Listen,' Bea barks. 'Don't go putting yourself down, Annie. Just go out with Reef, throw caution to the wind and have fun. You're young and you can, so do it. I need someone I can live my life vicariously through. Goodness knows it's late in the day for me to find a footballer to date. Don't start this romance on a negative footing, you never know where it could lead.'

Bea's romances have varied from the love-them-and-leave-them to swoon-worthy tales of elopements and forbidden love. She's passionate and falls in love easily but falls out of it just as effortlessly. But I don't have Bea's knack for going with the flow. I take things too seriously, overanalysing everything. I don't want my love life to be all about flings, nothing serious. In a few years, I'll want to have children, settle down. I don't tell this to Bea who is already moving on to more chapters in the on-and-off relationship she has had with Bertie. They'd met in their late twenties, but Bertie was already at the start of a long engagement to a titled young woman whom Bea says she mustn't talk about. She is a heated ball of excitement, regaling me with stories about parties on a yacht in Henley-on-Thames with Bertie and about a sweaty club in Soho that she and Bertie ended up at on an impromptu trip to London. The next day, they'd both arrived at his sister's wedding in Hereford, their clothes reeking of cigarettes and Bertie without his morning suit but in a pair of tight-fitting, flared trousers he'd bought in Carnaby Street. The very same sister whose funeral she would be attending the next day.

Bea orders a food delivery from the local Thai restaurant and we chat into the evening until my cheeks hurt with laughter. Bea walks me to my Toyota Yaris, rubbing at her arms beneath the silky kimono as she waits for me to start the engine and drive home.

In bed, I toss and turn because I can't get images of Bea trying to seduce Bertie in my shoes out of my head without laughing all over again. I hope she doesn't sprain an ankle. Reef and Noé are also on my mind because Reef had called yesterday to invite me to lunch with him and Noé on Sunday. I'm so nervous about it but I hadn't revealed to Bea how much so after the ticking off she'd given me. And then there's Anton the builder who is starting work on the kitchen on Monday, and I'm embarrassed about having him back in the house now that I've made it awkward for him to say anything about my artwork. My ridiculous shyness made me overreact.

I sit up in bed with a jolt, rubbing my temples and squeezing my brow as if that can stop my mind working overtime. Maybe I should blame Bea's stories for overstimulating my brain. I squash my temples with the heels of my hands. I fling the covers aside, jam my feet into my snow boots, pull on my padded coat and a bobble hat. I close the front door gently behind me, not that I'll disturb anyone, and I trudge down the road in the wee small hours of the morning to nowhere in particular, Mum's voice singing, *How High the Moon* in my head.

11

You Can Depend on Me

Noé sticks to me like glue from the second I arrive for lunch with him and Reef at their sprawling country house deep in the forest. Bea told me all about the house, said it was more of a mansion, or a small palace, especially if you took into account the acres of land surrounding it. She had looked up photographs of the house online, and with a little more digging from a male friend in estate management, she'd found out the breathtakingly steep price tag that went with it.

Reef called me during the week and had put Noé on the line. He told me they'd been doing lots of shopping, all for him. I'd imagined their shopping trip, Reef trying to get his son settled into his new part-time home by kitting out his wardrobe and buying enough toys and games to fill a room wall to wall and from floor to ceiling. I could see Noé cycling around the corridors, bashing into immaculately painted skirting boards and the whole house being redecorated after each bike ride. I wouldn't mind a no-expenses-spared kind of life.

Noé wasn't cycling indoors when I rang the doorbell. Reef had opened the door to a magnificent and highly polished hallway and Noé was on a sparkly hoverboard with enormous wheels. He'd stood balancing on it as they both grinned a warm welcome to me. I'd smiled back in my thick padded coat carrying a Sainsbury's bag for life containing a box of my homemade cranberry cookies. Noé had rotated for several seconds before jumping off, the board whizzing across the wooden floorboards and into an open door. It had smacked into something with a soft thud in much the same way Noé had run into me, leaning his head into my middle and wrapping his arms around my hips. I'd kissed the curls on the top of his head and he'd taken my hand.

'Noé said we should have pizza,' Reef says.

'Lovely,' I say, remembering our meal in Birmingham. 'Pizza is my favourite food.'

The kitchen is silver, pale green and white. It's a large square with glass doors onto a concrete patio. The ceiling window reveals the white and grey of the sky and there is a hint of movement in the clouds, the rain of earlier having left speckles on the glass. Thankfully it has stopped raining. I'd driven through flooded roads. Wide potholes concealed by last night's rain had caught me out when I thought they were just puddles, and the wheels of my little car had taken a bit of a beating.

On the island near the glass doors, there are uncooked pizzas on baking sheets. Reef can cook? There are at least three large pizzas waiting to go into the hot oven that warms the room with a comforting glow. The square dining table is laden with shiny cutlery, bowls of fresh salad and baskets of bread. A bunch of grapes sits in the middle of a silver platter, berries of all kinds surrounding it as do edible flowers, and I start to suspect that Reef has had help here. The dinner plates are big and round with a pale yellow design swirling through them. There is juice in a jug, bottled water, wine glasses and tumblers.

'You and Noé have been busy.' I smile at Reef. Noé holds my hand tightly and it feels hot and tiny in mine.

'We're busted, aren't we?' says Reef. 'Okay, so I had a caterer in but we did choose the toppings, so I hope you like them.'

'I'm sure I will.'

'If you're ready, I can get a couple of these in the oven. Apparently they'll need twelve to fifteen minutes each.'

'Best to start with one,' I say. 'They're enormous. Even I might struggle.'

Noé and I settle at the table and watch a clueless Reef trying to help a sizeable pizza with substantial toppings into the oven. Noé and I play a game of stacking hands on the table and he giggles with chalk white baby teeth, the bottom two incisors having made way for when his permanent ones come in. I move my hands faster and faster and he finds it hard to keep up, chuckling harder all the more.

'Winner,' I shout and he shouts, 'Again!' We continue for several minutes while Reef opens a bottle of white wine and fills our water glasses and a juice glass for Noé. When I can smell the pizza is ready, I watch Reef looking at his phone while he darts around the kitchen in pursuit of something. Oven gloves, I suspect, but he has no clue where anything is. The gloves are dangling from the oven door and I laugh inwardly at what it must be like to be left alone in a house to cope for yourself when you're obviously used to having someone else cook and clean for you since becoming a multi-millionaire.

Reef's beginnings were not humble, as such. His father was management in a building society, now retired, and his mother still runs her own nutritionist practice. He has a married younger brother and they both attended the local high school where Reef achieved average grades before being approached by Aston Villa and encouraged to enter the football academy system. He took five GCSEs while learning the skills that led to his playing centre forward for England for over fifteen years. All of these statistics were easy to obtain online. Reef didn't talk much about his family or upbringing on our date, and come to think about it, our conversations have been pretty shallow. I wonder how much I'll discover beyond the muscles and the man bun. Both he and Noé are sporting those today.

Reef serves the pizza straight from the oven to the table.

'Careful, it's hot,' he says to his son who sits up straight and nods before repeating the caution to me. Reef and I steal a grin between us because Noé sounded just like Reef.

I watch Reef struggle with a shiny, new pizza cutter and desperately try to hold back from offering my services. In the end, the temptation to intervene is too great. Noé is bewildered and Reef can't figure out how to cut in a straight line.

'Do you mind?' I ask, standing.

'Go for it,' he says and hands me the clammy handle of the pizza cutter.

We eat while Noé tells me all about how his daddy has to find a tutor for him because it's not holidays yet and he should be learning more things. A fact that has him screwing up his face because who wants to do school work when you have acres of land to explore on a hoverboard?

'He's always been homeschooled,' says Reef. 'And I've got strict instructions to make sure that continues while Natalia is away.'

'Well, it's not long until the Christmas holiday and then you can play and have fun,' I say to the little boy with tomato sauce on his chin. I wipe it with a serviette.

'And then I have to go back to Mummy,' he says with a sigh. 'I don't know where I'm going to live at Christmas.'

I say nothing but stare at Reef whose cheeks are turning pink.

'Mummy has to decide.' Reef smiles glumly, and I can sense the tension he must have in his relationship with Natalia.

'Mummy's boyfriend is American so maybe I have to go there.'

'Don't worry,' I cheerily say. 'Father Christmas knows where all the children are, so wherever you are, his reindeer will fly there, too.'

Noé puts a well-bitten piece of pizza on the table and rests a greasy hand on mine. 'You know there's no such thing as Father Christmas, Annie, don't you?'

'Oh I do, but I just didn't know what … if …'

His eyes are full of pity as he tilts his head to the side.

'It's okay,' I tell him. 'I do know, I just forgot for a moment. Sorry.'

'Natalia didn't want to fill his head with fantasy and make-believe,' Reef says, looking down at the pizza crust he holds, and it reminds me of big frowning lips. 'I don't know.' He shrugs. 'Children can just be children, can't they?' He's not directing this at me particularly but a dark shadow veils his face. I don't suppose the tooth fairy visited Noé when he lost two of his milk teeth either, but he seems oblivious to it all as he reaches across the table and grabs for his juice glass with oily hands. The glass slips through his fingers and I leap up to save it from tipping over completely. There's juice on the table and I quickly mop this up with one of the fancy serviettes.

'Sorry,' says Noé. 'Sorry.' And his little face collapses inwards as if he's about to cry.

'You don't have to be sorry.' I sit back down and touch his shoulder. 'I can get you another glass and pour you some more if you'd like.'

He pulls his bottom lip over his top one and nods. His eyes aren't watery anymore, his sweetheart shaped lips bending into a grin.

'And is it okay if I don't have to eat salad, too?' he asks me with wide eyes. I look at Reef.

'Mummy says you have to have veggies or salad with every meal, son.' Reef winks at him. 'But this is a special one with Annie here, so you can skip it this time.'

Noé turns his large brown eyes to me.

'I think I'd better have a cucumber slice in case she finds out. Mummy doesn't like daddy's girlfriends and I don't want her to be angry at you.'

I reach over to a salad bowl, pick out a thin cucumber slice and hand it to him.

'There you go. Now we can finish our pizza.'

Noé runs happily along the grass after lunch, the only one of us dressed appropriately for a dank and miserable November afternoon in a bright blue padded jacket. Reef and I amble behind him along one of the many paths in the vast lawns that immediately surround the house. At the back of the house is a covered swimming pool. The pool house is partially surrounded by tumbling hedges and trees that grow tall and close. Cameras in drones aren't likely to get much of a view which might be the point. I wonder if Reef has security guards who might be taking the afternoon off because I'm here. The grounds are covered in clipped grass that goes on for miles in either direction. Not far from the house, I see a pond and possibly a summer house beyond it. Apart from the trees close by, there is a dense wood that maps the boundary of Reef's estate. He must have staff. Ground staff, a team of maintenance people and a housekeeper at the very least. I should be keeping every detail of this visit in my mind because Bea will quiz me about everything, but the reality is that I'm so taken with little Noé that all I do is focus on him. A feeling of warmth and joy swells my heart as I watch him and Reef playing with a remote operated plane which they drop in favour of a football lying on the grass. Reef weaves around his son's legs, dribbling the ball before grabbing Noé up and tumbling on the wet grass with him. I'm sure Natalia would have something to say about this. Noé doesn't care that his jacket is growing damp, he laughs hysterically and calls out to me.

'Save me, Annie!'

Reef sits up and looks directly into my eyes as I stoop beside them.

'Well?' Reef's voice has a huskiness that makes me blush. 'You like to be tickled?'

Before I can say anything, Noé jumps on top of me and I roll over onto my back. His fingers find my neck, my most ticklish spot, and I cry with laughter. Reef sits on the grass beside me and places a hand on my waist. His eyes are a deep well of emotions, and though I find it hard to read them all, there's tenderness and admiration in his eyes. Noé's spiky little fingers tickling my neck distract me and I look away from Reef. I grab Noé and roll him on to his back and tickle him as enthusiastically. His little body convulses with fits of laughter. When an uncontrollable rush of coughing erupts from him, I stop, my heart fast and out of rhythm as I pray I haven't brought on a fit or something.

'Come here you.' Reef brings his son to sit on his knee. 'Slow it down, just breathe, okay?'

Noé nods and sucks in air in a practised way. The coughs and splutters slow and subside completely.

'You okay, son?' Reef leans his face close to Noé and I frame this image in my mind. It's the perfect pose for a painting or a quick sketch if only I had my charcoals with me. I don't suppose it's a good time to ask if they would ever sit for me, and I haven't told Reef about my art or the fact that I'm already using little Noé as the subject for my next piece.

'Is that asthma?' I ask. 'Are you all right now?'

Noé leaps onto my lap and presses his face in my neck so that he's buried in my hair.

'He had it as a baby and grew out of it, but he has a few of these coughing fits now and again,' Reef tells me. 'He doesn't need an inhaler but he shouldn't get too carried away.'

I bite my lip.

'It's all right, Annie,' Reef says, gently. 'You weren't to know, and look at him, he's perfectly fine.'

'It is quite cold,' I say, still worried enough to want to call out a paediatrician for a second opinion. 'Maybe we should head indoors and get warm. I – er, did make some cookies and maybe –' I can't finish the sentence as Noé has burrowed his way out of my hair, his arms around my neck and his beautiful face so close to mine. His smile says, 'bring on the cookies', so I glance at Reef to check it's all right.

'Cookies?' says Reef. 'What do you say, bud?'

'Yes, please.' The missing teeth in Noé's smile only make him that much more adorable and I give him a squeeze.

'Let's go then.'

We walk back to the house.

'We probably all need a change of clothes,' says Reef.

I look down at the wet patches on my knees, feel the damp and dew on my seat, my hair and my jumper. I help Noé out of his jacket and Reef leads the way upstairs. Noé's teeth chatter as he bounces up the stairs beside me holding the banister and my hand.

'Go on, big man, you change your trousers and I'll find something for Annie to wear.'

In his bedroom, an enormous room with a king-sized bed and a mint and mahogany colour scheme, Reef pulls off his wet sweater and throws it on the bed. He has a skin-tight top on underneath. He pulls open a drawer and hands me a charcoal grey sweat top and bottoms.

'These will probably be enormous on you but you can roll up the sleeves.' He shrugs and goes to pull out a pair of navy joggers for himself and leaves the room. 'I'll see what the boy is up to and meet you downstairs.'

Once I've changed, I look into the mirrored doors of the tall, wide wardrobe and I'm transported back in time. Annie, the kid in her too big hand-me-downs, messy, wild-girl hair. Twerpy Annie, the Charity Shop Girl. I roll the cuffs of the jogging bottoms up several times so that they reach my ankles and look a bit like harem pants and fold the sweat top cuffs up to my wrists. I wonder if Reef had known childhood Annie he'd have teased me as much as the other children? I try to flatten my hair. Reef has seen me with mad hair, a yellow scrunchy and a crumpled dress, and yet he still seems keen. It must mean he's serious about wanting me in his life. Introducing me to Noé so early on has to be a sign that he sees something other than looks in me. Maybe he's fed up with the glamorous women; maybe this is going somewhere.

Downstairs, I'm grateful for the underfloor heating. Noé skids towards me in his socks on the kitchen floor, shouting my name before he drags me over to the Sainsbury's bag with the cookies.

'You look so cute in that.' Reef smiles. He walks up to me and strokes my hair before kissing my forehead.

From the table in the hallway, I hear Reef's phone vibrating and he disappears. Between us, Noé and I arrange cookies onto a plate. I push the uneaten pizza to one side and I pour him some milk. I can hear Reef in the background asking whoever he's speaking to if they're bloody joking. While Noé sits swinging his legs at the dining table and taking alternating bites from the cookies he holds in each hand, I brew some coffee and wait for Reef to return.

'Not too many of those,' Reef says to Noé when he comes back to the kitchen with a red face. 'Ah coffee, brilliant.'

'Everything okay?' I ask as I place mugs of coffee onto the table.

Reef steals a brief look in his son's direction. Noé is oblivious to the tension Reef emits, and the look of anger in his eyes, I'm ashamed to say, only makes him more sexy.

'That documentary I did in Birmingham, they need some overdubbing and to re-shoot one of the scenes. They want me to come now. That was Jack on the phone.'

'But it's Sunday.'

'They have a deadline for final edits. I tried to tell him I was … that we were … plus I've got Noé.' Noé's broad grin when he hears his name is full of delight and cookie dough.

'I could stay and look after him.' I can't stop the urge to want to help. Reef looks so lost and it occurs to me that not only does Natalia have to leave her son for her work, so does Reef, and my heart breaks for Noé. If he were mine, I wouldn't leave him for a second, but I'm not a celebrity mum, or any kind of mum, so who am I to judge? 'I'd be happy to.'

'You sure? I mean I could take him with but somehow I think he'd rather hang out with you.' Reef leans forward, his elbows on the table, the bite of anger completely vanished now. 'Just like I do. We need more of this.'

The temptation to touch his face is too much, but out of the side of my eye, I see Noé reaching for another cookie and I know Natalia will not approve. Even two might have been over the daily recommended dose.

'Not so fast,' I say, smiling at him. 'Let's stick to two for now and maybe we can find something to do while Daddy has to go out for a few hours.'

Noé and I watch Reef leave the house with a suit bag and a holdall, and from the window in the lounge, we watch him slowly drive away in his Mercedes.

Lunch evolves into a kitchen tidying party. Later, when Reef still isn't back, we make sandwiches and watch cartoons on an enormous screen in the TV room. When Noé can no longer sit still, we start an indoor game of chase and then hide and seek. Now I can't find Noé in any of the many large rooms in the house, either upstairs or downstairs. I start looking for secret passages in the library and the games room. As I call his name, I'm practically in tears. Try as I might, my self control is spiralling. Where is he? Has he gone outside, hiding in the vast grounds? It's already dark. Just before I burst into tears and call Reef to tell him that I've managed to lose his son, I notice a little socked foot poking out from behind the weighty curtains in the formal dining room. I pull the curtain aside and see Noé curled up like a contended, sleeping kitten. He lets out a blissful yawn as his thumb slips out of his mouth.

I carry him up to his bedroom, lay him on top of his blankets and curl up beside him, sniffing his coconut milk hair, my arm across his tiny body. I feel myself easing into sleep and, as with every night, I hope this is the night I will sleep until a reasonable time in the morning.

It's late, almost midnight when I hear my mobile vibrating and ringing from a place too far for me to reach. Where is my phone and is this a dream? Something soft stirs beside me and whispers my name.

'Annie? Is something ringing?'

'It's my phone. It must be Daddy.'

Noé follows me, eyes squinting in the half-light as we trot out onto the landing, and the phone stops ringing. With Noé as my shadow, I pad down the stairs and feel for my phone in my coat pocket. There are a couple of missed calls from Reef and I return his call immediately.

'Sorry, it's late,' he breathes and sounds as if he's out in the open. There are voices around him. I hear a car door close and an engine start up.

'You driving home now?' I ask.

He sucks in air and lowers his voice.

'It's just that Jack has set up this meeting. Arranged it because he'd forgotten I had Noé, the idiot. I did tell him I can't do anything until I sort out a sitter or something. So, anyway, one of the directors at Birmingham City collared Jack, wants a sit down to discuss my decision about the manager's job. The owners are taking me to breakfast. Jack told them I would be here in the city. A bit sneaky of him but they need a decision.'

'What will you say?' I don't have to be a football aficionado to know it would be a brilliant career move for him. A chance to plant some roots and the possibility of making history by turning the whole club around and getting back into the Premier League. The owners would probably up their offer because they really want Reef.

'I seriously don't know. I love the idea and it's a great time in my life to do something like this.' He lowers his voice even more. 'But to be honest, all I really want is to see you, see where this goes. And, of course, the job has to fit in with Noé and what his mum has planned. Is he okay? Sleeping?'

'He's right here. Can you tell him you won't be back tonight?'

I hand Noé the phone and it pains me to see his hopeful expression and the way it falls when he realises what's happening. Up to that point, he'd made himself giddy reaching up to speak to his Daddy. I can hear Reef sounding bright and cheerful on the other end and saying something about way past bedtime. Noé hands me back the phone with doleful puppy dog eyes.

'Again,' Reef says to me, 'I'm so sorry to do this to you.'

'We'll be just fine. I'll see you after the meeting.'

As I hang up, I visualise the bookings in my work calendar. I have at least three clients in the morning and I have no idea what time to expect Reef the next day. I look down at little Noé.

'Is he coming back, Annie? Because they always go and leave me.'

I crouch in front of him. 'Of course he will, Noé. We should get you into your pyjamas, shouldn't we?'

*

103

The early morning hours, while it's still dark outside, have me cradled into the tranquillity of their arms but sleep evades me. My mind won't allow these arms to lull me to sleep. I lie on top of the duvet in one of the guest bedrooms with the lamp on. The house rests peacefully in the depths of the countryside under a black sky where the occasional star sparks and dims and planets, unknown to me, blink momentarily. I see them all. I just can't sleep. Then, from somewhere in the house, I hear a noise that makes my heart stop for a second. It can't be Reef. I steel myself to leave the room, looking for something heavy to throw at whoever is running around the house, opening and closing doors.

I peer over the balcony down to the ground floor to see Noé darting out of the television room and into the kitchen. There are one or two lights on downstairs but most of the rooms are in darkness which makes me think he might be sleepwalking. Or sleep-running. I run down the stairs quietly.

'Noé,' I whisper, just before he heads to the front door. 'What are you doing?'

He looks wild and wired, his curls bubbling around his tearful face.

'Is Daddy coming soon?'

It's as though the whole conversation about Reef being here the next day hadn't happened. He must have forgotten since falling asleep after our crackers and hot chocolate supper.

The poor child, he has probably run the whole length, breadth and depth of the house looking for his dad and was on his way to look for him outside.

'Come here,' I say, kneeling in front of him. 'Remember, Daddy has a meeting to go to and he'll come home after. It's not that long to wait, so let's try to sleep. When it's light out, I want to have a go on your hoverboard because I think I could be pretty good on it. If not, could you teach me?'

He nods deeply and allows me to take his hand and lead him up to his bed. I do what Mum does to help me sleep. I sing to Noé. My voice isn't as good as Mum's but I remember the words to *Dream a Little Dream of Me* and then *I Only Have Eyes for You* until he finally drops off to sleep.

Noé sleeps peacefully as I lie, peacefully, beside him. I realise I know more about this little boy than the father I'm supposed to be dating.

12

Me and My Shadow

There's nothing in the house that I can tempt Noé with for breakfast. Not even pizza is an option or my offer to make cinnamon whirls. I found the recipe online in my desperation to tempt him to eat. It's pretty obvious he's missing Reef though he hasn't said as much. He's said very little apart from, no, I don't like it or no, I don't want it.

Nothing in the whole of this sprawling kitchen is of any use to Noé, and I'm losing the plot because I haven't had a shot of coffee, I have appointments I need to cancel and I'm supposed to let Anton in to start work on the house. I quickly shoot him a text and try to put him off until Tuesday saying that I'll pay for his hours. He replies saying Tuesday it is and don't worry about the money.

'I've got it,' I say at last to the hangry child who has his forehead against the patio windows. He turns and leaves a greasy smudge there. 'If there's absolutely nothing here you fancy, how about we go and pay a visit to Rhiannon? Remember her? She was my friend you met last Sunday.'

'The lady with cookies?'

'That's the one. She has a café full of cookies and lovely things to eat. We can go there now.'

He shrugs an "okay then". His mouth turns down while I zip up his padded jacket, pull the door closed and lead the way to my car. At the end of the drive and on the other side of the tall gate, I see a cluster of cars and people chatting away casually. Noé is bolstered up on a cushion in the passenger seat. He has a seatbelt around him but I'm probably violating child car seat laws. I slow down when I get to the security keypad, but I don't open the gate because whoever these people are, they are so close to the iron rails they're bound to lose teeth if I tap in the code. I get out and walk up to the gate.

'Excuse me,' I say to the two people closest. I see they have cameras and I realise they are hoping to snap photos of Reef, possibly Noé. 'I need to get out so I'll have to ask you to move.'

'S'all right, love. We were told Reef Mayer has a new girlfriend from around here so…'

'So you want her picture?'

They look into the car at Noé who is peering out at them with big eyes. They barely look at me in my thick coat, no make-up and hair piled into a tall haystack on my head.

'S'all right,' the same guy says to the others. 'It's just the nanny. Move back.'

'Thanks,' I say. 'Really kind of you.'

'No worries, mate.'

Now it's clear that I'm not paparazzi worthy, I drive away. I *am* Reef's girlfriend, I want to say to the photographers who have their backs to me and are lighting cigarettes. I can't fight the feeling that Reef's urgency to have me as his girlfriend could be because I'm not flashy, glamorous or famous and probably useful because I won't draw media attention. I'm feeling decidedly plain and decidedly uninteresting. I look in the car mirror and attempt to make my hair sit better but I'll hit a pothole if I carry on. I glance quickly at Noé to make sure he hasn't slid off the cushion after the last bend in the windy road to town. He stares up at me curiously with a finger wedged up his nose. He promptly pulls it out and says, 'Eugh. What do I do with this?'

Having a child wave a slimy bogey in your face when you're not your most confident self and you've never been asked to deal with a bogey crisis in you life is not easy. I don't want him to think I'm disgusted, though I'm trying not to wretch.

'Put it out the window,' I say calmly as I wind along a wet country road. 'I'll open it.' But Noé has already attempted to put it out of the window while the window is closed and the bogey, still on his finger, smears its way upwards as the window lowers. He leans forward trying to free his finger of it, depositing the remainder on the top of the open window. He sits back with a satisfied smile. Who would think that a small, babyish button nose could contain the snot of a group of grown men?

'Well done,' I say, patting his head. 'Here.' I lean down to grab a tissue from the well at the foot of the gear box, eyes on the road. We begin to near the town centre and I park as far from the practice as possible and hurry Noé down to Rhiannon's so I can start to cancel my clients. It's such short notice everyone will be angry with me.

It's fairly busy at Rhiannon's and she's serving a customer as we arrive. It doesn't stop her being welcoming and cheery.

'This is a lovely surprise. Sit yourselves down, my lovelies, I'll be there just now.' She turns back to her customer as Noé and I make our way to a table near the back. Someone is humming in the kitchen. The tables are laid with menus, salt and pepper shakers and tiny vases of primroses. Classic FM is playing in the background and the smell of breakfast cooking makes me light-headed.

'What do you think you'd like?' I ask Noé as we sit down and I hand him a menu. 'You can have anything that is breakfast and isn't too sugary.'

Noé looks at the man opposite us reading his phone while devouring a sausage sandwich that leaks tomato sauce onto his knuckles and then back at me. We make a telepathic pact. This is the breakfast we both want.

Just then, Rhiannon comes over to give us an official welcome, which means a squeeze of my shoulders and a patting down of my hair before grabbing Noé's cheeks with both hands.

'You are just so precious, I could eat you.'

He pulls a face at me and we both giggle.

'What brings you here this morning?' Rhiannon asks me.

'We had a hard time choosing something from the breakfast menu at home so we thought we'd do something different. The sausage buttie looks good so we'll have two, please.' I wink at Noé and he concurs with a rapid nod of the head, sending his unkempt curls into orbit around his crown of hair.

'Coming up, my lovelies.' Rhiannon can't resist giving Noé an extra tweak of his cheeks and a kiss of his curls. She looks at me curiously so that Noé can't see.

'I'll tell all at knitting later,' I say.

I get on with the business of cancelling my clients and trying to rearrange bookings while Noé happily creates a scene involving a dog and a little boy, using the salt and pepper cellars from the table. The little boy, who is the salt cellar, is so pleased to have got a dog, the pepper grinder, for his birthday and is allowed to take him to all the places he stays with his mum and dad in the various parts of the globe that his parents have houses. I pretend not to listen in on his conversation but I recognise this as his story. Next I text Amira to say I won't be in, and then I text Reef to tell him that Noé and I will be hanging out at my place after breakfast. He doesn't reply, but whenever he turns up, I hope it's before knitting club as I have a lot to discuss with the ladies.

13

Taking a Chance on Love

At the window in Rhiannon's Eatery, I sit and chat merrily away to the Monday Afternoon Knitters about what I should wear to Becs Sprigg's engagement party. I'm also unravelling the beanie hat I've hardly touched since last week. They're excited for me to have finally decided to go to the party, Bea more so because I'll be going with an A-list celebrity. I try to play down this fact as I'm nervous enough as it is. Under the watchful eye of Judith, I wind the yarn that was the start of my hat back onto the spool. It's crinkly as it's being unravelled for a second time and is a darker shade than the rest of the ball.

It was Noé who'd reminded me and Reef about the engagement party. He'd been staring at the strawberry magnet for the longest of times, calling out the letters of the spirally wording while Reef and I talked about his meeting with the owners of the football club. He'd promised to have a decision to them by the end of the week. He said it was a massive decision that he didn't want to rush into.

He'd arrived at the door with a package containing a remote control truck for Noé, smelling of aftershave and wearing a suit that looked nothing like the one he'd packed the day before. His thigh touched my knee as he sat very close, apologising for leaving me in the lurch and thanking me, as he clasped my hand, for being such a wonderful person. Noé, in his excitement, completely forgetting how much he'd been pining over Reef, had leapt up, grabbed his father's hand and led him out to the garden to try out the truck, discovering after frantically pressing the buttons of the controller that Reef had forgotten about batteries. So instead, Noé had introduced him to Rosie the cat from next door who had slunk over earlier and stayed put in the seat of a rickety garden chair, obviously curious about my house guest. Having got bored very quickly by the A-lister, the cat dashed home, so Noé took the opportunity to proudly lead Reef to my studio to show him the sketch I had started of him. The one I'd drawn from memory and intended to paint at some stage. Reef had looked at me in disbelief.

'You never told me you were an artist. Like proper.'

'Well, not proper, not really.'

'Annie, these are seriously good.'

I'd blushed fuchsia and ushered them out, diverting the conversation to football of all topics because I knew Reef would take up the mantel. Within seconds, he'd forgotten about my studio and was talking tactics regarding the match on Saturday between West Ham United and his old team, Aston Villa. The claret and blues had met again and he was surprised he hadn't been asked on to *Match of the Day* to discuss the old rivalry. He was convinced that Gary Lineker had it in for him after a loose comment he'd made about the BBC presenter and which he hadn't meant anything by. My eyes had glazed somewhat and that's when Noé had brought up the party.

'Of course,' Reef had said. 'It's soon. Looking forward to that. Are you?'

'I am, but have you got a sitter for…?' I signalled over to his son who was then resting his chin on his elbows on the kitchen table as we spoke.

'I'd better look up an agency. Oh, and I need a tutor too, don't I?' Reef took his lack of organisation regarding his son's care arrangements in his stride.

'I can find a local person to look after Noé,' I'd said, looking at the boy whose eyes were growing large as it dawned on him he was going to be left with someone else. I'd thought of Rhiannon straight away.

I'm unravelling wool as I relay this to the Monday Afternoon Knitters and Rhiannon is more than happy to look after Noé.

'For goodness' sake.' Judith has grown tired of seeing me dismantle what could have been a very nice beanie under her guidance. 'What do you think you're doing? Giving up on that hat again?'

'On this, yes,' I say. 'But I've got a new idea in mind.'

I produce a printout of a knitting pattern from online and hold it up to them. The three pairs of glasses are adjusted. No one speaks as they look at the happy child in a multicoloured cardigan holding hands with a man in a matching sweater.

'See, I was thinking about knitting something for Noé,' I enthuse. 'It would be a wonderful achievement but I'd need a lot of help. It doesn't have to be exactly like this. A jumper, instead of a cardigan. I've got experience of those.' I move on quickly before anyone mentions the shapeless pile of rubbish I'd knitted last winter. 'I want it to be Fair Isle, I want to learn cable stitch, I want buttons at the shoulder, I want it to look professional and it has to be a perfect fit.'

113

'That's a tall order, Annie.' Judith purses her lips. She peers at me over her glasses for a full minute of quiet contemplation trying to establish whether my faculties are in place, but this doesn't put me off one bit.

I hold up the printout to them again because they need to appreciate how happy the boy in the picture is. No one is knitting, no one is talking, all eyes are on me in the stillness of the coffee shop.

'Looks lovely.' Rhiannon's dulcet voice initiates the shuffling of bums on seats and the clacking of needles. 'More tea, anyone.' She leaves the table and quickly starts another brew, though no one has finished the cup of Earl Grey she poured a second ago.

'Okay,' says Bea, 'before Judith tells you that this could take you years to accomplish, I'm just going to say, you'd be better off going for a colourful scarf. It's quite an achievement changing yarn in the middle of a piece. Why not start there and see how you go?'

'Because I think this would really suit him.' I look at the little boy in the pattern again. He looks just like Noé. He even has dimples like the cute one Noé has on the side of his chin. 'I thought, you know, row by row, you guys could help me.'

'And when did you want to present this masterpiece to little Noé?' Judith's fingers are a blur as the wool whisks around the tips of her knitting needles. She doesn't drop a stitch.

'Christmas?' I say in a humble tone.

'Which?' Judith stops knitting. 'You mean the one in five weeks or a future one?'

'Okay, forget it,' I say.

'Why ask for the moon...?' Bea says sympathetically. 'He'd probably be much happier with a computer game or something like that. A thing he can hold, drop or break but that he can do something with.'

'All right. I understand.' I look at the unravelled wool on my lap and begin to cast the stitches back on.

'So now that's all decided, let's determine when we're going to go shopping for your party dress,' says Bea.

'Yes, please, that'll be great. I'll check the diary to see how I can fit it in around patients.' The stitches are growing on my needle, looking rough and loose. I suppose if it doesn't fit as a hat, I could always make it into a tea cosy, or something.

'Fabulous,' says Bea. 'I'm an expert shopper as you know. Let me know when you want to go. I'll come over first thing and order us a taxi. We can do lunch. You know Reef is going to look like a catwalk model so you've got to keep up.'

Rhiannon has set out more tea and some toasted scones with butter and jam condiments alongside them. I ignore my knitting for a scone and Bea frowns. I know she expects me to starve myself down two dress sizes before we go clothes shopping but there's no chance of that happening.

'I was wondering,' Rhiannon says in her timid voice, the one she uses when she has a serious question to ask but doesn't want to upset anybody, 'I thought it was rather strange, Reef leaving you with his little boy like that. It's either very trusting of him or a bit...'

'A bit like he's taking you for granted.' Judith drops her knitting onto her lap again. 'I'm glad someone brought it up, Rhiannon. You have to be on your guard with these people.'

'What do you know about *these* people?' Bea exclaims. 'You've never moved in the same circles as the stinking rich and famous. You gave your life to one man, and when he passed away, you went with him.'

I have never seen Bea this riled up, nor Judith so tongue-tied.

'Ladies, please.' Rhiannon has her hands up and uses the voice she orders people around with. 'I was asking Annie a question. An important one.' She turns to me. 'I just don't want you rushing into anything. We promised your mum we'd watch out for you, but if you think I'm overstepping the mark, then you just say so.' She stares hard at Judith and Bea, both as cool and still as mannequins since they'd snapped at each other about Judith's late husband. The tension bears down and my mind whirs with the sound of past conversations between these two, the mystery of Bea almost missing Judith's wedding, the fact Bea doesn't have a keepsake of the wedding and how she could speak so coldly about Judith's dead husband. I feel the oppressive air fill my lungs and I can't exhale it because the questions would stream out with them: *What is it with you two? How can you stare at each other like that?* I don't want this to be the day everything blows up, not when I'm feeling this happy about my future. I want the three of these ladies to be a part of that future and I can't imagine them apart. I swallow and timidly raise a hand.

'Look, all of you,' I say. 'I understand your concern but I'm loving being in their company. Noé has brought that old house to life and I'm really looking forward to the party now that I have Reef. And I do, sort of, have him. He wants to get serious and what's wrong with that? He's a really good person and you should see him with Noé, it's incredible to

116

watch. I don't feel as if I'm being used. I'm enjoying this, all of it.'

'Of course you are, darling.' Bea angles her body away from Judith and towards me. Her face warms with a smile. 'And you should jolly well carry on enjoying it, you lucky girl.'

Judith tuts and gets back to the baby dress she is knitting. 'As long as you're happy, that's all I care about.'

'And I'm more than happy to babysit!' Rhiannon hands the plate with my half-eaten scone to me. 'I've got my grandchildren that weekend. The parents are going to the theatre so Talulah and Billy are staying over. Noé is more than welcome.'

'That'll be amazing,' I say, feeling the excitement for the party returning. 'At least he knows you and he really likes you a lot. Thanks, Rhiannon.'

'It's my pleasure.'

'So,' says Bea, taking her knitting up again. 'With little Noé tucked away safely and my expertise in shopping for a dress sorted, this is shaping up to be a wonderful night out for you. Now then, are you sure I can't come to the party?'

14

I've Got You Under My Skin

I'd left Rhiannon's Eatery on a high, but the friction between Bea and Judith niggled and gnawed away as I crawled into bed after midnight, only to be awake again just before three in the morning. I'd reached for my phone to see how many hours of sleep I'd managed. Having given up on the idea of falling back to sleep, I went trudging out into the wintry darkness to walk, count sheep, count my blessings, summon sleep – a coma would do – and managed an hour or so back in my chilly living room after a mug of chamomile tea and a biscuit. I'd come across Dez and Phoenix who had been in the doorway of Sainsbury's inside the precinct and had stopped for a chat. Dez was still awake and had sat up when he'd heard me on the slope down from the car park.

'Annie Mac?' he'd said. His voice gravelly with concern. 'Do I really have to tell you again that you shouldn't be out here?'

Phoenix's long body was sprawled flat on a piece of cardboard. He'd opened one eye and sat up before burrowing his nose into my gloved hand. We'd chatted, just for a few moments, before Dez sent me packing, telling me it was lovely to see me but to hurry home. I had done, but had dallied as I got close to Judith's house.

After my shower, Anton arrives. It's good to see his bright face and wide smile as he passes me in the corridor. In his heavy, dusty work bag, I spot scrapers, boxes and metal things that look like instruments of torture. He also has a big, yellow toolbox with him that bumps my knee.

'Oh, sorry, Annie.'

'It's okay and sorry I had to put you off yesterday. Something came up and someone needed my help.'

Anton stops to look back at me.

'Sounds mysterious.'

'Oh, my life has no mystery at the moment.'

'No? Seems a shame. We all need a bit of mystery in our lives.'

I follow him into my kitchen where he drops his tools with a clomping sound onto the old tiles.

'I thought I'd start with measuring up the windows, then we can get those on order,' he says, looking up at them from the middle of the room. 'I'll start making good the walls in here while we wait for those and then I'll hire a window fitter.'

'Of course. I'm leaving it up to you.'

I'd cleared and packed away all the things I could. All the everyday things you leave around thinking you'll come back to soon, only to find them still sitting there a few days on, untouched and not required for the foreseeable. Like clothes brushes, nail kits, a bottle of bleach, a sweater you needed when the evening became chillier and you were watching television long past bedtime. A magazine you'd seen something interesting in but hadn't time to read, and later you wonder why you thought it was so important in the first place. I'd even tidied away Becs' invitation. Now that I knew it was all confirmed, I'd moved it to a drawer in the kitchen and thrown the magnet in with it.

'I have to go to work now,' I say. 'I haven't got my knitting circle after so I won't be back too late. What do I do? Leave you a key?'

Anton tries not to smile too heartily as he says, '*Knitting* circle? *You*?'

'What's wrong with knitting circles and what's wrong with me being in one?'

'I don't know. I thought it was for, like, older people?'

'Not everyone who knits is old, and knitting circles aren't for old people, just people who like to knit.'

'Fair enough. Sorry.' He stumbles on his words. 'I just hadn't imagined you as a knitter.'

'You've been imagining me?' Now I want to smile.

'Well, yeah. Of course. Ever since I saw the paintings I'm not supposed to talk about, or the fact you have a natural flair for art.' He breaks eye contact to check out his work boots now that he has touched on the taboo. 'But I couldn't help wondering how a person can be so talented and be so humble at the same time. If I was that good, I'd be bigging myself up.'

I sigh. It sounds like I'm bored with hearing this from everybody, but I'm not. And I'm not bored hearing it from Anton, I just don't know what I can say that won't come across as tetchy and sensitive just because compliments like his embarrass me. I want to dissolve the building tension in the room, but all I can do is stare down at Anton's work boots, too.

'So where's work and what is it you do?' He gives me one of his killer smiles. The atmosphere immediately lightens.

'Here in Ross. I'm a physiotherapist.'

The lines on his brow twists.

'What's wrong with physiotherapy?' I exclaim.

120

'No, nothing. It's just, I thought you'd be a curator in an art gallery or an art teacher or something … something…'

'Something better than a physiotherapist?' I pick my lunch box up from the table. Leftover pasta and two apples.

'Sorry, I didn't mean to annoy you again.' He looks at my lunch this time, my eyes probably too full of fury for him to handle this early in the morning. He's already annoyed me by going on about my knitting, now he's criticising my job. I like him, he has a good nature, a nice smile, but he seems to get under my skin with his observations about my life. A life he knows nothing about, mind you. And so what if I have no mysteries? That's none of his business.

'I can let myself out.' He fiddles with his fingers in the awkward silence.

'What?' I sigh. 'You don't have to leave because you don't approve of my job. I still want the house redecorated.'

'And it will be. But I'm not leaving right now. You asked about leaving a key. I'm just saying I'll let myself out at the end of the day.'

'Oh.' I shuffle my feet and hitch the lunch box onto my jutting hip. Now he has the cheek to check out my hips. I can tell he is. 'Fine, then. Let yourself out.'

'I will.'

Anton will be around for several weeks. He won't be finished before Christmas and might be here until the new year. I just hope he can keep himself to himself and stop getting on my nerves. At the front door, I stop to put my lunch into my bag and grab my coat. I turn to see Anton with his back to me, peeling off his heavy jacket. I do up the buttons on my coat and feel for my scarf on the hook, my eyes still on Anton. I wrap my scarf a million times around my neck and watch Anton rummaging in his dusty bag. Bent

121

over, his jeans cling and contours appear. When he stands and turns my way, I blink several times and look around my feet as if I've lost something.

'You off?' he says.

'Yes.' It comes out in a snap that isn't intentional.

'Of course you are. You said.'

'Yes, well, see you later. Or not. If you're still here. How many hours do you do? Sorry, wait, I didn't mean that to sound like that. I think I'll be home by six. You can help yourself to anything. Tea, lunch, whatever. There isn't much or perhaps you brought lunch.'

'I did but I'll help myself to coffee or something if that's okay.'

'Oh, yes, yes of course.' If I could nod any more enthusiastically my head would roll off. I open the front door and leave Anton to it. He doesn't know whether to smile or wave or just say see you later. He does a half-hearted version of each at once. I slam the door as I leave and have no idea why. My builder thinks I'm prickly, easily annoyed and bad tempered. That's a great start to a relationship that will last right through the winter.

15

Prelude to a Kiss

It's Thursday evening. I haven't seen Reef since Monday and I'm fiercely missing Noé. His cute little button nose is right there on the canvas in front of me. I stand observing the sketched outline of the boy looking up from the milk white background of the canvas, his large eyes gazing softly into mine and the gentle curve of his cupid mouth. His smile is tentative, the way it was the first day I met him, but now I know how close we are and how I've grown to love him. I have to make this come across in the final painting. The only colour so far is on the T-shirt he wears. His curls look shiny and as full and bouncy as I could make them. I'm struggling to find the right blend for his skin tone. It has to be just right. Clear honey and soft sand mixed together and it has to glow.

A gentle tap on the studio door breaks my concentration.

'Annie, er, sorry. I'm finishing up now.'

I open the door to find Anton holding his hands together and backing away into the dark corridor.

'You're going?' I ask. I close the studio door behind me. 'Did you fancy a tea or anything before you set off?'

'Wouldn't mind a coffee.' Anton follows me to the kitchen where he has done a great job of clearing away his mess, though the taste of dust hangs in the air and the feel of it on every surface will linger even after I've wiped it away. He's straightening up my tumbledown kitchen: plastering,

123

smoothing, sanding, taking tiles off and making good. In only a few days, a lot has changed and my new windows will be arriving soon.

'You sure you want coffee?' I ask while filling the kettle. 'It's a bit late, isn't it?' He's smiling as I turn. 'What?'

'Oh nothing,' he says, pulling up a seat at the kitchen table which has newspaper covering it.

'No, tell me.' I sit opposite.

'It's us.' He chuckles. 'I think we got off to a bad start. I know I should have minded my own business about your art studio, but it just seems as if...'

'Go on.'

'Well, we seem to be rubbing each other up the wrong way somehow.' He holds up his hands. 'Maybe I'm reading this wrong but I get the feeling I annoy you.'

I look down and shake my head. The kettle clicks but I ignore it.

'You don't annoy me. I annoy myself. I've been told about this. My mum, my sister, they say I don't know how to take a compliment. Especially when it comes to my paintings.' I can feel my cheeks heating up but I have to come clean with Anton.

'I guess that explains a lot. I didn't pick up on that. Sorry. I wouldn't have kept going on about it if I'd known. I genuinely thought I'd turned you against me or something.'

It's quiet as both of us look around the kitchen. I'm sensing he's searching for something to say, the same way I am.

'No, of course you haven't,' I finally say after leaving him thinking the worst.

'Thank God for that,' says Anton. 'By the way, the reason I'm having coffee is because I need to stay up late.'

'You have a second job?'

'No, it's not work. It's my mum. She's not been doing too well and I'm staying at hers tonight. The nurse won't be there so…'

'That's really good of you.'

'Well, it's Mum, you know? She was always there for us. Brought me and my sister up on her own. She's, *was*, a nurse back in the day, so you can imagine what it was like, trying to raise two kids on a nurse's salary. It was tough for her.'

There's another silence as Anton looks over at the kettle and then down at his hands, long fingers clasped in an arch, resting on newspaper. From his demeanour, I can tell he and his family struggled a lot and I feel compelled to tell him more about mine. Something about Anton makes me want to reveal more of myself in a way I can't with Reef. At least not so far.

'My mum didn't have it easy, either,' I say looking at his hands. They fold on the table and he gives his full attention. 'She raised the two of us, me and my sister, on her own, too, and she was living with a … well, a mental illness.'

'I'm sorry. So did that mean you and your sister had to look after her?'

'A bit, yes.' I put my head down, trying not to tear up as I remember those years. My earliest memory is of me aged two when my father died after a recurrence of throat cancer. For years later, on the anniversary of his death, Mum was her most withdrawn. She didn't make any sound, but the tears fell so fast she ran out of them while Cat and I hugged each other on the living room sofa. I'm not sure I understood what was happening when my Dad died. I felt sadness but I cried because Cat did, and she told me to do it quietly so Mum wouldn't be doubly sad. As we grew older, on the anniversary of Dad's death or whenever Mum was lost to us, we'd climb into the grand old oak in the garden, sitting among branches that cradled us like hugs. We'd sit in the tree and eat crisps. Cat would tell me her ambitions. They'd change frequently from teacher to astronaut and from tree surgeon to prime minister. As teenagers, we often had to call the library to make excuses for Mum being off work. Sometimes we sat her in the kitchen so she could watch us learning how to bake casseroles, playing her jazz music at full volume, singing all the words we knew.

'Coffee,' I exclaim. 'Sorry. Forgot.' Anton must be wondering where my mind has crept off to and how bad things must have been for us. I don't want that. 'Coming right up. Instant okay?' I'm whizzing around trying not to delay him. 'Unless you just want to shoot off.'

'I've got a minute or two, don't panic.'

'I'm not. I'm just… Oh, I'm snapping at you again. Why do I do that?' I remember how he drinks his coffee and place a hot, black, steaming cup in front of him and a sachet of Stevia. 'I stole this from work because I forgot to buy sugar and I knew you took it in your coffee and I was aware that you would have had to drink bitter coffee this week and that wasn't fair. I should have been more thoughtful.'

'Don't beat yourself up, Annie? I shouldn't take so much anyway, my teeth will rot. Just chill.'

'I know. Another of my failings. You've caught me out again. Can't take a compliment. Wound up. Can't sleep.'

'Yeah, I noticed the sleep brews you have in the cupboard. What's all that about?'

'I'm a bad sleeper, that's all.'

'Do the teas help?'

I sigh a short laugh. 'Not in the slightest. I've wasted so much time and money trying to find ways to fall sleep or

126

stay asleep. I've tried sleep routines until they came out of my ears. In a way, I've resigned myself to my insomnia, but yet as soon as I notice a new sleep app or a magazine article, I'm back on the case. I go to bed late and wake up far too early, hours before I need to get up, and then I can't drift off again.'

'That's an overactive mind, isn't it?'

I look down at the empty space in front of me. I've forgotten to make myself a cup of tea.

'Something like that.' I look over my shoulder at my sleep cupboard.

'So, do you go into your studio? Paint? Draw? When you can't sleep?'

'That just makes me more awake and I don't usually feel inspired to create much when I wake up in the early hours. I'm usually fed up and too exhausted to hold a paintbrush.'

'There must be an answer. I suppose you've already tried sorting out the things that are on your mind and keeping you awake.'

'That's just it. I can't exactly nail anything down. It's all just one huge jumble in there and I don't know where to start.'

'Start with one thing.' He shuffles closer to the edge of his chair. 'No matter how small. When something pops into your mind, grab it and face it and tell it to leave you alone. Or you let go of it.' He takes a few gulps of his coffee and puts the mug down. 'I must sound like an idiot. You've probably tried this before and I'm probably winding you up again.'

He isn't, actually. I can tell he cares.

'I walk,' I say simply.

'Sleepwalk?' I like the way his frown lines come together on his forehead.

'No, I mean I go out and walk. Sometimes, when I can't sleep, I get up, put my coat on and walk.'

'You mean like in the dead of night?' His eyes are nearly out of his head. 'I don't like the idea of that. I hate to think what could … I mean, Ross isn't exactly a crime hotspot but even so. Can't you just watch TV or read a book?'

I can't help grinning at his concern for my safety.

'It's not funny, Annie.'

'I'm not laughing. It's nice that you care about me, my not being able to sleep, I mean. Seriously, not being able to sleep, or stay asleep, is the bane of my life. I just got so desperate in the end I developed a hatred for nighttime, pyjamas, my bed, even scented candles. It was like I needed an escape from the whole idea of sleep. So I decided to walk. I don't know, I thought if I could convince myself that sleep didn't matter, that I didn't need a whole night of it, then I wouldn't get so worked up and just fall fast asleep.'

Anton leans his elbows on the table.

'I can't imagine what it must be like to be sleepless.'

'Sleepless. That's a good way to describe it. I never liked the word insomnia. Sounds too medical and disease-like. Anyway, I don't go out walking so often as I did. It worries Mum and I don't want that.'

'Of course your mum is worried. I am, too.'

We both pause at that, my cheeks glow and Anton's eyes dart sideways.

'I suppose your mum must have suggested sleep remedies before,' he says.

'It'll sound ridiculous but I used to call Mum when I couldn't sleep and … and she'd sing to me.'

I can tell this amuses him but he tries not to let on. 'Like lullabies?'

'Jazz standards, actually. She knows them all.'

'You like jazz?'

'Love it. Well, the singers and big bands, some modern stuff too.'

'Your mum has good taste. Speaking of…'

Anton chugs down the rest of his coffee as if it's throwing out time at the pub. He stands, half smiling at me as my eyes follow his large frame to the sink where he runs water into his mug. I leap towards him.

'No, no. You don't have to do that,' I say. 'I'll sort it for you.'

I've grabbed the cup now, by the handle, while Anton's fingers still lace it. He leaves his hand there. I'm holding my breath as he leans his face right down to mine.

'Thanks,' he says softly.

I look into his eyes and feel myself being pulled towards him, moving closer like a magnet to metal. He doesn't move his face and when I look at his lips they are parted, just slightly, but so are mine. And then I notice his eyes. They are smiling and in that moment I believe he is laughing, mocking me. I must look ridiculous. I straighten and draw away.

'What's wrong?' he asks.

'I thought … I mean, I … I'm supposed to be seeing someone. Going out with. Dating. A guy.'

Anton stands upright.

'You don't sound too sure about it.'

Now we let go of the mug. It tumbles and rolls across the metal surface of the sink. We watch it and turn to each other.

'It's new,' I say. 'I've been on one date. Well, two, I suppose.'

As I speak, Anton backs away from the sink, moves over to his work bag and pulls at the zip. It won't fasten because it's overfilled with his tools and equipment. He grabs the yellow toolbox from its position outside the kitchen and I follow him to the front door. He turns and shakes his head.

'That was weird,' he says. 'We went from bickering to having a nice conversation and then…'

'I'm sorry, I don't know what happened. I shouldn't be kissing you of all people.'

'Thanks a lot,' he exclaims but grins broadly to show he's not put out. I shake my head, inwardly chastising myself for my choice of words.

'I suppose I'll see you tomorrow,' I say and unlatch the door for him.

'Sure. See you tomorrow, Annie. I hope you can sleep a little longer tonight. Enough for you not to want to go out for a walk in the dark at least.'

I pull my lips in and nod as he leaves and I softly close the door. I have a feeling I'll not be able to sleep at all. Not when all I can think about is the kiss that almost happened.

16

Night and Day

Anton kneels on the kitchen floor, digging away and pulling up the antiquated tiles with a metal tool and his bare fingers. The noise this makes sounds awful and feels as if he is ripping pages out of the story my family wrote within this very kitchen: the time Cat taught me to tap dance with silver buttons superglued to my plimsolls; the time she stomped from one end of the kitchen to another when Mum said she couldn't go to Ann Beckett's sixteenth birthday party because there were too many big boys going and Ann's parents wouldn't be home; the time Mum danced and sang '*S Wonderful.* She moved like Audrey Hepburn dancing with Fred Astaire after she and I had just watched him singing that song in *Funny Face.*

Anton's work is noticeably louder than Mum's old CD player which he has on, a Sarah Vaughan album turned up full, making the speakers tremble with distortion. Anton had sniffed at the battered and aged CD player earlier but not at the takeaway meal I'd brought home for us to share.

'You can't play Sarah in this thing. It's pre-war. It'll ruin it.'

'Don't be such a snob. It works fine.' I'd reeled kitchen paper off the holder for us to use as napkins. 'I know it's old but Mum was keen to leave it, and some of her music, to keep me company.'

'Company or a bloody racket,' he'd said, looking for a non-existent equaliser to adjust the sound with when the player has only on/off, play/stop and volume controls.

Supper was nice. We'd sat quietly, neither mentioning the night before. I'd asked about his mother and discovered she had a heart condition that the doctors could do very little about apart from prescribing drugs and ordering her to get plenty of rest. She'd had to take early retirement from Hereford Hospital where she'd worked as a specialist nurse practitioner for fifteen years. She'd been a nurse for over thirty years. Anton's eyes had glistened with sadness when he'd talked about her and the fact that she never ranked any higher in her career and would have loved to have done. I could tell he loves his mum.

Now, as I sit in the living room, pretending to read a book, I listen to the ripping up of floor tiles, Anton's puffs and sighs and his occasional expletives when the tiles won't come up as they should, and I'm hoping he's being careful and won't hurt himself.

The phone rings and I see Reef's number come up. He's been busy for days so I haven't seen or heard anything of him or Noé all week. I'm coming close to finishing my painting of him. I'd mixed together the perfect skin tone and I was happy with the way I'd captured his dimple. When I felt overwhelmed by the painting process, I sketched a picture of Noé from one I'd taken of him in the garden when he last visited. Noé sat cross-legged on the grass and Rosie was sprawled over his thighs looking like a huge fluffy cushion, one that purred and whose ears twitched towards me, warning me not to come too close. Noé was the one she wanted to hang out with.

When I answer the phone and say hello to Reef, I hear Noé chuckling and telling me in a giddy voice that it's him and not Daddy speaking.

'I can tell,' I say with a laughter in my voice. 'How have you been?'

'I don't know,' he says as if he's singing a line from a nursery line. Reef says something in the background. 'I'm fine, Annie.'

'Good. I'm glad to hear it. What have you been up to?'

'I don't know. Well, getting a teacher and getting pizza. Can you come to my house, please?' He holds the 'ea' in please as if it's coming out of a long, squeaky tube.

'One day,' I say, aware that Reef hasn't called since Monday and I'm hoping against hope that he won't cancel our date to Becs' engagement party. 'Can I speak to Daddy?'

There's a shuffling sound and I hear Noé squeal at something and his footsteps thudding across the wooden floorboards.

'Hey, you,' Reef breathes down the phone. 'I've missed you. I know it's been less than a week, but still.'

'I sort of have my hands full at the moment, anyway. They've started work on the house.' And by "they" I mean Anton, but I don't want to let Reef know I'm alone with a man in my house. 'And you must've been busy with Noé, right?'

'Tell me about it. I had to find him a tutor. I was getting to it but Natalia called to say she'd arranged interviews and the tutors, who incidentally have to speak Spanish, French as well as English to keep up with his language skills, were all lined up to come here. She gave them interview dates without checking with me, so I had to stay here and sort all that out. I mean, I thought I was on it but turns out I'm dragging my heels.'

'Natalia said that?'

'I know, right? And she not only arranged the interviews with an agency, she also arranged to be a part of them via Zoom. There was Natalia lying on a massage table in her hotel with a physio bloke rubbing her calves, the poor tutor sitting on the edge of the sofa trying to answer Natalia's questions while little Noé had his face up in the camera asking his mum when she's coming home? It was embarrassing. And like you said it's only weeks before regular schools pack up for Christmas holidays. I can't see why she won't let the kid have some time off. Have some fun. I've got practically a whole floor of new toys for Noé to play with. I know what I'd want if I was six years old.'

'Maybe she thinks he needs consistency.'

'Consistency? Consistency would be her staying in one country long enough for him to know where his socks are kept. She has no idea.'

This sounds like a well-worn rant on Reef's part and I don't feel at liberty to comment. I just think that what Noé needs is a routine so he knows which parent he's living with, when and for how long. Not to feel as though he is being left behind all the time. I remember the fat tears rolling down his cheeks, shiny even in the dim hallway, and the despair of being left alone overnight with someone he'd known for two seconds. I swallow my opinion down hard. In the end, it's up to them to decide. I can hear running and playing in the background, Noé telling Reef to make Annie come for pizza and to bring Rosie.

'Hey, Annie, I'm all done here. I'll see you in the morning?' Anton says and ducks out to gather his things.

'Who was that?' says Reef, in a not so casual way.

'My builder,' I say. 'Finished for the day.'

'It's late,' he says. 'It's evening not day.'

'True but he wants to get a head start on tomorrow.'

'So he's there again, tomorrow?'

'Yes. They are.' I feel as though I should protect Reef from knowing that it's just me and Anton.

'Noé keeps asking to see you, so how about we come to you tomorrow night? Bring pizza?'

'Is that our thing, now? Us three and pizza?'

'Well, why not? It's the boy's favourite food at the moment.'

'Um…' I hear the front door close and the house is quiet again. 'Yes, that would be nice. Really nice. We could make our own pizza. I'll make bases and Noé and I … well, the three of us could do the toppings together.'

'That's a brilliant idea.'

'What time will you come?'

'I don't know, five o'clock?'

'Perfect.'

After I end the call, I send a message to Anton asking if tomorrow he could be finished, cleared up and gone by five. He answers in the affirmative and I feel a sense of relief that he and Reef won't run into each other. I haven't done anything seriously wrong. I didn't give in to temptation and kiss Anton and I'm not exactly engaged to be married to Reef. So why do I feel like I'm in the throes of a wild affair?

Gripped by guilt and panic, I have a lavender-scented bath and try to settle my rambling mind by taking deep breaths. After drying off, I put on some fleecy pyjamas, pull all my hair into a pineapple and tie a silk scarf around it. For good measure, I rub lavender on my temples and climb into bed.

After more deep breaths into my stomach and some audible sighing, I try to relax my body for sleep. How much of it or when it will come is anyone's guess. I give up trying after fifteen minutes of pillow pummelling and rolling from side to side to get comfortable. I suspect my pineapple bunch is a mess and my hair probably looks like a bird's nest. I get up. Instead of heading out, I sit up and start a video call to Mum. It takes a while for her to answer, and when she does, Cat is beside her and her two children are running amok in the background.

'Hey Annie,' Cat says. 'You look like Marge Simpson. When are you going to do something about your hair?'

'Thanks Cat, not everyone can be blessed with your perfect hair.'

'Whatever. How are you, sis?'

'Not bad. I can see the children are fine. No school?'

'Teacher's training, so no.' Cat rolls her eyes and doesn't turn to acknowledge her kids, even though one of them is screaming and being chased out of the room by the other who is waving a foam sword.'

'And you're still up, Annie.' Mum pushes her face close to the screen, lines converging into the middle of her forehead. 'No sleep for you again?'

'Just take some drugs,' says Cat, and both she and Mum settle back into her wicker sofa. They look beautiful, dressed for summer, bronzed by the 22°C average temperatures for November. Cat's long hair is plaited in one braid that sits in front of her shoulder. She looks younger than the last time we spoke, fresh, with no make-up and one of her spaghetti straps dipping off her shoulder. Mum wears a floral summer dress of dusky pink and cream. Her thick and wavy hair is mostly grey now and past her collar. There are laughter lines visible along her cheeks and the sides of her eyes. They used to look like worry lines when she was here but Mum seems to be in a much happier place now. Cat messaged me about the great medical care she is having, how good she is at keeping up her medication and how she finally talks about the future in a positive way and looks forward to things at last. One of those is me having a good, long sleep.

'It's fine, Mum. Being up all night is kind of me now. But it might be nice to hear you sing again.'

There is a loud bang from elsewhere in Mum's house. Cat leaps up and runs out through the open door to the kitchen demanding to know what on earth is going on. Mum draws closer and her sunny face fills my screen.

'You look worried, my love,' she says. 'Are the ladies looking after you okay?'

'They're all amazing and they're always there for me.'

'I worry about you. How are the renovations going?'

'Really well. The builder Bea suggested is brilliant, just as she said. I'm definitely in safe hands.'

'That's good to know.' Mum's face freezes for a second as I begin to tell her about Anton really liking my artwork, that we didn't hit it if off at first, but I don't tell her about the almost kiss.

'By the way, Mum,' I say as light and as casually as I can, 'I went on a date.'

'You did?' The picture stutters again and I'm not sure if I've missed her next question. When I see her smiling, I decide it's better to play things down.

'He's nice, good-looking but it's early days.'

'That all sounds positive, darling. Keep me posted, won't you? What's his…'

137

We hear Cat in the background shout at the children. 'Maybe I need to intervene,' says Mum with a sideways smile tugging her cheek. Mum's accent is spread with a heavier helping of Adelaide than it was before, even Cat sounds Australian, but then, with all her theatrical ways, it's what I'd expect of her. She comes back into view now.

'I don't suppose you want me to package my two up and send them over to you for Christmas, do you?' she says as she flops into the sofa and Mum adjusts the position of her phone.

'Only if you can come too. I miss you all.'

'I miss you too, sis, but close your eyes now. Get some sleep. You look old.'

'How did I get to have such a lovely sister?'

'Just luck, I suppose.' She blows a kiss and heads back to her children.

'I love you, Annie,' Mum says. 'But do settle into bed and rest.' Mum looks at her wristwatch. 'It's gone midnight. Put on some music and drift off.'

'Will do.'

Lines appear on the screen and a jagged still of Mum blowing a kiss is the last I see of her. She'll get back to the grandchildren. It must be their lunchtime.

In the YouTube search bar I type *Jazz Music for Sleep* and click play on an eight-hour recording which lifts me into a state of calm. Calm enough to smooth over the cracks left by my sleep demons. And as the sultry tones of a tenor saxophone plays *Until There Was You*, I fall asleep with images of two men moving like clouds through the other thoughts in my mind. I manage three hours of a deep, heavy sleep until I awake in the wee small hours of the morning. Everyone on my side of the world is fast asleep.

17

Smoke Gets In Your Eyes

As if it were the whistle for kick-off at the FA Cup final, Reef knocks on the door promptly at 5.00 p.m. He kisses me gently on the cheek while Noé squeezes my hips and I pat the soft curls of his hair. He lets go and shouts, 'Rosie,' before hotfooting it down the corridor to the kitchen.

'Rosie won't be out today,' I say to Reef as we follow behind. 'It's too cold for her and too dark.'

Reef's fingers find mine and we hold hands, watching Noé's head bob up and down, jumping to see out of the kitchen door window into the shadows.

'What happened to your kitchen?' he exclaims after deciding Rosie isn't worth all the effort.

'I'm having the house decorated,' I say. 'Let me take your coats.'

Noé waits long enough for the sleeves of his puffa jacket to peel away before he scoots out of the kitchen and charges up the corridor to the coat hooks by the front door. Reef hands me his and I hook them next to my padded coat where they hang in a row looking like a family of three out holding hands.

'Okay!' I clap my hands together. 'Let's get this pizza party going.'

'I didn't know it was a party,' Noé exclaims.

Reef takes in the cemented kitchen floor and the work Anton has done trying to level the walls. If this were Reef's house, he'd probably stay in a hotel or go on a long holiday somewhere fabulous while the work was done. I can't imagine he'd have lived in any place where the walls were stripped bare and everything was coated in dust. It had taken me ages to clear it and to clean the kitchen table for us to make pizzas. The bases are already rolled out and I've made a tomato sauce.

'Let's all wash our hands, then,' I say and help Noé wash his. He reaches his hands as far forward towards the running water for us to at least manage to get his fingertips clean.

'I'm just going to watch,' says Reef and puts his hands behind his back. I beckon him over to the sink.

'If you're going to eat, you have to help.'

Noé jets between the sink and the kitchen table singing *Daddy has to help*. I lean my hip against the sink, watching Reef. He pretends to be hard done by as he washes his hands and I pull a face at him. As our smiles grow wider, I'm halted by the image of Anton and me by the kitchen sink, his face drawing closer to mine, his lips parted. I hand the dish towel to Reef and rush to grab Noé and carry him by his underarms back to the kitchen table where the bowl of homemade tomato sauce waits to be spread over the pizza bases.

'Let's start.'

Standing on a kitchen chair, Noé manages to get tomato sauce on the table, his nose and the floor. Some of it lands on the bases and I spread the rest over the thick, elastic-textured dough.

'Right,' I say. 'Next the toppings. Who likes ham?'

We weigh down three thick-crust pizzas with tomato slices, olives, ham, cooked beef and chorizo. Next is the grated cheese. I look at an excited Noé and wonder how much of it will land on the floor, along with some of the toppings, and how much of it will end up on the pizza.

'Maybe we'll ask Daddy to do the cheese,' I say.

'I'm an expert with grated cheese.' Reef chuckles and begins layering it onto the pizzas. I look away from his face and to his hands as I'm remembering again how close I came to kissing Anton and I don't want Reef to see this on my face. He'd sounded jealous yesterday evening when he'd thought I was alone in the house with a builder. I made sure I'd ushered Anton out by four o'clock, just so there'd be no chance of them meeting. I tell myself once more that I haven't done a thing wrong. Nothing physical, just thoughts. If I talk to the ladies from the knitting circle about these thoughts, Bea would advise that I date them both. Rhiannon would sit me down with some thick-cut sandwiches and cream cake to contemplate my feelings over a pot of tea. Maybe I'll talk to Judith separately. Surely she'd be able to guilt-trip me back to having purer thoughts about my builder.

I look at Reef standing back to admire his handiwork, forgetting that this is a millionaire celebrity I have in my broken-down kitchen making pizza with me. He's taking me to the one party I've been to in centuries and I'm only a physiotherapist. No one special, not famous, not anybody. I'm actually very lucky and I should remember that.

I realise Reef is speaking and Noé is patting my shoulder, saying, 'Wake up, Annie.'

I gather my thoughts and place one pizza directly onto the shelf in the oven.

'Can I look for Rosie while it's cooking?' asks Noé.

'I think we should go in the living room and stay warm. That's probably what Rosie's doing now.'

'Can we do painting instead?' Noé asks. He opens his chocolate-coloured eyes wide and, despite my insecurities of what I've got set up on the easel, I give in to him. He leaps into my arms and I stumble back.

'Easy, big man,' says Reef. 'No rough stuff in here.'

'It's fine,' I say, carrying Noé who is clinging so tightly I can only just breathe. 'We have to remember the pizza. We've only got ten minutes to get started on a painting.'

Reef reaches around me to open the studio door. With the picture of Noé facing us as we enter, Reef inhales in shock and Noé swings around to see what the fuss is about.

'It's me!' he shouts and peels away from me, landing to the floor as if he's jumped from a speeding car. He almost knocks down the easel as he gathers his balance to look up at the painting. Reef strolls over to it with his hands in his pockets.

The painted Noé smiles back at us, his dimple having taken me several attempts to recreate. I look down at real Noé now and see I've just about captured it. He looks up at me, delighted.

'Can I have this?' he asks, shyly.

'You hold on a minute,' says Reef. 'It's up to Annie who she gives it to and she might want to keep it.'

'I would like to,' I say. I take a step back to see, after about a million times of staring at it, if I have the proportions accurate in relation to his background. As I made the sketch by memory with a little help from the photos I took of him when I was babysitting, I had to improvise the background, placing Noé in front of the old oak in the garden. I have

142

painted that tree a hundred times so it was easy to fill in the detail by looking at sketches of the tree I'd already made. It's a summer picture with Noé in a T-shirt, jeans and his Converse trainers standing on rich green blades of grass, white daisies growing near the roots of the tree the way they do in actual summer. In my picture, Noé smiles as though he is happy to see me, and I'd love to keep the picture because I know one day he will go back to his mother's house and I won't see him often, or at all, depending on where things go with Reef. The thought of not seeing Noé, to watch his gappy smile fill out and to watch him grow taller than my hip, makes me homesick.

'Maybe I'll paint you a different one,' I say. 'A smaller one you can have in your room.'

'Paint it with Rosie in,' he pleads.

'Well, I sketched a picture from the photo of you with Rosie on your lap. Perhaps I could turn that into a painting.'

'You don't have to do this, Annie,' says Reef. 'Noé, you have to ask Mum first if you can have a painting.'

I remember how exacting Natalia is when it comes to her son. She might not want my amateur artwork on walls that I can only imagine are filled with pictures by famous artists, and if she wants one of Noé, there's no chance she'll ask me to paint it.

'I know,' I say, bending down to talk to Noé, 'why don't we have a go at painting portraits of each other. I've got a folding table stacked up in that corner, I could set it up right here. I've got lots of paper. Afterwards, you can keep yours at Daddy's house so you can see them whenever you want.'

'And you're Daddy's girlfriend now so I can see you whenever I want.'

This seems to please Reef, who grins at me like the cat who got the cream. I, on the other hand, feel as though someone has turned up the heat dial and my cheeks are the hotplate it's connected to. Since meeting Reef, all I've thought about are the "what ifs". What if he is as serious about me as he says he is? What if this is it and finally I have a relationship worthy of an Instagram profile? And then there have been the "I wonder when" times when I wonder when we'll get a chance to kiss again, to sleep together, to take photos for my Instagram feed.

'Okay,' I say snapping a finger and shifting my thoughts back to the here and now. Noé is looking up at me with expectant eyes.

'Reef, could you move those canvasses to the wall next to the door and I'll get the table. Noé, you stand over by the window and make sure I don't bump into anything while I get the table out of the corner.'

I lift the table over my head and Reef takes it from me and rests it on its side in the small space by the door. It's a tight squeeze when we open it and Noé has to sit on a cushion while Reef and I stand, and I get to mixing some old powder paints that were deep inside a cupboard. With Noé's help, we mix the only three powder paints I have left: yellow, blue and black. Next I find us all some paper and we're ready to go.

'I think we've forgotten something,' Reef says suddenly. 'The pizza.'

'Pizza!' Noé and I shout, looking at each other open-mouthed.

I rush out of the room with the two of them close behind. I fling open the kitchen door to find no signs of smoke floating out of the oven and no smell of burnt pizza. We've been lucky.

'Hang on,' says Reef. 'Was the oven actually on?'

With the oven gloves at the ready, I open the oven door.

'Um, no. I forgot about that bit.'

Noé, in fits of giggles, asks if we can still eat it.

'I'll put the oven on now,' I say. 'It'll taste better cooked.'

Noé skips out of the room, still giggling and shouting, 'Okay,' over his shoulder. As I go to follow, Reef takes my hand and spins me to face him.

'I'm off to Paris tomorrow.'

'For work?'

'Natalia wants me to bring Noé back to her. She's missing him.'

'Oh, I see. That makes sense. So you'll miss the party next Saturday.'

'I'll be back in time for that. I'm not staying out there.'

I pull my bottom lip in and try not to pull a face.

'I know,' says Reef. 'I'm sorry, but I'll literally be taking him to see his Mum and more or less coming straight back. Only problem, in true Natalia style, is she wants to rethink the plans for the holidays that she only just made. We'd already decided she was having him for Christmas and he'd spend New Year with me. Now she wants to discuss with Noé what he wants to do and where he wants to be.'

'Of course,' I say, but inside I wonder why she would leave such a big decision to a child.

'But I'll definitely be back for the party.'

And "what if" she misses you too and wants you back? And "what if" I never get to see Noé again?

Reef touches my chin and bends closer to kiss my lips. I don't have to wonder about this anymore. A kiss. At last.

And I don't want it to end. The thought that I might lose him before we've really begun makes me realise I really do feel for him and the Anton thing was just a stupid slip up. I put my arms around Reef's shoulders and he pulls me closer. We stop when a little voice from the corridor is coughing and spluttering and saying, 'Yuck,' over and over again.

We find Noé rubbing his mouth with the back of his sleeve.

'What happened?' I ask, but I can see right away what he's done.

'You're not supposed to drink the paint, kid.' Reef picks him up and carries him over to the sink. Cupping his hand as he holds Noé around his middle he tries to get Noé to gargle and spit, but all that happens is that Noé throws up in the sink.

'Better out than in, right?' Reef tries to make light of it as I hand him a dishcloth. I know what he's thinking – Natalia will kill him. But Noé seems to be all right, his eyes were watery and now they are clear and smiling.

'Paint tastes horrible.' His voice is a whimper but he smiles up at me. 'There's still some left for painting.'

'We shouldn't have left you,' I say.

'He'll be fine,' Reef says, seeing my concern.

We do the best job we can of cleaning Noé up, cleaning his vomit out of the sink before we head back to the studio. Minutes after starting our paintings, I remember the pizza. Well, actually, I smell the pizza and it's burning.

I pull open the oven door, fanning the heat away from my face.

'Anyone like burnt cheese?' I ask, and Noé throws up on the kitchen floor.

18

Desafinado

The Christmas lights have been up in the centre of Ross for weeks now. I missed the ceremony because I'd forgotten about it. I'd got out of the practice of doing anything community based ever since the pandemic. Back then, the town had looked deserted, smiles, if anyone bothered to smile, were hidden behind masks in a town where nods of the head and smiles were de rigueur. I remember the eerie quiet and how I hardly recognised the people who had braved it to the massively long queue outside of Sainsbury's in the hope they might find flour lurking among the empty bottom shelves in the baking aisle. It all seems so long ago now and a bit like a dream until I see the odd person still sporting a mask, albeit one of those scary ones with a drawn on smile on the front.

As I pass Specsavers, Phoenix walks up to me and nuzzles the palm of my hand. His lead is dangling down beside him on the ground. 'Hey, you. What you doing out on your own?'

He looks thinner than usual and he doesn't yelp a greeting. His owner, Dez, walks slowly behind him and greets me with a nod. He isn't wearing a warm hat. The top of Dez's head is bald and his remaining hair is fully grey now, uncombed, long and straggly as usual. His face is drawn, his skin has a greyish hue, the whites of his eyes look yellow.

He is only in his fifties but today he looks as though he's been around for closer to a century. The air is biting, as it has been for weeks, and I want to knit him a hat. I want to tell him he should be wearing one at least but he doesn't look as if he is connected to his surroundings today. He looks disoriented, not grounded, not part of the town.

'Annie Oakley, how are you?' His greeting, usually bright and cheerful, is flat and forced and all my fears about him living on the street and not getting proper health care weighs heavily on me.

'Oh, you know, same old same old. Is everything okay, Dez?'

'All's good, babes. Just been doing a bit of Christmas shopping.' He holds up a blue plastic bag from the late night grocery shop, a few bottles knock together from within it. I wonder if there is anything wholesome in there for him and for Phoenix. I so want to take him home to feed him but Dez never accepts and I've been close to tears at his stubbornness, so I'm forced to say nothing. I can see by the way he shifts his eyes away and turns his body sideways to me that I can't mention the taboo subject today: he's not in the mood. I can't be too pushy today anyway. My kitchen is not cooking friendly at the moment because of the stage Anton is at and I'll be having dinner with Rhiannon and her husband tonight.

'I haven't even thought about Christmas shopping,' I say instead.

'Gotta go, babes,' Dez says and picks up Phoenix's lead.

They leave me staring at them as they head in the direction of the library. It'll be closed now, and Dez will settle down there in the corner beside the locked glass doors and no one will ask him to move on and no one will offer to take him home for dinner. I keep looking over my shoulder at Dez's lanky outline and Phoenix's slow, thin body as I head towards Rhiannon's Eatery for a session of knitting. I'm greeted by the smell of buttery toast and the coffee that still fills the air from the brews of earlier.

Rhiannon leaps up to greet me, as usual. What is unusual is the deathly quiet coming from the window table of the coffee house. Instead of the clacking of needles and the hum of conversation, usually lead by Bea, knitting needles are propped lifelessly on top of works in progress which sit limply on the laps of fellow knitters, Bea and Judith. Judith sucks hard on an imaginary lemon and stares at Bea. Bea stares back, fake lashes unblinking and lips pursed as equally tight as Judith's.

'What's happened?' I say at the side of my mouth to Rhiannon.

'Nothing, dear, just a little misunderstanding.' She folds my coat over her arm and also stares, at the other two. Green and red from the Christmas lights reflects off the coffee shop windows and tints the white and silver in the women's hair. I wonder why Bea hasn't already smoothed over the situation. She never leaves it long after one of their rows before offering the peace pipe, which in Bea's case would most likely be filled with marijuana.

This is it, I think to myself. *This is the big one, the unresolved history between the two women is about to be revealed. And where else but at one of the knitting circles.* I don't move, apart from stretching my mouth towards Rhiannon so I can whisper down to her.

'What do we do?'

In a loud voice, Rhiannon says, 'Nothing, we do nothing. In fact, if these two are going to carry on like children, then there'll be no knitting today. We pack up early and I'll take you back to mine to get the supper on. I've got peppered salmon waiting for us in the fridge. Some baked potatoes and some broccoli. How does that sound, my pet?'

'Sounds great,' I say, finding it hard to drag my eyes away from the staring contest heating up at the coffee table.

'Well, ladies,' Rhiannon bellows, still holding my coat over her arm. 'What's it to be? Am I locking up or are we knitting?'

Bea and Judith speak simultaneously. One says, 'Locking up,' the other says, 'Knitting,' but I'm not sure who says what.

'I have a good mind to dissolve this knitting club altogether.' Rhiannon, who never speaks much louder than her dulcet Welsh tones will allow, is quite out of breath from raising her voice. But she continues to. 'You can settle this like grown-ups or you're both barred from the group.'

Bea and Judith stop sucking lemons and look at her in indignation. Now they are playing three-way eye ping-pong and I become dizzy trying to work out who is outstaring whom and how they can keep this up without blinking.

'Okay,' I say and sit down. Rhiannon sits, too, with my coat on her lap. 'I'm sure whatever has happened between you both can't be so bad it should end in this … in this sort of animosity. If one of you could just apologise.' I look at Bea.

'Why are you staring at me? I'm not the inflexible one.'

'No one said–'

Before I can finish, Judith and Bea begin a quarrel about holding too tightly to things and choking the life out of everything. The truth is about to land and I don't know if my mediator skills are up to much. What if I learn something I

150

don't want to hear? What if I secretly take sides? I wish so much that Rhiannon wasn't part of the fracas.

'Please,' I say, 'one at a time.' I point to Rhiannon. 'Go.'

'Okay,' she says and clears her throat. 'Bea wants to change the name of our knitting circle and Judith doesn't like the new name.'

What? I think to myself. Is that really all this is about or is it a metaphor for something worse?

'Why do you want to change the name?' I dare to ask.

'Because it's old and it's fuddy-duddy, like some of the members in it.'

'I'm only a year older than you,' hisses Judith. 'And I'm as hip as the best of them.'

'Hip?' exclaims Bea. 'No one says hip these days. What do people say now, Annie?' They all stare at me.

'I'm sorry, I haven't a clue.' They each sigh or puff in exasperation and lean back in their seats. Surely they must have noticed I'm not "hip", "street", "chill" or "calm". Just a dork who wants her seventy-year-old friends to kiss and make up.

'What is the new name, by the way?' I think I might regret asking but it's out now.

'Well, I thought,' Bea says and dramatically picks up her knitting needles, 'that we should call ourselves Spool and the Gang.' She looks at me brightly, urging me to concur.

'Um, like the band?'

'Yes, like the band but obviously not exactly like the band because it's Spool instead of Kool.'

Admittedly, I do like the name, but I can't admit that I do because Judith will be upset the longest. And, look, they've made me take sides.

'Well, you know, if you've been going all these years with one name, why change now? The Monday Afternoon Knitters is a great name. *I* think.'

'There,' Judith says proudly. 'If it ain't broke…'

'Oh whatever.' Bea's knitting needles click rapidly and she huffs every time she wraps the wool around the needle for the next stitch. 'You'd know all about broken things, wouldn't you?'

'Well, I've put up with you all this time.' Judith huffs and proceeds to knit with vigour.

'Is that it?' asks Rhiannon. 'Are we okay again, ladies?'

Bea and Judith look at each other just briefly and something passes between them, the unknown truth behind their occasional tiffs and spats. I don't suppose I'll ever find it out but I can feel stories of their past playing out between them via their extrasensory link. I have to hold my breath because it really is a lot, the silent exchanges between them. I steal a look at Rhiannon, but she rises quickly from where she is perched on the edge of her chair.

'I'll get you some tea, pet,' she says, not looking at me once. 'You must be gasping.'

I open my mouth to speak but nothing comes out. Before I leave the circle after knitting another three rows of my beanie hat, I am still none the wiser but I know three things: Whatever they are harbouring, it is big, they definitely don't want me to know and I'd do anything I could to help them resolve the problem.

*

Rhiannon and I drive in silence back to her house. She swallows loudly, blinking through the large glasses she

152

wears for driving but leaning close to the windscreen as if the glasses are not helping at all. I look at her periodically, expecting her to say something about earlier. For a woman who is generally so chatty, it must pain her not to be able to make a single comment about the history between Bea and Judith, but she's obviously been sworn to secrecy. I've yet to earn my place of trust and be allowed to know what on earth has happened. Mum swears blind she has no idea what I'm talking about. In the years she'd been a member of the knitting group, she never once cottoned on that something was awry about their set up. I put that down to Mum having so many secret worries of her own that she couldn't have noticed what I'd sensed not long after joining the Monday Afternoon Knitters.

Rhiannon parks in front of her garage door and leads me straight to her large kitchen at the back of the house. She calls something out in Welsh to her husband, William, who answers in Welsh. I hear them mention my name and Rhiannon's husband calls, '*Noswaith dda,*' to me, which I understand so I call, 'Good evening!' back to him.

'Right,' says Rhiannon. 'Peppered salmon here we come. I'll microwave the jacket potato if that's okay. It's fast and I'm guessing you must be hungry.'

'Well, you know me.'

I watch Rhiannon whizz around her kitchen in an apron with hundreds of apples printed on it that I didn't notice her put on. She moves her cuddly form in a fast and efficient whirr of white curls and apples. I go to ask if I can help set the table, but before I can finish the question, Rhiannon has set three places as if she'd whipped out a magic tablecloth already laid for a party of three. The broccoli is on the boil, and before I know it, she's calling William in to join us at the table.

'You sit yourself down, my pet. You need food down you. You look thin.'

'I'm hardly thin,' I say, but I do as I'm told.

'I told your mother that I'd make sure you ate well and looked after yourself. It wouldn't harm you to put on a few pounds.'

I'm pretty sure Bea would have something to say about gaining extra pounds before Becs' engagement party. I'd made a date for our shopping trip this coming Saturday, the actual day of the party. Rhiannon places a plate of peppered salmon, broccoli and a massive jacket potato dripping with butter, without having asked if I wanted butter, in front of me. She has halved another potato to share with William who doesn't stand on ceremony but tucks in straight away. For pudding, there is apple crumble and custard. *Hello size sixteen.*

It isn't until I'm helping Rhiannon with the dishes after dinner and I can hear William snoring in the living room that I dare to ask her about Bea and Judith.

'I know you don't want to mention what happened earlier, Rhi, but I wondered if perhaps some mediation could help them move forward. There's obviously something going on behind all the smiles and jokes we share on Monday nights. And I know they both meet up regularly during the week. They've been best friends since they were what? Seventeen? Eighteen? It would be a shame if they were to fall out now.'

'I do my best to keep out of it,' Rhiannon says, handing me a dripping wet dinner plate. 'They're old enough to keep a good lid on things to stop it all blowing up.'

'Maybe, but tonight things got so heated I didn't know what to do with myself.'

'You did just fine.'

'Sure,' I say, drying the forks. 'But that lid can't stay closed on top of a boiling pot.'

'Seriously, my pet.' Rhiannon stops washing up and turns to face me. 'There's a lot under that lid and you're best off out of it. Only know it's to do with a man. It goes back a long way and the women say they've made peace with it.'

'Well, that's not true.'

Rhiannon puts a wet Marigold finger to her lips. 'You know I can't say a word and it kills me to know what passed between those two. Do yourself a favour and don't bring it up. If they want you to know, it's up to them to tell. All right, my lovely?'

'All right.' I put a finger to my lips and smile.

Rhiannon chats merrily as she drives me home. She has packed a Tupperware container with a portion of apple crumble in it. I've sat with it on my knee and Rhiannon has told me of several ways I can enjoy it the following evening after dinner. I nod as if I'm listening but my mind is still on Judith and Bea.

It's cold and quiet as I let myself in. Anton would have left ages ago. There's a familiar smell of dust and the house has an air of a place that's lived in rather than a quiet cavern I come home to each night. It's as if he's still here, Anton, and I can hear him in the kitchen. Him being here during the day, the sub-contractors coming and going, makes the place seem lived in again and stops me feeling so lonely. I'll miss them when the house is finished.

At two in the morning when I can't sleep for thinking about my knitting buddies and their secret, I eat apple

155

crumble out of the Tupperware container with a large spoon and picture Rhiannon's finger over her mouth. *It's none of your business, Annie, just get some sleep.*

19

Can't We Be Friends

It's Saturday morning and the dark circles under my eyes are going to need heavy duty concealer before Becs' party tonight. I've dosed up on caffeine, to the point that I feel strung out and unable to blink my eyes. Bea will be arriving for our shopping trip to Hereford and I've had less than two hours' sleep. Apart from the dress, Bea has convinced me that I'll need a few beauty sessions. She'd sent a list of personal questions yesterday via text to establish when I'd last been tweezed, waxed, plucked or shaved then she'd made a string of appointments for me, one with a brilliant hairdresser she knows in the centre of the city.

'Snap!' Bea says as I crawl into the passenger seat of her navy blue Audi sports car. We are both dressed in skinny jeans and fur-trimmed jackets. Class and good breeding exude from Bea's outfit, mine screams Primark. I can't help comparing her slim legs to my lack of thigh gap. She has added a splash of colour by way of a handknitted red scarf, artistically swathed around her neck. It covers half of her chin and her lipstick matches it exactly.

Unlike me, who has been analysing the relationship of my knitting friends since Monday afternoon and losing hours of sleep over it, Bea is relaxed and assured in her perfect foundation and driving gloves. The drama of Monday's knitting circle is back in a strong box and locked away, just an echo from the past.

After the prodding, preening, waxing and threading is out of the way, I tie my hair back from my face and I'm ready to hit the shops. We bounce from store to store, Bea in a wave of energy and adrenalin, me on a caffeine high. The hunt for *the* dress is under way. I'm excited about tonight. Reef and I haven't spent much in the way of alone time together. As much as I adore Noé, I haven't got a handle on the real Reef yet and tonight will be an ideal opportunity to find out more about him. Conversation on our first and only date centred around his career and his celebrity rather than it did anything more personal. Reef didn't ask a lot about me and my personal life, but maybe he thought there was no rush because he's made it clear he wants a relationship with me. That said, in a short space of time, I have gleaned a lot about his relationship with Noé's celebrity mother, Natalia. She is in complete control and he won't do anything to upset her.

Hanging over her arm are at least three dresses Bea thinks I should try on. All are pretty daring, sexy, very little in the way of support for my 34DDs, apart from hope and double-sided tape. Bea's insistence that I'll be the belle of the ball leaves me weak, and I shudder to think what would happen if I went braless in one of these dresses and Reef insisted on dancing to all the party bangers with me. Bea, of course, is expecting that Reef will be stripping my dress off later tonight with his ultra-white teeth. I'm not opposed to this idea. Let's face it, I haven't had anything stripped off lately apart from the drab wallpaper in the kitchen.

By the time we get to the changing room, petite Bea is hidden beneath the pile of silk and satin dresses she has draped over her arms.

The girl at the changing room door looks down her false lashes at us, so thick and brushlike I wonder how she can see.

'Only six items,' she drones.

Bea shoves all the dresses into the shop assistant's body who then dumps them all onto the counter and tuts loudly.

'Just count them into piles of six, would you?' Bea says with a smile. 'We'll let you know when we're ready for them.' I love the way Bea dismisses the girl's sullen, bad behaviour with her brand of "the customer is always right" bad behaviour. I wouldn't have the nerve. I also wouldn't have chosen so many outrageously gregarious dresses in as many bright colours and, as I spot from a couple of the labels, in a size smaller than my actual one.

'Should we just whittle it down now?' I implore.

'No, we can't,' Bea says, marching through the changing room, peeping into all the vacant cubicles until she finds the one she likes. 'I've picked out some absolute stonkers and I don't want you leaving here without the best there is. It'll take time but it'll all be worth it. You'll see.'

The effects of caffeine are waning and I could do with a spot of lunch. I'd skipped breakfast so I'd have a flattish stomach, but it gurgles and I silently ache for a hot croissant. I just have to hold it together long enough to try on the whole dress department.

'Here,' says Bea as she ushers me into the farthest cubicle. She grabs the first six dresses from the sales assistant who is managing to smile and grimace all at once. Bea waves her away with her turquoise nails and turns to me with the dresses. 'Now then, there you go. Try each of them on and then come out and give me a twirl.'

I hang all six dresses up on the rail in my changing room and stare at them. I run my hand down the front of one, a deep blue party dress with a low neckline and fitted bodice. It's beautiful but it isn't going to suit my figure. I try it on first to get the agony of stepping outside in an ill-fitting dress out of the way. Somehow, the zip manages to do up at the back and I can still breathe. I poke my head out of the curtains to make sure Bea is the only one in the waiting area. She's sitting on a cosy chair at the dressing room door beside a tall, oval standing mirror.

'Well?' she says with wide eyes. 'Let's have a look at you.'

I step out gingerly and attempt a twirl, my arms crossing in front of my stomach.

'Turn around properly,' says Bea. 'Raise your arms and do this.' Bea pirouettes and lands facing the mirror with one leg in front of the other, hands fanned on her hips, her chin tilted upwards. 'You know I did a stint of modelling once,' she says, looking at herself in the mirror. 'It was when I ran away to London for the second time. Before I met my third husband, Latimer. What a flatulent pig he turned out to be. A drunk, too, although he managed to keep that all under wraps until after the honeymoon. Up to this day, I cannot understand how a person could keep two weeks of wind at bay. Still, the Algarve was delightful. And now you, my darling.'

I try to walk and turn the way a catwalk model would. The way I saw Natalia De Veras do at Paris Fashion Week in some old footage on YouTube.

'That colour isn't as good for you as I thought,' says Bea, now standing with an arm across her body supporting the other as she cradles her chin between her thumb and forefinger. 'Next one?'

'Okay,' I say obligingly, and suddenly I feel like Eliza Dolittle.

The next six dresses are just as catastrophic as the first and my body is struggling to cram itself into the amount of fabric that goes into making them. Some are a generous twelve but mostly I've been lucky to get some of them past my shoulders or over hips. I wish Bea would accept that I'm a size fourteen.

Suddenly, I hear raucous laughter coming from the cubicle beside me and I have a terrible feeling there must be a hole between the two changing rooms and I'm giving the neighbouring occupant a good laugh.

'Bea?' I call through the wall just in case she is trying on the dresses I've discarded. But the person doesn't have the same laugh as Bea and now it seems as if she is talking into her phone. She's trying to show whoever she is speaking to the clothes she is trying on.

I step out of my cubicle in the thirteenth dress. It smoothed upwards past my hips with ease without the sound of static over my underwear. The zip seemed to glide up easily and, I thank God, we've managed to find another generous size twelve. Bea stands beside the tall, oval mirror, her hands clasped under her chin, her smile of pride and overwhelming joy pulled so high up the sides of her face she could be a smiley face emoji. I stare into the mirror to see what has caused such a change in her demeanour. The dress is silver, sleeveless and falls to my shins. Its skirt swirls as I sway from side to side, my hands on my hips. I dare to turn sideways onto my reflection to see what I look like from the back. I've got the hang of posing now that I've been coached

161

by Bea. The deep V at the back of the dress certainly is flattering. The fabric falls delicately over my wide curves and makes me look a lot slimmer than I actually am. This is probably one of those trick, skinny mirrors, but as I swing back around to check out the front again, I can't help but grin happily at what I see. The spray of sparkly crystals on the bodice are not at all as pathetic as I'd first thought when I'd taken the dress off the thick velvet hanger. In fact, they are subtle and stylish and I would never have chosen this dress for myself in a million years. Bea was right, she does have an eye for these things.

'That's the one,' comes a voice from somewhere. A pretty face peers out from the curtain of the changing room next to mine. She's off the phone now and beams admiringly at me in the reflection of the oval-shaped mirror. I immediately recognise her from somewhere and swing around. She is wearing the dress I first tried on, only it's a size smaller and fits her perfectly.

'It absolutely is the one,' Bea says, standing between me and the other girl. 'We can call off the search.'

'You certainly can,' says the girl in the dress that looked awful on me. She steps out fully from her cubicle. 'You don't remember me, do you?'

She smiles excitedly and almost bounces on the balls of her bare feet, and I can't help doing the same, only I have pink ankle socks on. It's Jade Lewis from school. The vivacious girl from my biology class and, at the time, one of only two girls of colour in the entire school. Her hair was thick and yanked into two bushy pigtails back then until the day she came into school with a head full of thin braids reaching her waist. Some of them were beaded in the school colours, cobalt blue and grey. She'd caused quite a stir and I had always found myself drawn to her outgoing personality. She fizzed and sparkled back in those days, and I would stand at the edge of the conversations she was having with her friends, trying to summon the gumption to join in. It's not that I was unwelcome to. In fact, Jade often nodded and smiled at me as if she'd wanted me to join in. At the time, Jade had been part of, or the leader of, a group of really cool girls. But they were the cool girls who didn't try hard. Coolness exuded from them as they walked around school, gleaming, knowing all the bands that no one else had heard of, excelling at sport without showing off and having high grades but not coming across as nerds.

My group of friends, led by Becs and Zarina, were also considered cool because they had matching socks, hair clips and school bags for every day of the week. They wouldn't consider going out with a boy less than a ten or was at least three years older than themselves. Cat had been right about Becs and Zarina, they must have allowed me to join their gang through pity considering none of my hair accessories came from the same shop as theirs and that I only had one school bag. And, quite possibly, I was allowed to stay in their friendship group right through to A levels just to make them look even prettier and cooler than they were.

Jade hugs me.

'Anne, right?' she says, pointing a questioning forefinger at me.

'Yes, well, Annie actually. And Jade, isn't it? Of course I remember you.' Not least because I longed to make friends with you but was too shy to leave the safe quarters of the benches by the netball courts where Zarina, Becs and the rest of their gang hung out at break times. Jade's group played music in the playground through the speakers of their MP3

163

players. They made up dance routines and sang the latest songs. They dressed up their school uniforms to make them look stylish and had no problem dating boys in the same year from the boys school next to ours.

'It's lovely to see you, Annie.' Jade smiles as though there had never been any dividing lines in the playground. Probably in her mind there hadn't been. She and her friends weren't out to impress anyone, and while I look back on some aspects of my childhood and adolescence with sadness and regret, I bet Jade has nothing but fond memories. I used to try to slink off to the library to avoid Becs and Zarina's constant pressure to buy the right shoes, coat or school bag to meet their exacting standards.

I remember my manners and make the introductions.

'And this is my good friend, Bea,' I say to Jade with a slightly awkward feeling in my stomach. I've just told the coolest girl in school that I now hang out with a woman in her seventies.

'I have to say, you look absolutely stunning in your dress,' Bea tells Jade. 'I had that one earmarked for Annie but it wasn't quite her style. You both look amazing, I must say.' Bea casts an approving eye over us both. 'Going somewhere special?'

Jade mocks a frown. 'Hardly. Just some engagement party of an old school acquaintance. I have no idea why I was invited.' Jade shrugs.

'Not Becs Sprigg's party?' I ask.

Jade nods, a delicate laugh bursting through her lips. 'Not you, too? But I suppose she was a friend of yours. She's been following my Insta and trying to invite me to drinks and things since she discovered I lived in London.'

I have a sinking feeling in my tummy. Jade is in London now, of course she is. I'd already started fantasising about having a friend my age and planning to get her number.

'I suppose since Becs found out I was moving back here and she was having her party here that she somehow felt obliged to invite me,' says Jade.

'You're moving back to Ross?' I say a little too eagerly.

'Well, nearer Much Marcle,' she says. Close enough. 'Mum's health is a bit...' Here she gestures the idea of up-and-down with her hand. 'I work freelance as a data analyst, mostly remotely, so I don't have to be in London particularly.' I'm disappointed that Jade isn't a music industry mogul or chief editor for a fashion magazine or running a multi-million empire.

'I'm sorry about your mum,' I say. Jade's phone buzzes from the cubicle.

'That might be her now. I've been showing her my outfits and so far she thinks I should buy them all.'

'Not surprising,' says Bea. 'You look like a model. You'd look great in anything.' A statement that leaves me uncomfortable when I see Bea look quickly over my curves and back at Jade's washboard stomach and gym-sculpted arms. 'Why don't you join us for a late lunch, Jade?'

'I'd love to but I should get going. I've got a few things to buy for Mum and then I have to tackle all this.' She points to the high afro puff in her hair. The curls glisten, the sides smoothed to her scalp with gel and I can't see why she would have to change a thing. It looks perfect for a party and suits the dress she's wearing. Her hair looks like it behaves. Mine takes on a life of its own.

'I'll see you later, then?' I say.

'Definitely.' Jade jogs back to her changing room, pulls the curtains closed and shouts. 'Better call Mum back. See you tonight!'

'Great,' I call to the curtains and have a hard time trying to curb my enthused grin.

'Right,' says Bea, looking at the gold Cartier watch on her wrist. 'Next, lunch and then the hairdresser and then you're ready. Big night tonight.'

I don't want Jade to think I think going to Becs' party is a big night for me. I want her to think I've only just managed to fit it in last minute and couldn't care less if I had to miss it. After all, she hadn't been in the least bit excited about it herself. I am so pleased that Jade is moving from London and will be local. She has practically invited me into the cool girls' circle by breaking the ice like that. I can chat to her later, make friends properly. How cool would that be to have a friend who doesn't talk about osteoporosis. I'm looking forward to this party even more.

20

The Way You Look Tonight

I'd spent ages at the hair salon in Hereford, feeling hot and flustered as the hairdresser launched into the taming of my hair as if she were on a mission. I have to say, after all her effort, my hair looks much the same only cleaner, full of product and, admittedly, a bit glossier. Bea insisted on paying for the entire shopping trip, including a lavish lunch at an Italian restaurant. I had it on good authority, that is Rhiannon had once told me, that out of the three of them, Bea was responsible for my social engagements. While Mum had asked Rhiannon to make sure I ate properly and looked after my health, Bea was charged with seeing to it that I didn't spend all my time locked away in my studio, only leaving to go to work and go to Morrisons. As well as the knitting circle, I must take part in local activities, keep up with popular culture and find a boyfriend, for goodness' sake.

It hadn't occurred to Mum that Ross was devoid of eligible bachelors. The average age is about sixty-five from what I can see, which is a godsend for someone like Bea, but for me, not so much. I'm pretty sure it was Bea's intention for me to have taken a liking to Anton, which is why she'd insisted I call him to work on the house, but she must have thought I'd struck gold landing a date with a celebrity. She'd talked about it non-stop during the outing earlier. I'm surprised she didn't brag about who my date was to the woman in the nail studio, the one in the hair salon or the overly keen girl who'd done my facial and body treatments. Perhaps if we'd let her in on the identity of my celebrity date, she would have softened and not gone about the obliteration of my unnecessary hair with such determination, burning wax being her favourite form of torture. Every chance Bea got, she stressed how important a date with a man of considerable means and social standing was and how I shouldn't, for Christ's sake, make a pig's ear of it and, as often as I could, I must at least sound interesting.

'Are you saying I'm not interesting?' I had asked over lunch.

'I don't mean it like that, darling,' she'd said as she sipped Bollinger with her spinach gnocchi. 'But most men don't hang around waiting for your good points to show themselves. I'm just saying, best foot forward and all that. Be on your A game.'

'I don't have a game,' I'd replied as I stared into the garden salad she'd ordered for me. 'Let alone an A one.'

'Just smile a lot and wear good underwear. If all else fails, be a vamp in the bedroom.'

I'd stared blankly at her.

'Goodness me, do I need to spell it out? You do have some tricks up your sleeve, don't you?' She'd leant forward, grey eyes wide open. 'Tell me you do have *some* experience in these matters.'

'Yes, thank you Bea. I know where everything goes.' Knowing where things go is about all the experience I'd had, but there was no way I'd subject myself to more stories about Bea's sex life than I'd already endured.

In Mum's old silk dressing gown, the one with the large butterfly on the back, I carefully apply my make-up. I'm following a video for a no-make-up look that seems to require more make-up than I have in my ten-year-old make-up bag, the plastic lining scored with eyebrow pencil and eye shadow brush marks. My mascara, in fact everything apart from the shimmery lipstick Bea bought for me today, should have been replaced, along with the make-up bag because I'd had it all since my eighteenth birthday.

My good underwear still looks good. The moths have been kind from what I can see. Next, the dress. I slip it on with care as I've already done hair and make-up. Reef is due in twenty minutes, so there's plenty of time to deal with casualties if my hair goes awry or I get lipstick on my teeth. None of this happens and I'm just slipping into my shoes when I get a text from Bea:

Just a last minute check to make sure you have topics of conversation lined up, haven't damaged your dress or have lipstick on your teeth. Just be yourself x ps and have fun darling xx

Reef gives a loud rap on the door which shakes me back to earth as I'm already worrying that none of this feels like fun to me. I'd wanted to go to Becs' engagement party on receiving it, but at the same time, I hadn't wanted to go. I'd been so nervous about meeting the old crowd again, knowing that they'd all moved on in their lives and I wasn't so sure I had. I'd worried myself silly about running out of things to say to any of them. Mostly, I was afraid of going on my own, without even a friend to take with me. Fear and worry has caused a lot of heartache in my life, especially the worry I might end up like Mum and retire into myself and never come out of the cocoon of gloom that Mum used to sink into. And though Cat had told me there was no chance I would turn out to be like Mum, I couldn't shake my doubts. Which is why, since my teens, I'd forced myself to be involved in life and lively things. Even when Becs and Zarina talked about going to parties, parties I was sure would leave me cold, I'd made myself go with them. I made myself strike up conversations and I convinced myself I'd had a good time. At university, I didn't have a Becs or Zarina and I'd told myself I needed to try harder, be more assertive. But the friends I made at university were very casual and I haven't stayed in touch with any of them. In the end, after my studies, it was back to just Mum for company. Eventually, I'd fallen out of the habit of going anywhere. That's why I'd stuck that magnet on the fridge door and that's why I'd clung to the notion that I could get back out there and make new friends. That invitation had brought out the emotions from the past, the best in me and the worst in me. I'd talked myself into thinking that I could go on my own. Maybe I'd meet somebody. Make a friend. What a maize of thoughts that invitation had created.

I smile as I open the door because now I am going to the party with someone, and not just any someone. A celebrity footballer. It doesn't matter that I know nothing about football and don't particularly like it, a celebrity footballer likes me. And he's my date. For Becs' party.

'Am I on time?' Reef leans on the threshold of the door like a good-looking gigolo in a romantic film, smelling of aftershave, teeth gleaming, and I look for an animated star to sparkle off them. His wide smile fades as he looks me up and down. I touch my hair, the front of my dress, look down at my shoes.

'Something wrong?' I ask and bite my bottom lip.

'You're joking.' He steps inside and shakes his head. 'Everything is all great. I mean, you look great. Beautiful actually.'

I sigh with relief and look at us in the hall mirror over Reef's shoulder. His broad silhouette blocks most of me but we look so good together. It slips my mind how unalike we are. He's confident, good-looking and poised. I'm jittery, nervous and absolutely average. But my dress has made a difference, my hair and probably my make-up, and Reef Mayer has noticed.

'Should we get going straight away or… ?' he says.

I don't understand what the 'or' is that Reef is referring to until he starts running his fingers up the side of my bare arm and tracing them along my collarbone and down my chest. Oh *that*, I think to myself and picture him ripping off my good underwear with his teeth.

'I think we ought to go,' I say, dancing around him to reach for my padded coat. 'Or we may never make it.'

'Well, if you're sure,' he says and helps me on with my coat. Why didn't I think to buy a dressy winter coat?

We pull up outside Glewstone Court Country House. Lights shine onto the white walls of the middle section of the two-storey building, onto the stone fountain near the entrance and spills in a semi-circle onto the pebbled drive. The right and left wing of the house have bricked walls with large windows, the ground floor of one of the wings illuminated by a warm, yellow light, the other side in darkness. The tall hedges are hard to make out until the headlight of Reef's car touches them. A man whose face looks ghostly white in the beam of the headlights points us in the direction of the car park. He does a double take as he notices who the driver is. My heart pounds loudly in my chest. I'd thought about how impressed everyone would be if I walked into the party with Reef but I'd forgotten that it would also mean a lot of attention coming my way, and I'm suddenly aware that I won't be able to handle it. Reef comes to my side of the car and opens the door. My first instinct is to throw off my old coat and walk in as the new improved me, but the biting wind that whistles up my bare legs as I step out of the car reminds me that it's the dead of winter and I'd probably catch my death if I did.

Reef's warm hand envelopes mine as we walk back to the house. My heels sink into the shingle in the path and I step daintily over it so as not to land on my face. Reef seems to glide on an invisible carpet and pulls me along to the entrance where there are stone pillars and double doors opened wide onto a small, brightly lit hallway. Inside, a grand, shiny oak staircase spirals to the upper floor. I notice that the two suited staff members at the door, who had asked to see invitations from the three girls ahead of us, stand aside for Reef as he steps up to the entrance. I'm slightly behind him, scraping a piece of shingle off the sole of my shoe onto the step.

'It's you, isn't it?' one of the doormen asks.

Reef looks back at me and I stand to attention at his side.

'I didn't bring the invitation,' I say meekly.

'You don't need one,' both of the doormen scrabble to say. Neither has looked at me and are ushering Reef into the hallway where music pulsates through from a back room. The people in the hallway are pointing their phones at Reef. He turns to me.

'Oh no. I wasn't expecting this,' he says.

I'm about to ask what he did expect when Becs and Zarina come flying through from the back room, a blast of music heralding their arrival.

They both shriek my name as first Zarina and then Becs throw their arms around me and pull me in for air kisses and brief hugs in which there is little to no body contact below the shoulders, just lots of perfume. Becs and Zarina stand hungrily in front of Reef. I try to make the introductions, but a small group of people have gathered in front of him. Reef smiles at me but his eyes are asking how long we need to stay. I'm thinking that perhaps it would have been better if we had stayed at mine – Reef could have been exploring my good underwear by now. Instead, I'm being jostled further and further away from him while Becs is exclaiming what an honour it is to have Reef Mayer at her engagement party as if she'd orchestrated the whole thing.

'Um, Reef,' I say, but no one hears me. A bit more loudly I say, 'Reef, could I introduce you to Zarina and Becs whose party it is?' This is a bit of a redundant question as Becs has already announced to Reef who she is. She spots me on the periphery and swishes a pointing finger at me.

'And you, you dark horse.' She brushes past everyone to grab my shoulders. 'I don't hear from you in ages, you don't RSVP and here you are, showing up with Reef Mayer. Don't tell me he's your brother.' She turns to Reef, as does everyone else.

'No, he's my…'

'Annie's my date,' says Reef, and suddenly all eyes and cameras are on me as if I'm supposed to make a speech.

I frown, I shrug my shoulders and open my mouth to say something – I'm not quite sure what – when Becs grabs hold of the shoulders of my padded coat.

'Well,' she says in a very loud voice, 'don't just stand there. Come in and have some champagne. You and I have a lot to talk about.' She looks down at my coat and quickly removes her hands. She spins around and calls over the bobbing heads. 'Could someone take this?' She looks at my coat again. 'This, please. Would you? Thanks.'

A doorman pushes through the gathering crowd. Each time the music booms more loudly from the main room, a few more eager people come out and congregate in what is a pretty hallway but not big enough for the whole party to spill into. Some people are standing on the stairs and holding up their phones from there. Reef helps me off with my coat and hands it to the doorman. He offers me his elbow as he leads me to the loud room. Becs rushes to my other side and hooks an arm through the crook of mine. It's very awkward for the three of us to get through the door in a line but somehow we manage it. Becs grabs a glass of champagne being carried on a tray by a gliding waitress. She hands it, right past my face, to Reef.

'There you go, Reef Mayer,' she says

He holds up a hand and says, 'Driving.' She proceeds to drink the champagne herself and giggles helplessly.

'We've got a buffet later. Drinks are on us and we brought the DJ from our favourite club in London. Isn't he great?' she asks while spraying my face with champagne spittle and jiggling her hips. Standing in front of a large sash window, facing his hi-tech equipment and the rest of the room, the DJ bobs his head and fiddles with a mouse to line up the next song. Very few people are dancing, mostly they are hovering and staring at Reef.

'Don't just stand there, go on and enjoy yourselves,' Becs sprays. 'We'll catch up later.' Then into my ear she

174

whispers. 'And you can tell me how you got hold of Reef "The Body" Mayer, you naughty girl.'

For the next few minutes, I'm standing next to Reef, sipping the champagne he has swiped from another passing tray and handed to me. But we're unable to conduct a conversation because he is constantly being accosted from the other side by people who just love him in the adverts, love his ex-wife, love his son, thankful for the penalty against Chelsea in the cup final and want to congratulate him on becoming manager of Birmingham City. He hadn't told me he'd accepted the job, I only knew he'd gone to discuss it when he'd left me to look after Noé. I expect he thought I'd caught up with it on the news or his Twitter feed. I don't follow either so I wish he could have told me. It's obviously big news.

'Birmingham?' I ask when I can finally get close enough to him to ask.

'Oh, yes. That. Didn't I mention it?' He screws his face. 'I thought with a bit of stability in my life I could see more of Noé.'

'That's nice,' I say, but really I'm hoping it means I can see more of Noé. He's safely over at Rhiannon's house, probably having a bedtime story read to him alongside Rhiannon's grandchildren as we speak.

'Fancy a dance?' Reef asks, but just as I'm about to answer, Becs strong arms Reef and yanks his ear towards her mouth.

'Um, Reef Mayer, could you come over so can I introduce you to my dad? He's a massive fan.'

'Oh, I…' he says, and then I see him disappear in a puff of party smoke, and he's gone before I can tell him that I'm not much of a dancer but that I'd love to.

'Annie?' I turn to see Anton standing just inches away. It's weird not seeing him in jeans or dungarees. He's in black trousers that are narrow at the ankles and his highly polished shoes end in a slight point. Under his black, formal jacket is a crisp, grey shirt, the top button undone. He's clean-shaven which complements the new skin fade in his hair. He moves closer and bends to smile at me. I try to form a sentence by opening and closing my mouth like a damned goldfish. Why can't I just say hello?

'You're here.' It's all I can seem to muster under the circumstances. I'm dying to ask how he knows Becs, why he knows Becs and is it too late to change the colour of the wall units.

'So are you,' he simply says and looks out to the ballroom floor. There is a handful of people dancing to *Happy* by Pharrell. The DJ is looking at his laptop screen and chewing gum. There is a group by the bar and people in black aprons are laying down food onto a long table against the wall. Around the perimeter of the room are eight large dining tables covered in white tablecloths, glitter, glasses, bottles and bowls of snacks. Reef is at one of those tables while a man in a suit whose sleeves are too long, presumably Becs' dad, holds court. Reef seems unable to get a word in but he smiles graciously and nods from time to time. People are clicking his photo and asking for selfies, and people are even taking pictures of people taking selfies with Reef. It's all pretty chaotic but Becs seems to be having fun. Zarina has her arms draped around her husband who can't seem to get enough of Reef Mayer, either.

'You didn't tell me you were coming to this,' Anton says close to my ear. 'And you didn't let on you were going out with Reef Mayer.' He smiles and I'm hoping to God he doesn't go and ask for a selfie, too.

'And who are you here with?' I ask.

Anton looks around just as the doors open and a beautiful black woman, in the dark blue dress she tried on at the store in Hereford earlier, steps in.

'Her,' he says, being nonchalant. How he could be, I don't know. She's probably the most attractive woman here. Effortlessly making her way over to us in the same flying carpet motion Reef had earlier, only in high stiletto heels, is Jade. She smiles and walks up to us and I'm filled with such envy to know that she is here with Anton – even though I'm with the most sought after man in the whole party.

'Annie!' Jade hugs her long arms around me and pulls me in close, kissing both my cheeks. 'You look amazing. Doesn't she, Anton?'

I half turn to Anton and can barely meet his eye now that I know he's dating Jade. I'm quite annoyed at him for trying to kiss me when he has a girlfriend. Perhaps he thought it was okay because it was obviously a long-distance relationship until now, now that she is moving back to Herefordshire for good.

'She does look nice,' Anton says.

'*Nice*?' Jade flicks Anton's arm. 'Talk about understatement. That dress is so beautiful on you and your hair looks ... well, you just look, wow.'

I don't feel wow. My head is spinning and my tummy is knotted. I really like Jade and hoped we could become friends, but how is that going to happen when I have a crush on her boyfriend and was a breath away from kissing him not so long ago? Maybe I could brush that aside, the way Anton has, and I mustn't forget that I do have a date myself.

Though you wouldn't think it. Reef hasn't looked for me once. The image of him removing my good underwear with his teeth looks increasingly unlikely. Instead, I have a vision of putting them into the laundry basket myself and someone playing *Taps* on a bugle like they do at the end of a military funeral.

'Bloody hell,' Jade exclaims. 'That's Reef Mayer.' Not her too. But there is Reef, burrowing his way back to my side. His face looks serious, anxious, and he takes my elbow and squeezes it.

'I'm really sorry, Annie, it's Noé. Something's up. Rhiannon called.'

I wave weakly at Jade and Anton as I allow myself to be hurried back into the hallway and out of the main doors. The night air covers my shoulders and arms, pebbles from the pathway stick into the soles of my feet as I chase after Reef. He aims his keys at the car, and the locks click and the lights blink on and off.

'What happened?' I ask.

Reef has already started the engine and reverses out just as I close the door. I click on my seatbelt and stare at the side of his face as he looks over his shoulder and manoeuvres out of the parking spot and races towards the driveway. He makes the parking attendant jump as he revs up the engine. My head bangs the back of the headrest and I turn my eyes to the speedometer. We're already doing seventy and we haven't hit the road yet. My heart beats uncontrollably and I'm fearing the worst. Did Noé take a bad fall? Is he ill? Did he run away? I'm so scared and so upset because I arranged the babysitter, so if something terrible has happened, I'm to blame.

178

'Can you direct me from here, Annie?' Reef's urgency shakes me back to the here and now. 'I had Rhiannon in Google Maps but there's no time to check that now.'

'Just follow the signs to Ross and I'll direct you when we're close.'

I dread to look at the speedometer now, but I shoot directions at Reef as we get closer to town and direct him to Rhiannon's house in nearby Weston under Penyard.

I leap out of the car when we arrive. Rhiannon is standing in the doorway wringing her chubby hands, but she's smiling. Reef is already passing her before I can close the car door and bolting up the stairs.

'It's fine. He's perfectly fine, my poppet,' Rhiannon says when she sees my face.

'What happened?'

'He just missed his dad. He fell asleep fine and then woke up. Strange house, I suppose.' Rhiannon leads me to the living room and sits me down but I look desperately towards the open door. 'He was just a bit worried Reef might forget the address. Started crying and couldn't stop, the poor mite.'

'That's because they always leave him,' I say lightly on a sigh. I rub my face.

'What's that my pet?'

'His parents. He's either with one or the other. When he's with one he misses the other, but sometimes neither are around and he worries they won't come back. They're gone for days at a time sometimes. He gets so sad.'

'I'm not surprised.' Rhiannon is whispering because we can hear them coming back down the stairs. When Noé sees me, he leaps straight towards me and sends me backwards into the chair.

'Easy, big man,' Reef says.

'It's fine,' I say. 'Noé, you had us worried.' I stroke the cascade of his soft curls, wrap one onto my finger and inhale the smell of biscuits and soap that surround Noé. I love this little boy.

'I'm sorry,' he says standing in front of me, knees leaning against mine. 'You look pretty. Are you cold?'

I look down at the goosebumps on my arms. I've left my padded coat at the party, and during the drive over, I'd forgotten it was freezing outside. I was that worried about what had happened to Noé. My teeth are chattering and Noé wipes tears away from my cheeks with his fingers. I didn't realise I was crying, either.

'Don't be sad, Annie. I'm here now,' Noé says and leans in for another hug.

'I'm glad you're here,' I say. 'Really glad.' I look up at Reef who mouths the words *Sorry, Annie*, but I'm just so full of relief that a thousand Becs Sprigg parties couldn't compare to how wonderful it feels to have such a massive hug from Noé.

'You ready to go home?' Reef asks.

'I'll fetch his bits and bobs,' Rhiannon says over her shoulder. As she climbs the stairs, I can hear her telling the grandchildren it's time to sleep and no, we can't have more bedtime stories, well okay, maybe one.

Dressed in his cuddly jacket, Noé holds my hand in the back of the car. He pleads all the way for either their being able to sleep in my bed or that Annie comes home with them. Both Reef and I suggest that everyone will be better off in their own beds tonight. I give Noé a last kiss on his forehead and Reef leans back to hold my hand before I slip out of the car.

'I'll call you,' he says, but it sounds like a bit of an afterthought.

My teeth chatter and I can't open my bag or grip the keys properly to let myself into the cold house. I hadn't envisaged spending the last couple of hours in a flimsy dress on probably the most wintry night of the season.

I turn on the shower and deposit my good underwear, balcony bra and silky, skimpy briefs into the laundry basket. I have no idea when I shall require their services again but the hot water on my skin is so comforting. I stand under the shower for ages, determined I will sleep tonight, but somehow I don't believe I will.

21

A Fine Romance

'Annie! You're trending!'

A loud voice pierces the sound of a car in my dream cruising down a country road. I'm not ready for visitors.

I'd spent a large proportion of the night lying awake. Then I went to my studio with the intention of tidying up but couldn't help picking up a fine pencil and making some sketches. Anton once asked if I did any artwork when I couldn't sleep. I had told him that I can only focus on my art while fully functioning, but last night, I couldn't help myself. Through heavy-lidded eyes, continuous yawns and lots of heavy sighing, I completed four sketches. The topic of each was Noé. I'd begun to colour one of them in chalks, but my shoulders had slumped so far forward with fatigue I decided I was ruining the whole thing and took myself into the living room where I pulled a blanket around me and switched on my laptop. I'd sat in the cold on the Next website scrolling for padded coats like the one I'd left behind at the hall. I clicked on one for next day delivery and decided I would stay home until it arrived. I'd wallow in self pity for the shambles that was my date with Reef, thinking about Noé's little pink cheeks and eyes from crying because he missed his dad and his fear that one day neither of his parents would return to collect him.

I'd managed a couple of hours' sleep the whole night and now my morning dreams evaporate because of the brutal attack Bea makes on, not only the door knocker but the frosted window next to the front door, too. What is so urgent?

I get up, wrap the blanket around my shoulders and shuffle towards the front door where I hear two voices bickering.

'You don't have to get carried away. You'll wake the dead.'

'And you don't have to be so uptight.'

I unlock the front door.

'What's the time?' I ask with my puffy eyes partially open, chin jutting towards them.

'Have you not been on the World Wide Web, darling?' Bea declares as she pushes herself onto the mat and me out of the way.

'My dear, you simply must put the heating on,' says Judith, blowing onto her balled fists. 'It really is like a morgue in here.'

Without a word, I put on the heating as the pair set about making coffee and inspecting the chaos in the kitchen because of the work in progress.

Bea shoves her iPhone under my nose while Judith puts the handle of a coffee mug into my hand. The first sip burns my tongue and numbs the tip of it, so I quickly put the mug on the table.

'What am I looking at?' I ask as Bea scrolls Twitter without giving me a chance to take anything in, until... 'Is that me?' I splutter. 'Is that Reef?'

'Yes and yes,' says Bea with a girlish grin. 'Seems you've gone viral.'

'Do you even know what that means, Bea?' Judith asks. 'You know it's nothing to do with influenza, don't you?'

'I know that!' Bea snaps back. 'But look at all the likes, and one or two dislikes, you've generated. This is you and Reef at Becs' party causing an absolute riot.' Bea is overjoyed. 'Everyone is talking about Reef Mayer's new girlfriend.'

'What are they saying?' I try to grab the phone but Bea whips it out of reach and begins to read.

'It says, shortly after signing a contract to become manager of Championship side, Birmingham City FC, Reef Mayer has confirmed that he intends to remain in the Forest of Dean at his four-million-dollar house, now home to him and his adoptive son, Noé Laurent De Veras. Mayer's former wife, model and entrepreneur, Natalia De Veras, who has just released her latest line of yoga clothing, is reported to be in Europe as she trains for her forthcoming appearance on *Dancing on Ice Down Under – Celebrity Special*.'

'I didn't know she was making yoga clothes.' I sip more coffee.

'Forget that,' says Bea. 'Listen. Mayer, has been dating local nanny, Annie Lambert.'

Coffee sprays out of my mouth. 'Nanny?'

'Shh,' says Bea. 'It seems that not only has Mayer given up the glamour of his own modelling and acting career, he has given up his glamorous girlfriends for girl next door, Lambert. Onlookers say they left a party in a hurry because his son fell ill and was rushed to hospital. Mayer was reported to have said that family comes first and rushed away hand in hand with Lambert.' Bea makes a wide-eyed face to show her approval.

'That's not what happened,' I say, creasing my brow and trying to look over Bea's shoulder at her phone. 'Could I see the pictures of me?'

'They're not exactly flattering, my darling, so I wouldn't bother. Reef looks very handsome, though.'

'Of course,' I sigh. 'And what has Reef said about this?'

'So far I haven't seen any comments from him. I am following his Twitter and his Instagram.'

'None of this is true, well not really,' I say. 'First of all, why do they think I'm a nanny? Am I supposed to be Noé's nanny? It sounds like we're having an affair. And someone from the party must have exaggerated the truth. Reef had cameras on him all night. Can I see the pictures? How many are of me?'

'Please don't look, darling,' says Bea. 'Your cheeks look a bit flushed but you look super in that dress. Oh, how I wished we'd gone designer label, but never mind. You'll need to prepare a statement.'

'For the police?' I can't believe this is my life now.

'No, the press, you silly. They'll want to know all about Reef Mayer's new girlfriend.'

'I'm not sure I am, though.'

'Whatever do you mean?'

'I don't know if I count as a girlfriend. Not properly. I mean we've kissed but we haven't done, you know, boyfriend-girlfriend things.'

'You mean sex?'

Judith sucks a lemon.

'I mean candlelights and midnight walks. I mean one of us saying they want to take things a step further than making pizza and babysitting.'

'All of that will come, darling.' Bea waves a hand around like the queen greeting her public and puts her phone down on the table where Judith has been buttering toast and laying out the scraps from my fridge for a makeshift breakfast. Grapes and some cheddar cheese slices. I'm not hungry and I don't fancy the rest of the coffee.

'You'd better get yourself upstairs and take a shower,' Bea says briskly and flutters her hands towards the door. 'From now on, you have to look completely presentable at all times. You never know when the paparazzi will strike or if a reporter might turn up out of the blue.'

'I'm pretty sure–'

Bea places her fingers on my mouth.

'One always needs to be prepared in these circumstances. It was safe for me to jaunt around town when I was dating Tom Selleck but that was because he wasn't yet famous and our affair didn't make the papers. But since my date with the Earl of Harrington, I always look my best at all times and I know never to leave a house in the middle of the night wearing nothing more than suspenders and a fur coat.' She looks over at Judith who looks at me.

'Please don't ask her to elaborate,' Judith says. 'The full story will double your insomnia and then some.'

Bea laughs with a loud screech before ushering me up to the bathroom where I brush my teeth, wash my face and look for something to wear that could be considered presentable. My baggy tracksuit bottoms are out of the question. I opt for a shift dress and long cardigan and the comfort of some sheepskin slippers. I put on some lip gloss in case of photographers or reporters and join the women downstairs.

'Is that what you're wearing?' Bea trills. I look down at my clothes. This cardigan is practically new.

'Oh, just leave her, would you?' Judith says. 'She looks perfectly fine. You look lovely, my dear. Plain and simple, and there's nothing wrong with that.'

Plain and simple, I think to myself. 'Girl next door, Lambert'. I may as well be the nanny as I consider our nascent romance. I wish we could give the press something to really talk about. I wish I was a vamp, and I wish I didn't feel this sorry for myself.

Judith tries to reassure me that everything will work out for the best and that I'm not to worry or become stressed in any way. Both women finally leave the house without having touched any of the cheddar cheese or overripe grapes. Judith, according to Rhiannon, has been charged with keeping me balanced, emotionally, mentally and spiritually. With Rhiannon taking care of my health and well-being, Bea making sure I have a social life, Judith is the everything else. She is my moral compass, the person I discuss anything with concerning matters of business, the house or any legal problems. The person who helps me stay balanced and on top of everything. Judith always sits and listens to me, to my problems and anxieties. Actually listening, unlike Rhiannon and Bea, neither of whom realise I can think for myself. I can think, all right, far too much it would seem because all I can do now is worry about what the fallout another date with Reef will cause. I don't think that the three women combined can unravel the knot of worry that is tying me up.

My phone rings. There's a video call from Cat. She has a cheesy grin on her face.

'Hey, girl next door, how is life as a celebrity girlfriend and why am I only hearing about this now?'

I had played down who I'd gone out on a date with to Mum, swerved the fact that the date I'd mentioned so casually was with a celebrity. Not until I knew there'd be some kind of future in it. I didn't want her blowing things out of proportion and worrying that I might get let down by Reef and that he probably wasn't serious and had women lined up for every night of the week. Those were my main fears, but I tried to protect Mum from them all the same.

'Well, I did tell Mum I'd been on a date,' I say.

'Been on a date? You could have mentioned who with. Anyway, Mum is here and I've shown her the pictures of you. Why did you wear that dress?'

Mum leans her face into the shot.

'Are you all right, Annie? Do you need me to fly back and help you cope with this?'

'Cope with what?' Cat pushes half of her face into view. 'She's practically famous. What's to cope with? But you'll need new clothes. Something from the Victoria Beckham line.'

Mum nudges her and takes the phone away. She's walking towards her kitchen smiling sorrowfully at me as if I'm still ten and I've been crying because the girls at school have been laughing at my baggy clothes again.

'Tell her to do something with that hair.' I can still hear Cat in the background and Mum closes her kitchen door.

'Is he kind?' Mum asks as she sits at her kitchen table.

'He is kind, Mum, but we're barely dating. It's been blown out of all proportion.'

'But the news makes it sound as if he's changed his lifestyle for you. He must be serious.'

188

'Well, I kind of think he is. At least he talks as if he is. He can be very intense.'

'What does that mean? How emotionally attached are you to him?'

'I like him a lot. I really do, but if things are going to be this complicated…'

'If you like him, you'll work things out. It says he has a son?'

'Ah, little Noé. He's an absolute angel.' I can feel my cheeks grow warm and a flutter in my heart as I settle into the armchair in the living room.

'You've met him?'

'Not only met him, I've looked after him overnight when Reef had urgent stuff to do.'

'You babysat?'

'Don't say it like that. It wasn't as if I was being used. I loved every minute of being with him. Helping him get to sleep, making sure he had breakfast. We made pizza together, well we tried. And I had him in the studio with me because we were going to do some painting together. He loves the garden and Rosie. Rosie sat in his lap. She only ever hisses at me but she can tell what a gentle soul Noé has, and he truly does. I do feel sorry for him the way he's batted from parent to parent without any real structure in his life.'

'I imagine that's quite normal for some children. I'm sure his parents love him. I've seen his photograph, he's adorable.'

'He really is, Mum. I only have to see his toothless little grin and I melt. And he gives the best hugs.'

'I see.'

'What? What do you see?'

189

'Well, everything I asked you about Reef you've answered in a couple of sentences, whereas with Noé, well.' She sighs and shakes her head. 'You just have so much to say about him. It seems he's made more of an impression than his dad.'

I stop smiling for a second. Is she right? I mean, who can resist Noé? He's precious. But I do really like Reef. He's handsome, he's got a great body and he's a great kisser, too. I'm not sure that this is going to convince Mum I like him, so I keep it to myself.

'Reef and I haven't had the chance to get to know each other, that's all. These things take time and I'm really keen to see where it will go.'

'And he's worth all the media attention you're bound to get?'

'I can handle it. If there is any more. You know you can be making headlines one day and everyone swears blind they've never heard of you the next. But I'm not going to dump Reef and risk not seeing Noé because his dad is famous.'

'Can you hear yourself, Annie? It all comes back to the boy again. Now listen. I'm only a phone call away. If anything happens, any time you feel you can't cope, just call me.'

Cat bursts into the kitchen and leans over Mum's shoulder.

'Second thoughts, don't go Victoria Beckham. I think you'd be better in Alexander McQueen or something classic like Coco Chanel. And I suppose that dress didn't look too bad on you. Just get rid of the one you're wearing.'

'I will. Anything else?'

'No. It's late here and I'd better get going. Oh, wait. Mum asks how the decorating is going?'

'Great. The kitchen should be close to finished by Christmas.'

We're all quiet for a minute. I know that each of us is thinking about our past Christmases and how heavily the kitchen featured in them. It was the centre of our lives. Mum was always with us in body and mind apart from that one time. We always cooked so much food. Too much. We played all of Mum's Christmas jazz compilations so loudly we were sure the music and our singing could be heard all the way to the centre of town. We stuffed our faces for several days and watched all the Christmas films, even the bad ones. And we laughed. And we slept until late. I never had any problems sleeping then. By New Year's Eve, we were ready for our party. Cat would always make sure there was a theme. The last themed one we ever had, because she grew out of the idea by the time she was sixteen, was a royalty theme, and she made us crowns and we put on all of Mum's jewellery. As always, there were streamers, party poppers and trumpets and it all took place in the kitchen. Last year the three of us celebrated their Christmas online and I spent mine alone in the kitchen as I heated up a Marks and Spencer Christmas dinner for two.

Mum is saying that they'll ring off for now and that I need to think long and hard about what to do next.

'She'll fall in love with Reef Mayer's abs and live happily ever after, of course,' Cat says. She blows me a kiss and Mum puts her hand on her heart and hums the first lines of *Where or When* by Rodgers and Hart before closing the call.

Mum and Cat have breathed life into my deflated lungs, and my thoughts start to calm, even out. I send a text to Reef and he doesn't answer, so I go into the studio and spend the rest of the day finishing the pictures I was sketching of Noé and shading them in vibrantly coloured chalks. He smiles in all five of the drawings.

22

Sophisticated Lady

It's Sunday, late evening, and I still haven't heard anything from Reef. I've been grazing through the items in my cupboard all day. Returning to the studio again with Ryvita and a Cup-a-Soup, my phone buzzes and makes me gasp in shock, as if I've never heard of mobile phones before. I put my snack down next to my easel and grab it. There's a message from Reef. Finally.

Hi Annie, how are you? Crazy weekend. Listen, Jack says I should lie low for a few days till this dies down a bit but I'm missing you. Can we come over tomorrow?

I message back so quickly I mistype and my message is interpreted as *Yeti Pleasure,* so I message again saying, *I meant Yes, please. I miss you too. See you tomorrow x*

The next day, bright and early, Anton arrives for work unshaven and bouncy.

'Morning,' he chirps happily. 'No work today? Or late start?'

'Day off, thankfully, but I'll try not to get in your way.'

He shrugs, makes no mention of the me-and-Reef situation but begins to whistle along to the CD player in the kitchen before searching his bag for tools. I stand watching him, idly running a finger along the edge of the kitchen table, so tempted to ask how he enjoyed the party and how long have he and Jade been together. I wonder how they'd met and had it been before she'd moved to London. That's a long time to have a long-distance relationship. They must have known each other from when she was living here, or perhaps got together quite recently when she'd been visiting her mum. Who knows, maybe half the reason she's moving back is to be with Anton. I suppose it is still possible to become friends with Jade because I don't have to bring up the almost kiss. The only problem is, if I want to pursue a friendship, I'd have to go via Anton because I didn't have the time to get her number.

Anton turns because he can probably feel my eyes on him.

'Everything all right?' he says.

'What? Yes, yes. Fine. Coffee?'

'You're reading my mind.' He gets up, smiles and starts drawing lines and measuring where the splashback and tiles will eventually go now that I've decided which I want.

For a whole hour, Anton hasn't mentioned anything about the girl next door gone viral. It's clear he doesn't care about my relationship with Reef in the way I'm concerned about his with Jade. He is working hard on the kitchen when Reef knocks on the door in the late morning. Noé runs into my tummy and hugs me so that his little face disappears into the baggy sweater I'm wearing. Despite Bea and Cat's advice, I haven't dressed for media coverage. Not that I've left the house, not even a midnight stroll, especially as my warmest, most snug coat is in the cloakroom at Glewstone Court Country House. The replacement had been delivered earlier, but when I opened the parcel, it was bright pink. I'd obviously clicked the wrong colour in my sleepless state but decided to keep it as it might brighten me up.

'How you doing?' Reef asks when it's clear that Noé isn't going to let go of me.

'Well, I'm fine, it's just, I don't know what to think.'

'You don't know how to think?' asks Noé, looking up at me with big eyes before going back to snuggle into my sweater. Reef motions that Noé knows nothing about what's going on. We're still standing in the corridor, and Anton drags something across the floor which sparks Noé's interest and has him racing into the kitchen.

'Who's that?' asks Reef.

'Just the builder. He'll be fine with him.'

Reef doesn't look so sure, but we have a lot to discuss and I lead him into the living room where we sit together on the sofa.

'I've been fielding lots of calls about you. Well, my agent, Jack, has. He's been on the phone to me, asking what we're all about. Is it serious.'

'Oh,' I say.

'What am I telling people?' Reef moves closer and takes my hand.

'What do you want to tell them?'

'That you and I are together. That we're a couple.'

'Really?' I sigh with relief and smile up at him. He is serious. I knew there would be more to this relationship. It wasn't just going to fizzle out and leave me with nothing again.

'Of course,' he says. 'I mean, I've been telling you all along that I want us to be together. I wish you'd believe me. You're a special girl, Annie. I don't get why you don't know that about yourself.'

'I guess because the only person who has ever said that was my mother and she's kind of biased, so I'm not sure it counts.'

'Annie, you've got to start thinking more of yourself. You have to start believing that you're a really great person. You're kind, you're sensitive, you're talented and patient. Noé can't get enough of you.'

'Nor me him.'

At which point the cute boy runs in pulling Anton by the hand.

'Can I do builder work?' he shouts.

'Definitely not,' says Reef, rising and picking Noé up. 'You're destined for bigger things.' He allows Noé to clamber onto his back and hold onto him with his legs and arms as if he has now become Reef's backpack.

'I'll get on,' Anton says. He looks as if he has sagged in the middle after what Reef said and disappears from the room. I look at Reef expecting him to have rephrased it, he couldn't have meant to be insensitive, but he ignores Anton completely.

Noé leaps from Reef's back demanding that we do some painting and that he won't drink the paint. In the studio, father and son stop to look at the chalk pictures of Noé, all of them clipped to a string I've attached from the window pole to the light fixture.

'Is that me?' Noé jumps up, hands reaching upwards to grab the pictures.

'No,' I say, 'it's a little boy from down the road who looks like you.'

He giggles and insists it's him.

'What's the story behind these?' Reef asks.

'Well, they're not quite finished yet. But these are the places in Ross that Noé has been and where he's had fun and can know that he has a family here who loves him and where he can be welcome any time. This is Noé helping me make pizza in my kitchen because he always has a home here. This is him having breakfast at Rhiannon's Eatery because she thinks you're great,' I say, playfully prodding Noé in the tummy. 'And she'd want to look after you any time. This is the three of us in Daddy's garden enjoying tickles in the grass with leaves catching in our hair. And this is you driving in my car with me. We're happy because I've enjoyed all the times we've had together and I would take you anywhere you wanted to go.'

Noé's eyes are bright as he looks up at the pictures. Reef puts an arm around me and pulls me into him, very close.

'I told Mummy all about our fun things when I went to France with Daddy,' says Noé. 'She was talking to Daddy yesterday.'

'Oh?' I turn to Reef.

'It's all right, she was just curious about you after seeing something in her Insta feed. Wanted to know more about you.'

'What did you say?' I ask with a knot in my brow. Did he make it clear that I'm not the nanny?

'Just that you were nice.'

'I told Mummy lots about you, Annie, and she wants to meet you.'

There is a short ring on the doorbell that no one ever uses followed by one loud fist on the door. I'm not expecting anyone and assume it's someone here to help Anton. I get the shock of my life when I open the door to see Natalia De Veras standing there. She is the last person I expect to see on my doorstep.

Natalia pulls pink tinted sunglasses down her nose and stares at me from over the top of them. I suspect they must be for UV protection purposes as the sun is non-existent overhead. The sky is full of white clouds and very little light or movement. It's uncannily quiet in the small private road. Even though I see a neighbour cycle by, I can't hear the sound of pedals in motion, tyres along the gravel or the sound he makes as the words 'hello there' are spelt out on his lips. I glance at him for a split second, the only second I allow myself to look away from the intense and intimidating glare of Natalia De Veras. She is several inches taller than me. Her faux fur coat is unbuttoned and draped over her shoulders, and beneath it she wears a tight roll neck sweater and super-wide trousers held up by a thick belt which accentuates her trim waist. The huge belt buckle is silver with a cluster of emerald stones embedded in the metal. Natalia takes in a long, audible breath through her nostrils, and I believe she is about to blow all of this air into my face to revive me from the daze I find myself in. On an exhale, she states her full name as if it's the secret code to grant her access and I step aside for her. The fur of her sleeves brushes my face and, because my mouth is open, it makes me splutter and cough.

'What are you doing here?' Reef has stepped out into the corridor and he is bowled aside by Noé who trundles towards his mother with open arms.

'*Mamá!*' he exclaims in Spanish and stops dead in front of her with arms held up.

'*Mijo!*' she says and kneels in front of him, throwing off her coat in a swoop onto my feet before hugging her son into her mega-thin frame. She says several things to him. Some words in Spanish, some in French and then back to English, one eye on Reef. 'Are you safe, my love?'

'Of course, he's safe.' Reef steps forward and I see Anton craning his neck to look into the corridor before closing the kitchen door. 'Why wouldn't he be safe?'

Natalia rises from the ground like a superhero who has recently landed on her knee in slow motion, about to face the antihero. Reef.

'Isn't this the house where my boy drinks paint?' She waves a hand back in my general area, and I pick her coat up off the floor.

'Once,' says Reef. 'One tiny sip and he was fine.'

Natalia walks through the corridor, glancing into the living room door en route to my studio. I'm powerless to stop her, and Reef stands aside and lets her pass. She's like a tremendous force that knows no limits. She will go wherever she wants to go. No one can stop her. I don't suppose anyone has ever tried. Even I jog behind her carrying her coat like her eager lady's maid, not once mentioning that I don't like strangers wandering into my studio.

'This is unacceptable!' she declares as she, Noé and Reef disappear into my studio. I stand quietly at the door.

'Why does she have drawings of my son? Why has she been around him long enough to paint *this*? Where have you been while this is going on?' She doesn't even look at Reef as she questions him.

'I was here,' says Reef. 'Annie is an artist and she likes to paint.'

'I didn't approve this. And I didn't know she was significant to you. You didn't tell me. I thought Noé was describing his nanny, not your girlfriend.'

Again. Not his nanny. And I am his girlfriend if you must know, Natalia De Veras. She turns suddenly to me and I gulp.

'Should I hang this up?' I ask.

'I can see you have hobbies,' says Natalia, her head doing a swoop of the room. 'But my son is not one of them. When he is with his father, he is in his father's care and it isn't for you to arrange some babysitter to stay with Noé while you two carry on at parties.'

'Natalia,' Reef sighs, 'I told you it wasn't like that.'

'Whatever it's like,' she says to Reef but giving me her full attention, 'Noé was upset. He told me he cried for you. You shouldn't leave him with strangers. It's irresponsible and breeches our agreement.'

'So is this why you grilled me on the phone for Annie's address? Just to come here and start another row? And anyway, I didn't agree to your agreement, Natalia. According to the courts, when I look after Noé, I take responsibility of his care and I decide how that works. You can't do it from miles away. You can't know from miles away what he needs.'

Natalia spins around in the tiny space but creates a huge draught of Yves St Laurent air as she does.

'He needs love and attention, Reef. Love and attention, and he can't get that if you're gallivanting with some little girl.'

'Annie is not some little girl. She's my girlfriend.'

'She is,' says Noé, looking up at his mum. 'Don't be angry with Annie.'

Her large eyes slowly change direction, landing on me before her face has fully turned from Reef.

'You know it won't last, don't you?' Her voice is strangely quiet and the rest of her words get sucked into a vacuum the way the sound disappeared when I first opened the door to her. My head begins to spin as her mouth moves, and I swear she must be speaking her mother tongue because I

200

can't even lip-read what's going on. I feel pounding in my ears. I feel Noé's arms circle my hips and look down to search for his beautiful smile, but it's hidden by the massive fur coat I have in my arms that has no business being there.

'Noé,' I whisper and his face appears from beneath the dark brown fur. 'Take Mummy's coat to the living room and lay it on the couch.'

'Okay,' he obligingly squeals and leaves the room, half tripping on the coat and giggling as he goes. Presumably he's beside himself because three of his favourite adults are all together in one room. But he's the only happy one. Reef's face is red, his eyes glassy as he looks at Natalia. She squints as she looks at me.

'I'm sorry you feel, we haven't been looking after Noé,' I venture in a small voice. 'But all I've ever done is love that boy and try to make him happy.'

'And I haven't?' Natalia hisses. She smiles down at Noé who for the first time has picked up on the vibrations of the room. His eyes start to tear up and he looks wildly from one adult to the next. I kneel in front of him.

'Noé, could you ask Anton in the kitchen to find your coat and help you look for Rosie?'

I see Reef about to protest, but he backs down as I look pleadingly at him to please let it go.

Noé is quick to leave the room, and Natalia is quick to smirk and say, 'So now you want to boss everyone around?'

'I just don't think it'll be good for him to be in this kind of atmosphere,' I say, looking down to the incredibly narrow points of Natalia's shoes.

'And I think I've made it clear that I'm better equipped to know what is best for my boy.'

'Our boy,' says Reef.

'For now,' says Natalia.

They both look at me but I have nothing to say. They're right. They call the shots. I just wish they weren't being called in my studio. I see Noé and Anton chasing around the garden. I hear the bronze leaves crunch under their footsteps on the dry lawn outside. Noé giggles, calls Rosie, and Anton tells him, 'Let's go, I think I see her.' I want to be out there with them. Running around the garden in my pink padded coat, laughing and chirping and looking for a cat who doesn't like me. But none of that would matter because I'd be in *their* company and not in my studio where the toxicity levels are rising, and so is the bile in my stomach. I hate this.

'So, we'll pick up his things and get to the airport,' Natalia is saying, and I swing around to see water welling in Reef's eyes and his hands coming together in prayer.

'Don't do this, Nat. It isn't fair, not to anyone.'

'I want to see my lawyer. Revisit the court order because it's not working.'

'You do this whenever things don't suit you. Why can't you put him first for once?'

'How dare you?'

'It's true. All you want to do is punish me. As if everything is my fault. Look, Nat, when all is said and done, I love Noé and I want him in my life.'

'Stop treating me like I'm the monster. You were just as cruel. You left us alone for ages at a time.'

'I did nothing wrong. I had a career. I had obligations.'

'And one of them was to *us*!'

'You walked out on *me*!'

'I'd had it with you. I tried. I tried everything I could and you never saw that.'

'That's not true.'

'And here we are, still arguing, still hurting each other.'

'And Noé,' I say, and they both swivel to face me, finally remembering that I'm here.

'What?' says Natalia.

'Noé is hurting,' I say. 'It's crystal clear to me. He loves you both more than anything. He's so scared that you both might forget him one day that he cries and gets worked up about it. He's crying for help but you're both too wrapped up in your own drama to realise it.'

Since she's arrived, I've had two out-of-body waves. This is the third. An opinionated Annie has spoken for me and made two people very angry at her. But the words can't be taken back and they're just going to have to deal with it.

Natalia's face heats up, her colour darkens and the whites of her eyes seem more bright. Reef is red in the face, shaking his head. At me? Then something happens when the two of them lock eyes. I see a couple who have loved each other and love their son but they just don't know how to get on. Neither wants to give in to the other, and the tension in the room circulates like an aura around them and I'm shut out.

'Get our son,' Natalia bellows. The temperature in the studio changes in an instant, her voice like a glacier. 'We're leaving. I'll follow you to your house. Get his passport, he's coming with me. We'll spend Christmas with Alejandro and then on to Australia.'

'I was supposed to have Christmas and you have New Year. It was decided just days ago. Noé and I haven't been together for Christmas for two years. Natalia. No. You can't.'

Both Reef and I follow her out to the garden where she shouts for her son.

'Hey you!' she snaps her fingers at Anton and does a circular gesture with her finger to suggest he winds things up and delivers Noé. 'He's coming home,' she bellows in the crisp afternoon air, and white mist circles her angry mouth before she calls her son's name again. Noé stays put. Reef calls his son but still he doesn't move. Anton tries to angle him back to his parents.

'*Vamanos*,' Natalia cries, impatience making her sound less robotic. 'It's time for us to go.' Her son trots reluctantly to her side.

'Where?' asks Noé, looking from Reef to me.

'Mummy wants to have you for Christmas and New Year,' Reef says.

'But I was going to have them with both of you. A day each. Remember?' I can see the tremble in his lips and I hope to goodness he won't start to cry uncontrollably again. It will ruin the holidays for him completely if that's the way they are going to start off. My eyes glisten with tears and my throat is dry but I can't hold back.

'Please,' I say and everyone stares at me. 'Please don't punish Noé because of me. I paint pictures, I draw, that's who I am. If I'd known it was not acceptable, I never would have done them and you can take them, all of them, and do what you want with them. And I'm sorry I arranged the babysitter, too. It's just that Noé had met her twice and she's a very close friend of mine, so I knew he'd be in safe hands. Reef trusted me and I wouldn't have suggested a stranger to look after your son. I know you're good people and you love him, but if you go back on your promise, he's not going to enjoy Christmas. He loves you both so much and he'll be broken-hearted if you change plans again.'

Reef's eyes grow dark, his temples throbbing from clenching his teeth so hard. I can't tell if he's angry with me for speaking my mind or if he's still upset with Natalia. He lifts Noé up and buries the boys face into his shoulder, staring sadly at Natalia. She huffs and storms into the living room, picks up her coat and swings it over her shoulders like a cape. She goes to the front door, opens it without a word and Reef follows carrying Noé, who has made his body as stiff as a plank so that it's awkward for his dad to hold him. Noé's face contorts as I follow them along the front path, his arms are outstretched and reach towards me.

'Annie,' he cries, and I can feel the weight of his words and how they crash against my heart. 'Annie. I want Annie. Please.'

I hear his voice fade as the car door slams and Reef telling him everything will be all right. Reef looks straight at me, his bottom lip curled as he starts the engine. Natalia's is already revving and she speeds millimetres behind Reef's car as she follows him out of my road.

I'm cold and I'm shaking and I don't know what's happening. I wonder what I did. How I let this happen. Why didn't I just shut up and not make Natalia angry? I've lost Noé. I won't see him again and there's absolutely nothing I can do. I begin to tremble as I stand in the path, looking at the space where Reef's car was parked. I'm not sure how long ago they drove away, but the pain in my chest won't go and I feel colder by the second. A voice next to my ear whispers my name.

'You're shaking. Come inside and I'll get you some tea. Come with me.'

Anton leads me back into the house and sits me on the sofa. He pulls the blanket on the back of it around my shoulder and kneels in front of me, hands resting softly on my knees.

'Just let it out.' Then he leaves the room and I hear the kettle boiling in the distance, and I wish I could curl up and sleep. Until this pain goes away.

23

How Long Has This Been Going On

I send a message to Rhiannon with only one hour to go before the knitting group is due to start. I imagine Rhiannon and her assistant tidying up at the eatery, chairs pushed aside as the floor is bleached clean. Wiping over the laminated menus, and unsold food being collected for the food bank run by volunteers in the town centre. The last thing I want to do is go over to Rhiannon's Eatery later and join the Monday Afternoon Knitters as if everything is okay. When Anton came to the living room door and said he was leaving for the day, all I managed was a slight nod over my shoulder. I didn't even thank him for looking after me after I'd watched Noé being driven away without me even having said a proper goodbye to him. The only things I have left of Noé are the pictures I've drawn of him.

'They have to do things their way, Annie. But you were brilliant. I really think she'll reconsider.' That's what Anton had said after handing me a hot cup of tea.

'That Reef seems like a decent bloke. He'll find some way of getting the kid back here. Surely you can see him then.'

'She wants to keep me away from him. I just need to accept that.'

But Anton was undeterred. 'She was just blowing off steam. You know what famous people are like. It's all drama with them. She'll come around.'

I know Natalia is changeable. Surely she can't keep Noé in Australia, so far from his dad while she's ice-skating. She might send him back. Back to Reef's and then I'll see him.

'The cupboards will be fitted tomorrow,' Anton had said, hoping that would cheer me up. It did. I'm looking forward to it all being kitted out. Once it is, Anton will get down to the tiling and the final coats of paint. He says that doesn't take a lot of time. He'd left when all the tears were over and the tantrums no longer echoed in the house.

Half an hour after the knitting circle usually starts, the knitters arrive at the door with their knitting bags and baskets and Rhiannon has a big freezer bag with her. She has probably brought all the cakes in the café, including the ones that she would have donated to the food bank. Because I've cried off the knitting circle, Rhiannon will have assumed something dreadful has happened and I must need feeding. I've never missed a Monday afternoon since I started.

'That was a loaded message you sent,' Rhiannon says as each of the women come in and give me a warm hug when they see how pink the whites of my eyes are. After Anton left, I'd sunk deeper into sadness and rubbed my eyes so hard to stop me crying I may have burst blood vessels. My eyelids are puffy too and I know I look a fright. That's partly why I didn't want to leave the house in the first place. I wouldn't have been able to hide my feelings from the women.

I give them a tearful run down of what happened earlier and the women generously shower me in sympathy. I dry my eyes, determined that I won't sink into the depths of despair and would rather live in hope that Natalia will come around and not keep Noé away from his father, ergo, from me.

I sit on the foot stool, my knitting project on my knee, the twisty-looking beanie hat that is now about ten rows long, so more of a head band than a hat, and I try to concentrate on adding more rows by focusing only on the knitting pattern instructions. *Knit one row, purl one row. Keep knitting until the length is approximately 8 ins from beginning. End with wrong side row*. That's all I need to focus on.

As I screw up my face and try to place all my energy into this yellow, tangled mess of stitches and dropped stitches and discoloured wool, I notice how quiet it is. I look up at the women and they are working away. I stare at them all, minds on their work, eyes magnified by reading glasses, and that's when I notice a shiny tear trickle from the corner of Judith's eye. I quickly sweep the room to see who else has noticed, but no one has. I look back at my work, realising I'm about to do a purl stitch in the wrong row. I save it in time but I can't help sneaking another look at Judith from under my brow. I see another salty tear spill into a crease under her eye. She draws her lips in to stop the quiver in them.

'Judith?' I say, and the others both look up at her.

'It's nothing, dear. Nothing at all.' She takes off her glasses and wipes the tears away from her cheek, smoothing away the wrinkles temporarily until the next flow of tears.

'This isn't nothing,' I say, putting down my knitting and coming to sit next to her on the sofa. I put my arm over her shoulder and lean in close. Her perfume is lavender and her body feels a little frail under my touch, so I loosen my hold and place a hand on her lap.

'Whatever's the matter, Jude?' asks Rhiannon, a hint of disbelief as though she'd never known Judith to cry.

Judith shakes her head and looks down at the knitting on her knees. It's a chunky cardigan, a present for her sister.

'I was thinking about Annie, actually.' Judith looks at me and gives a weak smile. 'We were supposed to look after you. Protect you from sadness while your mother is in Australia but we couldn't stop this happening.'

'Well, how would you have known?' I ask and hug her close again.

'No one suspected Reef would have a nightmare of an ex, or that he'd be having custody battles,' Bea says. 'It doesn't mean it's over, Jude. Annie still has her man.'

Judith shakes her head. 'Of course, you're the expert on getting your man.' Judith dries her face and sniffs.

'Be careful what you say, Judith.' Something in Bea's eyes holds a warning. She doesn't want Judith to carry on.

'Wait one moment,' says Rhiannon. 'I understand why you're crying so much. This isn't all to do with Annie. It's the anniversary, too.'

'What anniversary?' I venture.

'It is twenty-three years to the day that my Richard died. I do get tearful, and when you described how they took Noé, I felt the pain of him being torn away from me all over again.'

Bea blows through her lips and looks short on patience. 'It's over twenty years, Judith. You need to move on from this.'

'Not all of us can be the merry widow,' says Judith, gathering up her knitting so that the arm I have around her is redundant and I move along the sofa and remain there, motionless, because the air is highly charged with uncertainty. I'm on edge – this reminds me of earlier when Natalia was raging at Reef. Noé, Anton and I stood outside

210

the waves of energy they created, unable to approach because of an invisible force.

I look at Rhiannon and I see her shake her head in an "Oh no, here we go again" sort of way. I draw in a deep breath of anticipation. I know this has nothing to do with the knitting circle name changing to one that sounds like a seventies funk band. This is the secret and I'm about to learn it.

Now I do go back to the foot rest, but instead of picking up my knitting, I sit on it, arms on my knees, and wait.

'There's nothing merry about being a widow,' says Bea. 'I know, I've been one. And you had some wonderful years with Richard, don't forget. Why can't you just think about the good times you had? Especially after what you did.'

What *Judith* did. I thought *Bea* was the one who'd committed the crime they're concealing. I guessed it had something to do with Judith's husband. I'd suspected an affair but maybe I was wrong. Rhiannon is winding wool around her spool, about to put her work away, and I wonder if I should too and if we should leave these two alone to thrash out whatever they have between them. But I'm pinned to the stool and a sudden move might be the wrong move. Maybe it's time the women got this off their chests.

'You told me you forgave me,' Judith hisses and makes a dramatic sweep of her head towards Bea.

'And I have, but you won't let it lie. You just won't move on. You keep needling away at me. Needling away as if I haven't said sorry enough. That I haven't atoned for what I said. And when are you going to realise, they were only words. I wasn't responsible for what happened to Richard. I didn't kill your husband. He died. He just died. People die, Judith, and we can't get them back. When we lose them, that's it.'

211

'But you didn't have to say those things.'

'I know.' As Bea stands, her knitting falls to the floor and I see the loop of a stitch roll to the tip of the knitting needle and gently slip off. 'Why do you insist that you've forgiven me when clearly you haven't. You've harboured a hatred for me and I'm the one who should be hard done by – not you. I'm the one who should have been Richard's widow – not you. You stole him and I forgave you, and you can't forgive me my anger, a few angry words? I didn't even mean them, Judith. For God's sake, will you wake up and see that holding so tightly onto the past is killing you too. I don't want to die a wizened old lady. I want to live life to the fullest so the four horsemen are chasing me down the high street while I'm running away with a bottle of Bolly in my hand. And where will you be, Judith? Shrivelled up and long dead because you can't move on.'

Judith's body shoots upward from the sofa. A tall, thin woman with hands balled into tight fists at her sides and a face so full of rage and colour it might explode from her shoulders.

'I loved him!'

'So you told me, years ago, when you stole him away from me.'

'You orchestrated that. You turned your back on him. He hadn't a choice but to seek comfort from me.'

Bea looks to me, points at Judith and swivels her head back to her.

'You're going to lie now, are you? Lie in front of Annie when you are supposed to be her moral guide and the person who keeps her honest and true?'

'Please,' I say. 'I don't want to be a part of this. This is between you two, or you three, and I think I should go.'

'You can't go,' Bea says through gritted teeth. 'It's your bloody house, my darling, and you're as much a part of this group as the rest of us.'

'But...' I try to protest. 'Mum doesn't know anything about the problem you're having. Why should I?'

'Your mother, God bless her soul,' says Bea, 'was far too fragile for this. We were *her* support system too, and no way was she ready to hear about what Judith had done. Otherwise, she wouldn't have appointed her your moral compass. Thought she was the upstanding one. But we all have our faults.' Bea sits now. Judith doesn't know what to do with her body. She wrings her hands, and it isn't until Rhiannon comes over to sit her down that she realises there is nothing more to do than to sit and listen to the words boiling up inside Bea. Bea turns to look at me and Judith's head bows downwards.

'I met Richard,' says Bea. 'I knew him before Judith did. She was going out with someone I'd arranged for her to meet. They were a good-looking couple, everyone thought they were going to get engaged, really excited for her because of that long engagement in her twenties that went absolutely nowhere. I'd turned thirty, been married twice already, wasn't going to bother again, and then I met Richard. He was gorgeous, and of course I introduced him to my best friend.' She throws a look at Judith. 'She said she liked him. I just didn't know how much.'

'Bea,' Judith whispers a warning for her not to go on.

'No,' says Bea. 'I have to say this. I consider Richard to be the love of my life.'

'But you didn't treat him like that,' Judith chimes in. 'You've never treated any man well.'

213

'It doesn't matter how I treated him. I loved him and I told you I did.'

'But you stood him up, went off to London with that boy, Toby. He was younger than you.'

'Toby knew all the best parties, the right people and I wanted to have fun, like I'd had in my twenties. Richard didn't know how.'

'So that was a reason to go off and leave him alone? Worried about you and what you were up to.'

'I was just a girl who wanted to have fun.'

'You were a grown woman who'd been married twice and should have known better.'

'Huh!' Bea turns to me now. 'Shall I tell you what this woman of supposed high morals did, Annie?'

'I ... I–' I'm shaking my head but Bea continues anyway.

'I arranged to meet up with Richard. I knew he'd bought me an engagement ring and I wanted to make amends for having waltzed off to London like that and give our relationship a proper chance. I called Judith from London, wanting to surprise Richard with a romantic dinner by the river, and I asked her to make sure he was there at a certain time. I got a hamper from Harrods and I drove up from London, ready to say yes, ready to settle down properly this time and live my life with Richard.'

'Please don't go on,' says Rhiannon. 'Annie is upset enough. She's not having a good time of things. Remember how it was for her mother when the stress got too much.'

'I'm not like that,' I snap. 'I don't do that and I never will. I can face up to things. I'm tougher than you think.' It's not that I ever thought my mother was weak, I just didn't want to go through all of those dark emotions that kept her chained to the spot, her bed, a chair, anywhere but with me.

I've always feared I had that side of her in me and I've fought hard to not let my insecurities enslave me. I'm me. I'm not her and I know I have to let go of that fear.

'Carry on.' My face is neutral, but my heart pounds in my chest and I feel it in my throat as I look at Judith. 'Judith, you need to listen. You need to keep an open mind and the pair of you have to resolve the whole situation. No matter how messy. It's the only way you'll both move on. What happened next, Bea?'

The women seem stunned by my outburst, but I'm determined that what happened between Reef and Natalia, rushing away with a screaming child, not having resolved a single thing, was not going to happen with my friends. I hear someone swallow and Bea continues.

'She went to Richard and told him I'd moved on and fallen in love with Toby. Said I was coming back to collect some things and then I would go back to London to be with him.'

'Judith,' I say. 'Really?'

'You have to understand,' Judith implores. 'Bea treated her men awfully.'

'That's not true. Not all of them.'

'But you did Richard,' Judith says with tears filling her eyes again. 'And I loved him. I loved him from the day you introduced us. I was used to having your cast-offs so I was willing to wait. Thought it would just be a question of time. I never expected that call saying you were coming back. That you wanted Richard back. We'd been getting to know each other. He was serious about me. He fell in love with me and we knew it was right. We knew we had to be together. So I … I didn't tell him about the call. Instead, I arranged for us to get away that day. A trip to my sister's in Monmouth and that's when we decided we wanted to be together.'

215

'I see,' I whisper.

'Then they spring an engagement on me,' says Bea. 'Next, a wedding, and they expect me to come.'

'But you did go in the end.'

'In the end, I wanted to be the bigger person,' says Bea.

'By putting a curse on my marriage?'

'Oh for crying out loud, Judith,' Bea exclaims. 'I have no power to put curses on people's marriages any more than I do of making a marriage work for myself.' She turns to me. 'I said to Judith that if she marries Richard, it won't last. He'll curl up and die before they even get to have children and she'll never find anyone else. But I was angry. I didn't mean it, Annie.'

'Of course you didn't. She couldn't have meant that, Judith. She came to your wedding. She wouldn't have done that if she meant all those things. Imagine how upset she would have been to see you marry the man she loved. You of all people know that Bea opens her mouth without thinking sometimes. No offence, Bea, but it's true. But Judith, surely you must know Bea loves you. I can see that. You must, too.'

'And years ago,' says Bea, 'you told me you forgave what I said.'

Judith shakes her head and tears fall on her lap. 'But I didn't. I couldn't. I love you, Bea, but I truly believe you ruined my life. I can't help it. I can't get rid of the bitterness because I miss him every single bloody day.'

Bea rushes to the sofa now and falls against Judith. She wraps her arms around her, holding her up because Judith's upright body has collapsed into itself.

'Judith, oh Judith,' Bea says with tears streaming down her face.

216

I go to kneel by the sofa where all three women sit in tears. I take Judith's hands and squeeze them.

'Mum asked you to be the one to take care of my mental health, the practical things, the legal things because she trusted you. Now, be honest. I know you and I know that you don't believe in curses.' Judith sniffs and looks at Bea. 'It's not Bea you don't forgive. It's yourself. You did something that went against everything that is fundamentally you. You lied to get Richard and that's what you can't forgive. But it's time to let go of all of that hurt and anger. Richard is gone. You had twenty-two years with a man you loved and who loved the bones of you. You told me that yourself, said it was a gift, and it really is.'

'It's more than I've ever had in four marriages,' says Bea. 'You once said you envied me. Well, I'd give up every man I've had, every wedding I've had, every party I went to, all the places I've been, just so I could have had a minute of what you had with Richard. You two were the making of each other. The perfect couple. You knew it and you made it happen, and I would have done exactly the same if the roles were reversed.'

Rhiannon has found some tissues in her bag and she hands them to Bea and Judith. The women dry their eyes and smile to each other. Their smiles grow wider. They begin to chuckle, laugh loudly and then uncontrollably until Rhiannon and I join in. Rhiannon, who has been wiping away tears all through the conversation, turns to me.

'I don't think we need worry about you anymore, pet,' she says. 'You were the calmest of us and said the most helpful things. You made these two come to their senses. Finally. It's more than I could ever do.'

217

'I only said what was in my heart. I'm no therapist. You two resolved this, I just encouraged you to do it before it went so far there'd be no turning back.'

'And finally we can look forward,' says Bea, patting Judith's lap. 'Can we?'

'Oh, we most certainly can.' She looks to me. 'Thank you, Annie. I'm sorry we've added to your problems. Can you ever forgive us?'

'There's nothing to forgive. Really. We're friends, and friends are there for each other in a crisis. You've all done so much for me in the past and helped me move forward in my life. So thank you.'

I keep a wide smile on my face as I try to keep my real feeling about moving forward to myself. While I'm so happy for Bea and Judith, all I see before me are the negatives in my life. The problems that I have going on. A heart I'm going to have to heal on my own. I'm just not sure I can.

24

Song for My Father

If there is one constant in my life, it's my disastrous sleep patterns. It has become the thing that defines me. It rules my life and sometimes stops me functioning. It isn't a particularly healthy way of being, but at a time when I'm discovering distressing truths about people I know, being raged at by people I don't and losing someone I wished I could hold on to forever, I can at least guarantee that I won't get a good night's sleep. I'm relishing pulling on my fur-lined boots, tucking pyjama bottoms into them and getting ready for a walk in the middle of the night because at least I can own that. Walking at night means I won't get let down because I know what to expect from it. Darkness and peace. No tears, no sadness, just cool air on my cheeks, the occasional lazy hoot of an owl, the bark of a fox and the rare rumble of a car engine in the distance. Maybe I see something in the shadows that stirs up my imagination and makes me afraid, but my fear is short-lived because there really is nothing to fear, out here on my own. The town is mine to walk through, breathe in and leave behind when I decide.

Zipping up the front of my ultra-pink padded coat, I'm happy that its first outing is in the dark where no one else can see or judge me in it. I unwind my ridiculously long scarf from a coat hook and wrap it a million times around me. It's like a cosy neck support that smells of my perfume and keeps me snug and warm. The gloves go on next. I remember I have a stripy pair that matches my coat, so if I'm going to be mugged or attacked in the middle of the night, as everyone fears I might be, I may as well be stylish.

As I pass her house, I notice a light on upstairs in Judith's window. The light is muted by the closed pink curtains of her bedroom where she is probably still thinking about the emotional episode of earlier. It's the most dramatic event in the history of the Monday Afternoon Knitters Circle, at least in the time I've been a member. Judith probably can't sleep off the heart-stopping scenes of earlier anymore than I can. It'll take me a while to get over the fact that Judith, the person I always thought to be upstanding and honest, told lies in order to get her best friend's boyfriend. I hope she learns to forgive herself one day. Bea has already moved on now that she is onto her next boyfriend. I wonder if Bertie, her date for the funeral, is likely to be husband number five?

I approach the town centre and head straight for the mall where I expect to find Dez and Phoenix. The temperatures are dropping and the predictions are that we will have a white Christmas. A bark echoes from the inside of the mall as I enter via Sainsbury's car park. Before I can see him, I hear Phoenix whimpering as if he's straining to come off his leash and rush up to me. He gives a happy bark as I approach.

'Annie Lennox. I thought that must be you,' says Dez, sitting up and leaning his back against the post office window. The list of people he knows called Ann or Annie seems limitless. He tells me whose name he has given to me if I've never heard of them. Annie Lennox needs no explanation. 'This boy knows our footsteps better than anybody's.'

They both look thin and grubby and should be fast asleep, but it's as if they knew I needed a friendly conversation as all I've had all day is tears and drama, and I'm drained. Phoenix nudges his nose towards me and I stroke his head.

'Look what I have for you.' I hand him one of the dog biscuits I've recently bought as a treat for him, but he lets it drop to the floor and moves it away with his muzzle.

'He's a bit off his food,' says Dez.

'I can see that.' I pet Phoenix again. I don't want to say that neither of them looks as if they have been eating and that I think they both need medical attention.

'Changes are afoot, Princess Annie. Changes are afoot.'

'What changes?' I kneel on the edge of Dez's cardboard box and he looks down at the encrusted blanket that covers his sleeping bag.

'I had a visit,' says Dez. Phoenix settles down at his side and lowers his head as if to sleep. 'A blast from the past came looking for me. Wants me to come home.'

'What?' I'm amazed because from what I know of Dez, he has no one in the world apart from his best friend. He told me he'd lost his job, then lost his home and then found Phoenix. He'd rescued the dog from where he'd been dumped as a puppy at a deserted building site on the outskirts of Bristol. They'd travelled from Bristol to Hereford and finally found their home in Ross. They've been a feature of the town for as long as I can remember. I hadn't imagined he'd still have links from the past because surely, by now, he would have reached out to them for help.

'Never told you this before but I was married once. Beautiful woman from long ago and we had a son.'

'You have a son? You're joking.'

'Oh, it's no joke. I didn't always look like this, I was quite a catch once.' He grins with yellowing teeth.

'Sorry, I didn't mean…'

'Just playing with you, Nightingale. I don't talk about all that because, well, you know me, I follow my nose and I don't look over my shoulder.'

'So, she wants to take you back?'

'*She* can't. She's dead. Things were never the same after that. I couldn't do anything. Hold down a job, look after my son. They had to take him from me in the end. The council. Care home. Said it was temporary until I got a new job but that never happened, did it? Evicted, I was, and the poor lad had no idea where I'd gone. I thought he'd forget I even existed.'

Dez surveys his corner of the mall with wistful eyes as I begin to realise that it's his son who has tracked him down. He obviously isn't happy to have been found.

'And so, what will you do about it, Dez?'

Phoenix has fallen asleep. Dez, in his fingerless gloves, rests a hand on the dog's head and scratches his brow. The movement makes Phoenix's closed eyes move back and forth as if he's contemplating the situation and might come up with an answer for Dez who does nothing but shrug as if he can't decide.

'How did he find you?' I ask at last.

'I have an idea. You know you asked where Phoenix and I had disappeared to when you didn't see us for a while in summer? Took a holiday, didn't I? Back to my old stomping ground, back to Bristol. I saw someone.'

'Your son? How did he recognise you?'

'Not him. Some old buddy of mine I had in a former life only went and recognised me. Called out to me. Desmond, Desmond, is that you, like? You know? We were both amazed to see each other. He knew all about my boy somehow and where he'd ended up. I'd told this mate of mine I was here in Ross before I realised he knew my son. He must have told him and the boy showed up in Ross.'

'Did he know how you've been living?'

'He knew, all right, and he wants to offer me a home. A room in his flat until I can get back on my feet.' He tuts as if this is nothing.

'That's amazing,' I say, coming to a cross-legged position. 'It's actually the best news I've heard all day.'

Dez smiles in response to my wide grin, but he doesn't seem to care that he's been offered a lifeline, a second chance.

'You don't want to go?' I ask. I wring my gloved hands together to bring some life into them. By now, my bones are stiffening in the cold and, once again, I wonder how Dez can spend a whole night out here. I think of the number of times I've offered him a bath, a meal, a room for the night, but he has never once taken me up on the invitation. This is my life now, he always says, and maybe that's what he's thinking now. But it's his son reaching out. Surely that must mean something.

'Had a bit of bad news, have you?' he says to change the subject.

'Something like that.' I huff because mainly I want to talk about Dez. I shouldn't be burdening him with my worries. But don't I always do that with him? He knows far more about my life than I do his. 'I may not get to see that little boy I told you about again, and I heard some alarming news earlier that has left me pretty shaken up.'

'I'm sorry.'

'I'll live. At least there was a resolution to the bad news. A happy ending. You might be denying yourself one of those, Dez. I'm sorry but I can't help thinking that you should give it a go. You know? Reach out to your son. He obviously cares enough for him to have told you to come home with him. Did he leave you his address?'

'The moon and the stars. The early morning breeze on my face. The space to roam as I please. That's my home. Not an address.'

'The freezing cold. Food that's days old and no medical care for you and Phoenix. That doesn't sound like home. Neither of you look well. And even if you can't stand living within four walls, think about how nice it might be for this fella. Phoenix looks so unwell.'

Dez leans down to kiss the top of Phoenix's head. The dog quivers but stays asleep.

'My son won't let me keep the dog. Not where he is. A two-bedroom apartment by the river. No pets. What am I supposed to do?'

'Find a kindly person to look after Phoenix for you. Maybe your son knows someone in Bristol so you could at least see him. Hundreds of people would take him in. He's a good dog. Well trained. Anyone would love him.'

'Would you love him?'

'I already do.'

We're both quiet and listen to the silence of the town. It's almost four in the morning. I'm cold and starting to feel sleepy. Dez leans his head back against the window and closes his eyes.

'I'd better go,' I say.

'You mind how you go, girl. Get off and get warm. You know you shouldn't be out here.' He opens his eyes and winks at me.

'And neither should you.' I get up and go to leave. I have pins and needles in my left foot and I stamp both feet on the ground which makes Phoenix sit up and bend into a deep stretch before lying down again.

'Um, Dez,' I say. 'I'd like to invite you both over for Christmas.' I quickly put up both hands before he lectures me about the wonders of the outdoors. 'Just think about it. You don't have to stay for the day. Just long enough to eat something or I'll fix you a bag to take with you. Just mull it over, Dez, and let me know. Please?'

'Will do.' Dez puts his hand up to wave me off. I take a few paces before turning back to see Dez cuddling his dog. 'Another thing to think of is your son's offer. Don't only think of yourself. Think about your son. Think about Phoenix.'

At the mention of his name, Phoenix whines. I wave briefly and leave the mall, heading up the hill to the market square, back to the path through the graveyard and back to my house so that, hopefully, I can grab a nap before I have to get up for work.

I do sleep, albeit shallow and fitful. My alarm sounds into the dimness of my bedroom. I contemplate the major dramas of the day before and hope that today will be a little easier. I gulp down dangerous amounts of caffeine and open the door to Anton who searches my face for remnants of Nataliagate, but he can't find any so he gives me a big smile.

'You'll have a new fitted kitchen by the time you get home from work, all being well.'

225

'Great,' I say, taking my big pink coat off the hook and wishing I'd returned it in favour of a sensible colour. 'I look forward to that. See you later, Anton.'

'Bye.'

I close the gate and turn Anton's words over. A new fitted kitchen, he'd said. All being well, he'd said. Considering nothing is well at the moment, I half suspect I'll come home to wall units in the wrong colour and to find I no longer have a fridge.

25

My Baby Just Cares for Me

Just as I enter the practice, I get a call from Reef.

'How is Noé?' I ask, plopping my bag onto my desk and sinking into the chair, still wearing my pink coat.

'Yes, he's fine. Well, he finally settled down and managed to stop crying by the time we got home. Sorry I haven't called you before.'

'Not at all. You must have had your hands full, packing his stuff and having to say goodbye.'

'No, he's still here. We're at the house. Natalia's here too.'

A heavy stone drops from my heart and lands in my stomach.

'Yesterday she said she wanted to leave straight away.'

'That was yesterday and Natalia can be as changeable as the weather. No, she's calmed down a lot. She's not so angry. And it's thanks to you, Annie, because of what you said. Made her have second thoughts. She has got a soft side, she just hides it a little too well.' His voice sounds soft as he says this. 'We're out in the grounds. Noé is taking her to the start of the forest where he saw deer one time. I think he's happy to have us both in the same place at the same time.'

And you? I think. *Does it make you happy that it's the three of you together*? I hold on to that thought.

'It must be wonderful for him,' I say. 'I just…'

'Just what?'

'I was just hoping that when Noé does have to leave, that perhaps he and I could say a proper goodbye.'

'Of course. Yes. And there might not be a goodbye. Natalia is talking about cancelling that ice-skating thing and settling back in London, or maybe even closer to here so that we can have something that's a little more grounding for Noé.'

'That sounds incredible.' Some of the worry that has weighed me down lifts. 'So you and Natalia are making plans together. I mean for Noé.'

'Don't worry, Annie, there's no chance we're getting back together again. Natalia and I are putting Noé first and sorting our own stuff out so that we can be better parents to him. She might have been angry yesterday but everything you said makes perfect sense. We haven't been doing right by our son. We were both being selfish, antagonising each other, and the kid was caught in the middle of it.'

'Maybe I should become a counsellor.' I laugh briefly and remember how grateful Bea and Judith were to me to have finally been able to voice the pent-up feelings they'd had from the past.

'What are you doing now?' Reef asks.

'I'm at work.'

'Any chance you can skive off for a day? You know, apart from that first night when you and I had dinner in Birmingham, we really haven't had any time alone together.'

'I know. It's been a crazy few weeks.'

'I want us to be alone together.'

'But Natalia is still here.'

'And she'll be looking after Noé. If we're out, he'll be happily settled with his mum, and you and I can … well, really get to know each other.'

228

My good underwear is washed and back in the drawer. I had seriously thought of putting them in a box and burying them in the garden, like a time capsule I could open when I was ninety and remember that time I used to have sex and that it nearly happened while wearing my good Per Una underwear.

'I'd like that.' I dismiss the capsule from my mind and begin to feel flustered in this padded coat.

'What about tonight?'

'Are you sure Natalia won't mind?'

'Don't forget she is seeing someone herself, and don't forget Noé already sees you as my girlfriend and we wouldn't want to disappoint a cute, innocent little kid, would we?'

'A very convincing argument, Mr Mayer. I'll book something for tonight and you can pick me up at seven. How does that sound?'

'Sounds like a date.'

I get through the rest of my day thinking about my impending date, which is a step up from thinking that the only thing I had to look forward to was a fitted kitchen. An actual grown-up date with Reef would make up for all the tears and heartache of the past few days. By the time I arrive home, I'm in the best mood I've been in for ages.

Anton's van is still there as I walk up to the house. I unlock the door and hear voices in the kitchen – one of them is female. I shake myself out of my padded coat and find it odd, but who says the kitchen fitter can't be a woman. To my surprise, not only have I got a wonderful, spanking new kitchen, Anton has his girlfriend here.

'Jade?' I try hard to fix on a smile when a million and one emotions are attempting to give me away. Slight anger that

Anton should flaunt Jade in front of me when I'm struggling to lose the undeniable attraction I have for him. Frustration because I really like Jade and it's going to be difficult to strike up a friendship with her under the circumstances. I think about the trouble liking the same man caused between two best friends. The only way a friendship with Jade stands a chance is if I control my innermost thoughts. Bury them and not let them breathe life. Perhaps that will be made easier after my night out with Reef when he and I can seal the deal as it were. I remind myself of what a catch Reef is, that I do really like him and I'm attracted to him and I'm desperate to sleep with him. I'll get Anton out of my system the minute that happens, and soon Anton will be finished in the house and I can move on and enjoy dating Reef.

'I know, coincidence right?' Jade laughs happily away. 'I meet up with you after God knows how long, in a dressing room of all places, not only are we invited to the same party but Anton is your builder. How mad is that?'

'Extremely,' I say, faking a laugh that sounds like Jade's.

'Well?' says Anton. 'What do you think?' He spreads his arms and paces backwards around the new kitchen. It's a total transformation. The light mint units are smooth and modern with easy sliding drawers and finished with shiny, gold handles. I wasn't so sure they'd work but Anton had insisted they were the business the evening we'd sat and pored over the choices online. The place really does look the business and this is even before Anton completes the finishing touches which I can already imagine. I've chosen the contrasting tiles he'll be fitting above the surfaces and around the window and then he'll paint the walls dove grey. It'll be absolute perfection. The whole place looks more spacious, and he has set up the table and chairs I'd bought from Ikea and got rid of the historic wooden one. The surface well-used by me, Cat and Mum over the years. The pastry rolling table, the homework table. The table for paintings and drawings, flowers in vases, full shopping bags, a goldfish bowl. Though the table had mostly been covered by a tablecloth, evidence of a life lived as fully as we could resided on the table. From the chips and chinks in the wood, from the wear and burn marks, the word "Poo" dug into one of the legs from when Cat sat under it for hours during one of Mum's dark moments. And God how wobbly that old thing had become. The chairs were just as bad. Just as close to collapse. I run my hand over the silky Ikea table and rock the back of a chair to see how sturdy it feels.

'It's beautiful.' I sigh and circle the room. I wish Cat and Mum could see it. 'Thanks, Anton. You've done an amazing job.'

'Well, I only assisted with the fitting so I won't take all the credit.'

'Speaking of amazing jobs,' Jade says, turning to me enthusiastically, 'I hope you don't mind. I had a little nose around when I got here.'

'Yes?' I say, dwelling on the word because I have a feeling I know what's coming.

'Annie, it's your artwork. What are all those amazing pictures and paintings doing covered up and hidden away in that little room? Why is your talent such a secret?'

I look at Anton who gestures that his hands are clean. This is all Jade. I know he would have told her how I feel about my studio.

'Don't blame Anton. He did tell me you had mad talent but he said you wouldn't want me prying. But I just couldn't help myself and now I'm absolutely stunned.'

'It's really kind of you both but it's really just a hobby.'

'I know, but your hobby could bring joy to others.' Jade is right up in my face and practically jumping with glee. 'Remember Lorraine Madden from school? Did you know she runs the exhibitions in the gallery in Market House in the middle of Ross?'

'Lorraine does?'

'Yes, she does, and I bet if I had a word with her, she'd exhibit your work.'

'It's not up to standard.'

'Isn't that up to the beholder to decide?'

I shrug my shoulders. I knew Lorraine vaguely. She hadn't been in my friendship circle but she was a good friend of Jade's. I look at Anton who has been busy trying to look elsewhere, but the grin plastered on his face gives away what he wants to say, and he can't stop himself.

'Do it, Annie. Let Jade at least ask her.'

'Gosh, the pressure. I suppose, if you really think it's worth it, then please, do ask her.'

Jade bursts into the studio and takes several photos of my work.

'What have I unleashed?' I say and turn to find Anton pumping a fist. Jade comes bouncing back.

'Do you have champagne or could we at least have some tea to celebrate your new units and your possible future as an artist?'

'Calm down, Jade, she hasn't said yes. And um … I'm supposed to be going out,' I say apologetically. I would love to have celebrated with them.

'Oh, are you off out with Mr Celeb?' asks Jade.

I nod coyly and feel my cheeks burn.

'We'd better get off,' she says, 'let you get ready.'

'Were you helping with the kitchen?' I ask. 'It's lovely to see you but I wouldn't have expected Anton to rope his girlfriend in to doing his work.' I grin at him.

'Girlfriend!' they say with the same inflection on the word "girl".

'Eugh,' says Jade. 'Anton's my little brother.'

'Not so little,' he says and wags a finger at her. 'There's not much difference in our ages. I was in the year below you guys, Annie. I went to the boys school next door.'

'Of course she didn't notice you.' Jade nudges my arm. 'You and Becs and that Zarina girl were always after boys in Year Thirteen, weren't you?'

'Well, not me so much. I didn't have a boyfriend at school.'

'That's a coincidence,' she says. 'Anton here didn't have a girlfriend when he was at school. That's something you have in common.' She sounds conspiratorial.

Just then, there is a loud tap on the door. If it's Reef, he's early.

I open the door to a huge bunch of flowers and behind them a sparkling set of white teeth. Reef's aftershave overwhelms the bouquet, and me too if I'm honest. He wears a light grey suit over a salmon pink sweater. His hair is loose and I spot a diamond stud in one ear. I hadn't even noticed he has pierced ears.

'I'm a bit early but Nats has taken Noé for pizza and bowling in Gloucester and I couldn't sit still.'

I thought pizza was our thing.

'Is it okay?' he crosses his brow because I haven't exactly welcomed him in.

'No, no. Yes, of course it's okay. Come in. Let me put these in water. I'm not ready but I can be quick.'

233

'You take all the time you need.'

Reef's voice dwindles when he sees I have company.

'Ah, Reef, you've met Anton. Anton the builder, this is Reef my ... my date.'

They shake hands. They hadn't done that the first time of meeting. They are squaring up to each other and squeezing hands for an embarrassingly long time. Reef looks down at Anton with a downturned mouth and Anton looks up at Reef with slanted eyes. Jade bursts into the middle of them and declares, 'Hi, I'm Jade. Sister of Anton. Friend of Annie.'

The men separate and Reef takes Jade's hand gently into his. Their chests extend towards each other and they could be looking into a mirror with their matching, wide white smiles. Jade is the image of Reef's usual girlfriend. Stunning, brown-skinned, long-limbed and oozing confidence.

'Yes, Jade is a friend from school,' I say and walk up to them just as they pull apart and look at me.

'And you and I have a lot of catching up to do,' Jade says, brushing my arm. 'But we'd better clear out and let you get on with it.'

Anton is already halfway down the corridor and I follow Jade out. At the front door, she leans very close to my ear and whispers something in the schoolgirl fashion that we used to when we were thirteen.

'My brother fancies you.' She winks, looks down the corridor and leaves before I can say another word.

I close the door and bolt up the stairs, shouting to Reef that I'll be five minutes. I turn on the shower, scoop my hair into a big pile and do the best I can to secure it with a towelling head band. I try to count the seconds in the shower so that I can be speedy and be out and dried before Reef gets bored. I can't seem to shake what Jade said from my mind. I'm mostly dry before I begin to slap moisturiser onto my body.

I pull open my lingerie drawer and locate my good underwear. "My brother fancies you" echoes in my mind and I pull up my knickers and fasten my bra. I look in my mirror and wonder what to wear. I'd hoped to have had time to figure this out when I got home, so I'll have to improvise. Out comes a pair of black jeans and a silky black, long-sleeved top. I jazz it up with long silver earrings and a matching necklace. I opt for high heels, a squirt of Daisy and a quick swipe of red lipstick which I throw into a small handbag for touching up after dessert. I'm ready.

I find Reef in the living room, his arms outstretched across the back rest of the armchair, legs wide apart.

'Amazing,' he says and rises from his chair as if he's in an advertisement. In fact, it's the exact same move I've seen him use in one of his Nivea for Men adverts, only in that one he was shirtless with a bath towel around his waist, telling the camera how smooth his chin is.

Reef kisses me and I see my lipstick has deposited itself on his lips. I wipe it away and he nuzzles his face into my neck.

'You smell nice,' he whispers. I bend backwards out of his hold and away from his kiss.

'We should go.' I smile, suggesting there is plenty of time for that later. He fakes a sigh of annoyance.

'If we must.'

At the door, Reef helps me on with my pink coat.

'Is this new?' he asks.

'Yes, I left my other one behind at the party.'

'Oh no!' he says. 'My bad. I dragged you out of there without even thinking. You should phone them and see if we could go and pick it up.'

'I'll sort it in the week. Not to worry.' But I can't help noticing the worrying look Reef is giving my pink coat as I reach for my scarf. 'Tell you what, I think I might wear something a bit nicer. It is a date after all.'

I try to make light but I can see the relief in his eyes as I pull a black three-quarter length coat from under the pile of old coats and jackets on the hooks. Some of them are Mum's and Cat's. He helps me on with the coat from TK Maxx which was trendy about four years ago. It's not as warm as the padded coat but looks far more presentable.

'Shall we?' Reef opens the door and lets me through. He remotely opens the car door with a click and we drive into Ross for dinner.

'I've booked us the swankiest restaurant in town,' I say as I settle into the leather seat of Reef's car.

We arrive at the restaurant and immediately Reef's presence causes a stir, only this time people are actually interested in me. I get lots of smiles. Two members of staff offer to take my coat. One holds the right shoulder the other the left and I feel as if I'm about to be torn apart like a loaf of bread.

'We had no idea you were coming,' the manager says to Reef. Would they have rolled out the red carpet had they known? A literal one. 'And congratulations, Mr Mayer. Manager of The Blues. Been supporting them for years. Let's get them to the Premier League, eh?'

'That's the idea,' says Reef.

The restaurant manager leads us to a table along the back wall of the dining room. It is subtly adorned by a variety of mirrors, clusters of silk ivy leaves and one or two shiny fixtures that house fake plant pots. The manager bows several times, calls Reef 'sir' and me 'madam'. A menu appears in front of my nose from nowhere and the manager hands Reef a wine list. He recites the specials and promises that someone will return to take our order. Two seconds later, a waitress smiles down at us, asking what we'd like to drink.

'We'll let you know when we're ready,' Reef says. She leaves with an 'Of course, sir'. Reef smiles at me. 'Any idea what you'd like to drink?'

I'm so shaken by the attention that we're getting, I wonder how Reef can be so casual. He puts the drinks list on the table between us and looks down at it. I'm looking at the number of eyes aiming our way and the way people are unashamedly pointing phones at us. Even the person behind the bar. The man at the next table, mouth agape, just stares at me until my cheeks are so red I want to pour the jug of water over my face.

'I might have a nice whisky,' says Reef, unperturbed. 'They have some good ones.'

'I'll have what you're having.' The fact is, I've been so busy looking at people looking at us that I don't know what there is to drink or if in fact I actually want a drink. Usually I settle for wine with my meal. I don't even like whisky. But Reef goes ahead and orders it from the obliging waitress. As I pick up the menu again, I feel my hands are shaking.

'Annie, are you all right? You look a bit…'

I lean forward to whisper. 'Everyone is staring. It's embarrassing.'

'What?' says Reef and pulls a face. 'I can't hear you.'

I try to mouth my feelings, adding subtle gestures with my eyes, but he looks confused and looks around the restaurant to establish what my problem is. Of course he can't see a problem so I give up trying to explain my discomfort as the waitress serves the whisky.

'Ready to order, sir? What can I get you?'

'Let's see,' says Reef. He begins to reel off a starter and a main course as if he knows the menu by heart or has eaten there so many times he's ordering his usual. I'm looking up and down the choices at a gallop, otherwise they'll both be waiting for me. I find something reasonable, a starter and main course, both vegan even though I'm not. I let Reef choose the wine.

I then find myself making small talk. I talk about how I'm missing Mum and Cat and have only ever met her first child, now she has two, and they're very loud but are absolutely beautiful, both with white blonde hair that probably won't stay that way. I talk about how pleased I am with my new kitchen and can't wait for it to be finally ready. I mention how many clients I have the next day. I talk about the beanie I'm knitting and how the name of my knitting club was going to change but that we're keeping it the same. I talk and gulp whisky while Reef savours his. I talk and gulp whisky after the starters arrive, and all the time Reef sits quietly with a slight grin.

'I'm talking too much,' I say. 'I always do when I'm nervous.'

'Why are you?'

'Because.' I draw out the word and look around at the diners who are finally having the decency to eat their food. 'I've never had so many people stare at me.'

'They're staring at you because you're beautiful.'

'They're staring at me because I'm with you and some of them may have seen my picture from the other day. I keep thinking that they might ask if I want to nanny their kids.

They have no idea who I am or what I do, but because I'm with you…'

'I'm sorry,' says Reef. 'But that's the life. Look, if it helps, I won't be renewing my contract with Nivea, so when people stop seeing me on TV, they'll start to forget and we won't have to put up with it. Club managers never get this much attention. Don't worry.'

'If you're sure,' I say.

Again Reef talks as if we have a future together. It's a comforting thought and I try to relax and accept the situation for what it is. I'm going out with a celebrity. A good-looking icon of British football and someone off the TV. I tuck into my meal and hope that I can wear this new me with a bit more confidence as time goes by. At the moment, I'm just so happy that Reef sees a future for us. I try to see it. See myself living with Reef in his manor house, walking around the grounds, eating out all the time, sleeping in the massive bed in Reef's bedroom. I can see that life for myself and it looks good.

Reef pays the bill and we leave the restaurant. Just as we do, a car screeches up and someone with a camera clicks away furiously in front of our faces. I try to stand behind Reef who holds a hand in front of his face while trying to cross the road to get to the car.

'Come on, Annie,' he says, and my heels make a clomping sound as I half walk, half run behind Reef.

'That's enough, mate,' Reef says. He ushers me inside the car. As he trots round to the driver's seat, the cameraman is clicking as if demented outside my window, his camera knocking the glass. I shield my face with my hand and bow my head. Turning to Reef to tell him to drive, I see he has

239

stepped back round to the passenger side and is wrestling the camera away from the relentless photographer.

Obscenities are being yelled and shouts of 'Be fair, mate, I have to earn a living' draw the people out of the restaurant. Now videos are being made of the three of us.

'Reef, let's go,' I say in desperation. The two men both have their hands on the camera and neither will back down, and Reef can't hear me so I jump out of the car.

'Come on,' I say and pull at Reef's elbow. At the same time Reef is letting go of the camera and his elbow launches towards me and makes contact with my cheek. For a second I see stars and I lose my sense of hearing. Then it comes back with a bang. The diners from across the road have rushed over to take better videos and photos, their exclamations like the buzzing of hornets in an upset nest.

'Annie! Are you okay? This is down to you, you idiot!' Reef points at the red-faced cameraman while he bundles me back into the car. Before he starts the engine and the man takes one more picture of me for good measure, Reef leans over and holds my hand.

'No,' he says.

'What?'

'Your eye. It's swelling up.' He pulls his bottom lip in and shakes his head.

'Really?' I whimper.

I pull down the car mirror to see for myself. It's swelling up all right. My left eye looks as if it's about to close. All of a sudden, my face feels hot and it stings. In fact it starts to hurt like hell. I slam the mirror closed.

'No!'

'Should I take you to A & E?'

'You're joking. And have more paparazzi taking pictures of me looking like this.' I let out a long angry sigh. 'Just take me home.'

'Of course.'

The car engine revs and Reef pulls off without indicating, without checking his mirror and before either of us have a seat belt on. I click mine on and touch my face. It feels as if it's even more swollen and it's hurting even more. To be honest, I want to cry. Reef is still apologising and eventually my anger at the whole situation begins to subside. At least we left with my coat this time.

Reef pulls up in front of the house and hurries to help me out of the car.

'We need to get something on that.'

'I must have something frozen,' I say.

I switch on the light in the kitchen and put my bag down on the new table. Reef moves the few items I have in the freezer around and comes back with a frozen mini pizza.

'Really?' I say and flop into the chair.

'I couldn't find peas and there isn't a steak.'

He kneels in front of me and holds the pizza against my face.

'Annie, please forgive me.'

'There's nothing to forgive.'

'I shouldn't have lost it. I knew you were feeling uncomfortable before and I just didn't want that guy making it worse. I got a bit carried away.'

'I should have blown a referee's whistle and had you sent off.' I want to smile but my face is achy and very cold.

'Nice one,' Reef says. 'But I was a bigger idiot than the guy with the camera. My agent is going to go spare.'

'This won't hurt your job at Birmingham, will it?'

241

'No, no. People know I have a bit of a temper. I had my fair share of yellow cards but I shouldn't have behaved like that. I just saw how upset you were and I saw–'

'A red card?'

'How you can joke at a time like this, I don't know.'

'It's fine.' I pull Reef's hand from my face. 'I just need to lie down.'

'Let me help you.'

'No, it's fine. Really. It was a lovely evening.' We both stand. 'But all I want to do is crawl into bed.'

'This isn't the night it was supposed to be. I'm so sorry, Annie.'

'Really, Reef, I'm okay. Let me walk you to the door.' I'm already walking along the corridor but Reef takes his time, swaggering up to me.

'But … I'm not ready to go. Because … I thought you and I would …' He begins to move closer, lips drawing towards mine, his hair brushing my swollen cheek. My cheek. How horrible must I look? I pull away and step back.

'What?' he says, stepping in closer.

'Reef, no. I must look like *Million Dollar Baby*.' I hold him back by his upper arms. I can feel the flex of his biceps and what a turn on they are, but I think about my swollen face.

'*Million Dollar Baby*?' he asks, still standing incredibly close. 'Who's that?'

'The film. You know, Hilary Swank plays a female boxer? She gets battered about in the ring.' I point to my face. 'Sorry, but I'm not really feeling like, you know? Not right now.'

'Of course.' He steps back and looks at the swelling. I haven't looked into a mirror since coming home but his face

242

tells me that perhaps the distorted look is enough to put anyone off sex. 'Look, if you feel dizzy or think you have concussion, call and I'll come straight round.' Reef is holding both my hands in his and brings them to his mouth. He kisses them gently and leans in to kiss my lips.

'I wish I could kiss this better.' He nods to my face and I turn around to look in the hall mirror.

'Bloody hell,' I breathe. 'I am *Million Dollar Baby*.'

Upstairs, I gently rinse off my make-up. The pain has eased and I'm not feeling so angry or so sorry for myself. The good underwear is settled in the linen basket as I climb into bed, and I swear they were playing *Taps* again. It's a jazzy version this time and the sound of the trumpet rings in my ears for ages and keeps on playing. It's a long time before I fall asleep, but after a few hours, I'm up again.

In the kitchen, I find a defrosted pizza on the table and pop it into the fridge before making some ashwagandah tea. It's only two in the morning and a long time before I leave for work. I rest my head on my hand at the kitchen table, waiting for my tea to brew.

26

Do Nothing Till You Hear From Me

Amira is winning points with her sons who no longer think her work as a physiotherapist is "wet" since the news about Reef's run-in with the photographer from last night made its way onto the breakfast news. The number of retweets were mounting and not showing signs of slowing down. Opinion has been split about Reef. Some think he was gallant, others think his actions were over the top, but I won't use the language that some people used. Amira's sons, apparently, think she's a "gangsta" by association.

I close my phone after having called both Amira and Bob at the practice to see if either can take any of my clients for this week. I've been pacifying and rescheduling everyone as I won't be leaving the house. It's not that I'm worried about public opinion. It's just that I look like I've gone in for some professional MMA without the training. My face is a mess and I've filled the ice cube tray in case of future swollen eye emergencies.

'Bloody hell.' Anton's expression as I open the door to him is priceless.

'Don't even…' I say, walking back to the kitchen where I have coffee brewing and a mini pizza baking in the oven for breakfast. 'Hungry? Fancy half a pizza with your coffee?'

'I'll say yes to coffee and I've already eaten, thanks.'

We sit silently at the table. Anton looks awkward and shifts in his chair.

'I'll be making a start on the tiles today,' he says. I can see he's trying to take a good look at my swollen eye but not catch my attention at the same time.

'It's not as bad as it looks,' I say and spring out of my chair to pour the coffee and get my breakfast out of the oven before it burns. 'I bruise easily.'

'And swell up a lot.'

I touch my cheek as I place a mug of coffee in front of Anton and return to the table with a hot but soggy-looking pizza.

'Don't mock,' I say as I begin to cut a slice of pizza. 'I've had to cancel all my clients and hide my face to the world. I'm hideous.' I start chewing and watch a smile grow on Anton's face. 'What?' I say through a mouthful of food.

'It kind of suits you. The kickass look.' He can't stop himself laughing.

'Yeah, I get my kickass attitude from all that knitting.'

'So knitting isn't as lame as I thought it was after all.'

'No it isn't. You should try it.'

'And you should try this.' Anton leans into his work bag and pulls out a plastic Argos bag. Inside it is a slick and stylish radio and CD player. I see the words "digital" and "Bluetooth" splashed on the box, and the player itself has a retro style.

'What's all this?' I say, taking hold of the box.

'Open it. It's a present for you. For your kitchen so that you don't have to play that naff one anymore and you can hear the music the way the musicians intended you to. Not warped and hissy.'

I can't help smiling as I open the box because I can see how lovely the player will look in the corner of the counter where Mum's old player sits.

'How much do I owe you for this?' I pull away the plastic covering the player.

'It's a present. I meant to get it set up before you came home yesterday but Jade was late picking it up and then you and whatshisname showed up so…'

'You shouldn't be buying me presents, Anton.' I look closely at his face. His eyes smile. He looks shy now, not so bold and not as cocky as I thought he was when we first met.

'It's okay, I can afford it,' he says. 'I have this client who's paying me crazy money to do up her house. So enjoy it.' He sips the rest of his coffee and gets up to start working.

'I really appreciate this. Mum will be impressed when I show her.'

Anton sits again and snaps his fingers as if he's forgotten something. 'She'll be even more impressed when she knows you've got these.' He pulls out a set of Miles Davis CDs from his bag, still in the plastic wrapper.

'These are also a present,' he says. 'They were recorded before his death. Only recently released.' He pushes them across the table and I reach for them.

'And you bought them for me?' I'm thankful but stunned.

'I know you and your mum are into vocal jazz, but I thought you might like to experiment with some instrumental jazz. Everyone likes Miles, but if you don't, I know a guy who's into this kind of thing.'

'Is he a good-looking builder who does fabulous work for people who pay him crazy money?'

Anton doesn't answer for a second. He looks deep into my eyes and leans forward in his chair.

'Are you flirting with me, Annie Lambert?'

'No!' I gasp. 'Definitely not. You were being playful and generous and I was trying to…'

'But you called me good-looking. I think that's flirting. It sounds like flirting.' He's trying to suppress a chuckle as he watches my cheeks heat up.

'I was just, I mean…'

'It's okay,' he says, standing and picking up my pizza. He takes a bite and puts the rest back on my plate. 'I'm teasing. I know you've got this big, mean ex-footballer who could probably knock me out if he wanted.' He takes another sip of coffee and then kneels next to a large plastic bag from Wickes and retrieves a box of wall tiles.

'He's not aggressive,' I say meekly. 'He's a really nice guy if you get to know him.'

Anton, still kneeling, turns to me. 'I don't think that'll happen. I can't see him moving in the same circle as builders, if you know what I mean?' Anton continues to open the box of tiles and takes one out to inspect it while whistling Miles Davis' *So What*. I might not know a lot of his music but this one I recognise. I open my mouth to apologise for Reef's attitude to Anton's job but my phone rings. I hurry to pick up in case it's a client returning my call.

'Reef, hi. How are you?'

'That's what I was calling to ask you. Has the swelling gone down? How are you feeling?'

'I'm feeling okay. It doesn't hurt anymore but I can't see my face getting back to normal for a few days. I cancelled all my appointments.'

In the background, Anton prepares the tools he needs for starting to place the tiles. Boxes and plastic rustle, his tools clunk in his toolbox. I walk to the sink to distract myself from what he's doing.

'It's probably for the best,' Reef says. 'Social media is going a bit crazy and I don't want people hounding you.'

'Are they likely to?' I look out of the kitchen window expecting to see photographers hiding in the bushes. All I see are the trees, bare branches swaying in a chilly breeze, a mist veiling the forest beyond. Only the hardy paparazzi would want to hang around someone like me in this weather.

'Hopefully not but Jack says I should keep a bit of a low profile.'

'He's right, I suppose. But everything will be all right, won't it? You didn't break the camera so it can't be all bad.'

'I don't think it's bad at all. These things do blow over, but Jack says to disappear for a while. So, um … I thought maybe it was best if … Nat and I are taking Noé to Spain to see his grandparents for a bit. She's cancelled the ice-rink show so she won't be filming or rehearsing anymore. We thought a bit of a family thing would be good for Noé. But Noé and I will be back in the UK for Christmas Day. We're spending it here and he's very excited to see you again. When we get back.'

I can't hide the fact that this news has left me flat and a little lost for words. I have a million of them doing a crazy tap dance in my head, but I don't know how to deliver them without sounding bitter and twisted. Thanks to me, Reef and Natalia seem to have become all chummy and making decisions together. I know a family retreat is going to be fabulous for Noé but I'm feeling so left out. Not to mention it's very irresponsible of Natalia to let down the producers of the ice-skating show so last minute. And what if they all decide to stay in Spain together for Christmas? My head

248

spins and I need to take a breath. I've gone from having fun with Anton to feeling like a catherine wheel in a firework display. I take that breath and count the moments of silence as I try to exhale without Reef hearing a quiver in my voice.

'I think it's a brilliant idea, Reef. Noé is going to have the best time. Give him my love and I look forward to seeing both of you soon.'

'Oh, me too, Annie. I'm really looking forward to seeing you. It's not long to Christmas. We can survive a couple of weeks.'

'Two and a half but, yes, of course we can. Besides, I'm going to be super busy with patients, especially as I'm taking this week off. I'll be double and triple booked for days, weeks, eternity. Busy, busy, busy. The time will fly by.' My laugh is close to hysterical.

'I'd better go. We're getting straight off to the airport now. So I'll give you a call when we land. Okay?'

'Absolutely. I'll talk to you soon.'

'Okay, bye, Annie. Take care.' He ends the call.

Take care? Isn't that the kind of thing your granny says when she packs you off for home after an afternoon of tea and biscuits? I take a calming breath, this time letting it out with a long "hah" sound.

'You okay, Annie? Trouble in paradise?'

'No, no. Everything's fine. They're taking Noé to see his grands in Spain but at least I'll see him soon.'

The last piece of pizza is cold and mushy and I swallow it down with a self-pitying gulp. Anton, very kindly, is ignoring the gloom I've cast on the kitchen and gets busy with a spirit level and a pencil. I clear the kitchen and wash up so that I can get out of his way. As I do, I summon up the good memories of Christmases spent with Mum and Cat.

This year, I'd imagined Reef and Noé being a part of my Christmas. I don't want to spend it here alone wondering if Dez and Phoenix might stop by for a mince pie or waiting to see if Reef and Noé come back in time. I want to fill it with people I care about. I dry my hands and send a group message to the Monday Afternoon Knitters Circle to invite them over for Christmas dinner. It's impulsive but it feels like the right thing to do.

Bea responds straight away, saying, *Yes please and can I bring a date?*

Judith says, *How refreshing. I'd love to come.*

Rhiannon offers to help with the cooking, and all of a sudden I have something good to look forward to.

27

The Best is Yet to Come

'So, I've got an early Christmas present for you, Annie.' Jade's voice on the other end of the line sparkles with excitement as she catches me on my way to the living room to think of all things Christmas dinner while Anton gets on with tiling the kitchen walls. 'I contacted the art gallery, spoke to Lorraine. She's well and truly into your work, and being a local artist, she loves the idea of an exhibit.'

'You're joking.' My first emotion is excitement, followed by pride, followed by complete fear. 'Just my stuff? No other artists?'

'She wants you, Annie. You and your wonderful paintings. But don't get too excited, it's going to be very low-key because she'll display in January when all the leftover art and crafts are still there from Christmas and there isn't an official art exhibition. It's too late to advertise anything proper because the diary is full up until next autumn.'

'Actually, that suits me. Something under the radar.'

'Yes, but it could lead to other things, and it probably will if I have anything to do with it. But for now, your paintings will be seen and they'll be up for sale.'

'I wouldn't have a clue what to charge.'

'Lorraine will help with all that. If we get the paintings to her just after Christmas, she'll have them installed for the whole of January. *Now* will you start believing in yourself?'

'I suppose I don't have a choice.'

'Happy?'

'I really am. Thank you so much, Jade. This means a lot. Without you, I never would have done anything like this.'

'I guess it won't hurt the sales of your paintings now that you're already a celebrity in Ross.'

'Oh no, you heard about the incident outside the restaurant last night?'

'Uh-huh. How are you after that?'

'Bruised and fed up thinking about it. I'd much rather talk about my art, believe it or not?'

We talk for ages about the exhibit and which paintings I'll use for it. Should it be all paintings or some charcoal sketches and some chalks too? Apparently, of the pictures that Jade had snapped in the studio yesterday, Lorraine adores the paintings of Ross by night. So I decide on a theme, the local area. I've got lots on the subject and the gallery isn't massive, so I can pick and choose what will go into it.

'Okay superstar,' Jade says, 'I'll ask Anton if we can borrow his van so that we can deliver the artwork. Talk to you soon.'

Subtle bangs and knocks come from the kitchen where I can hear Anton whistling while he works. He turns when he hears me enter.

'I just got off the phone to Jade. She spoke to Lorraine and she wants to exhibit my work.' My face is tight and hurts when I smile, but I can't help myself as I tell Anton all about it.

'That's brilliant. Well done, Annie.'

'I feel silly now for being so short with you about how private my art is to me. I'm finally coming round to the idea that that's a selfish attitude. I've been trying for so long not to be so introverted and here's a great opportunity to start.'

'I don't think there's anything wrong with being an introvert.'

I lower my gaze.

'I used to think there was,' I say. I look up to see nothing but kindness in Anton's eyes. 'It's just, well, because of the way Mum was, you know, becoming so silent at times, I'd worry that because of my art and my spending hours alone with it and the silent hours and everything…'

'I don't think it works like that, Annie. How your mum is, my mum's condition, that's a fact of their lives. We don't become our parents, Annie, not in that way. And just look at all the amazing art you produce in those hours of silence. The noise comes when we all get to celebrate just how talented you are. Just wait until you get your paintings out there. People are going to love you, love your art. Own it.'

'I will. I do. I'm proud of it. And talking of silence, let's get the CD player on so we can have music while we work.'

The music plays in the background and I leave the kitchen and studio door open as I begin to sort through my paintings. My mind goes into overdrive about the things that are happening in my life. Mum will be beside herself when she hears about the exhibition and when she hears I'll be entertaining in my new kitchen on Christmas Day. I haven't given much thought to presents for Mum, Cat and her children so far, but there is still time to post parcels to Australia. For Cat's children I'm sure I can't go wrong with toys and books, but what do I get Mum and Cat?

In the living room, I turn on my laptop for some inspiration. After half an hour, I realise the internet does not hold the key to the special present idea I can't come up with for myself. I stare at the laptop screen and screw up my face as I try very hard to decide what to buy. I pause before closing the laptop. I've resisted Instagram or Twitter for fear of seeing myself being elbowed in the face by Reef after our dinner last night. I sigh and tut but I open the Instagram tab anyway and log in.

There are lots of pictures from Becs' engagement party. So much has happened in three days that I'd almost forgotten about it, even after all that tense and emotional build up to it. I also see that she has been messaging me since the party:

Babes! Such a blessing to see you. It's been a minute. (Three prayer hands and three kissy face emojis.) With Reef Mayer no less. Sorry you had to rush off. Call me xx

Hi Lovely (Two kissy faces.) I hope you can come to London soon. Got to talk to you about Reef. What a guy. Spent ages talking to my old man about VAR xxxx

Hey Love when are you in London? (Two prayer hands, no kissy face emoji.) Doesn't Reef have a place there? I didn't know you were a nanny btw x

Hey you! (No emojis.) Hope you're getting these. Got a message from the venue about your coat. Told them to bin it as I'm guessing Reef will be taking you out shopping. BTW what happened to the kid?? xx

Our wedding is next September (One prayer hands emoji no kissy faces.) Should the invite say plus one or should I put Reef's name on it??? I'm so jealous love Becs x

There is only one message from Zarina:

You looked lovely on Saturday. Shame we didn't get time to talk (Sad emoji face.) Would love to catch up some time. Ps Reef Mayer! My God!!! x

Neither had actually asked after me personally and Becs had the cheek to throw away my clothes as if she were doing me a favour. I loved that coat, thank you very much.

I don't look at any other news about celebrities because what good would it do my already overthinking mind to see pictures of Reef and his ex-wife getting on a private jet with their son?

In the studio, I take down the chalk images I made of Noé. The fix on them has set and I decide to put them away in a folder. It's not that his image will make me miss him any more than I do. I can't shake the image of him and Reef with Natalia's Spanish and Moroccan family in Alicante. I know Reef says they'll be back in time for Christmas but I don't believe that for one moment. What little kid wouldn't want to be with his grandparents, the people who spoil you the most, for Christmas? Also, Reef doesn't take over from the caretaker manager of Birmingham City until late December, so he has nothing to rush home for. I take another self-pitying sniff and hide the drawings of Noé away. Then, an idea for a present for Mum and Cat comes to me.

I set out to paint a new series. Two small paintings that will hopefully be finished by early next week, in time for the parcel post deadline. I decide to paint a retrospective scene from one of our past Christmases, one for each of them. I want Christmas to be something to look forward to and not one in which my heart is in splinters. The paintings will be a celebration of the good times. And I do have good times to look forward to. I'll be joined for Christmas by people I love. Well, I don't love Bea's new boyfriend, I don't really know him, but she wouldn't have invited him for Christmas, of all things, if they weren't getting serious.

I start to sketch. With each stroke of the pencil as I draw the outlines of the pictures, I begin to unwind, relax and to not get so worked up about what Reef decides to do. This can't be the last I'll see of him and Noé, and I should just get on with everything else I want to do and not let time stand still. In fact, the time speeds by and I haven't moved from my chair when I become aware of Anton leaning up against the door frame, arms folded.

'Being in the studio suits you,' he says. 'You look much happier than you did earlier.'

'I am. I've got plans for a Christmas present for my mum and my sister. I'm doing a couple of paintings for them.'

'The ideal gift if it's painted from the heart by a great artist.'

I blush for a moment and then remember to accept the compliment.

'Thanks, Anton. The ideas are flowing so I'll probably be in the studio all day if you want anything.'

'I'm stopping for lunch and I was going to do coffee.' He gestures a drinking motion and nods to me, and I nod a yes please back. 'It's nice when you smile like that.'

'I didn't realise I was. Oh and I've made some plans for Christmas day, too. Really looking forward to it now.'

'Going away?'

'No, I'm throwing a dinner party.'

'Nice. Jade and I are having a quiet one with Mum before Jade goes back to sort out her flat in London.'

It hasn't left my mind what Jade said: *My brother fancies you*. But to look at him now, you wouldn't think it was true.

Either he's gone off me completely because of Reef, or Jade has blown things out of proportion. Either way, I'm not going to entertain the thought. Life is complicated enough at the moment.

From the kitchen, the volume goes up incredibly loudly and I walk in to find Anton chewing a bite from his falafel wrap, playing on an imaginary drum kit. He's getting so into the music he doesn't realise I'm there until I start to giggle.

'Ah, sorry,' he says. 'This album is crazy.'

'I could let you borrow it some time.'

'I was actually thinking of taking it back.'

'You wouldn't.'

''Course, I wouldn't.' He turns the music down. 'Here, this is for you.' Anton hands me a mug of coffee.

'Thanks, I'll take this back to the studio.'

He barely glances at me as I leave the kitchen: his eyes used to linger a lot longer on me. Maybe he'll be in the friends zone, along with Jade. Before entering the studio I watch Anton, now pretending to play the keyboard, and a warm feeling rushes over me.

I work on the sketches all day, and the one I've done for Mum, the Christmas she made duck for the first time, is close to being ready to paint. I remember what a spectacular winter it had been. Enough of a covering of crisp snow for me to make a small snowman with Mum's assistance. He had a red Lego brick for a nose and a top hat we'd found in one of the many charity shops in Ross. It had been a wonderful day. Mum had stayed on her medication all through the autumn and winter. She had just started working at the library. She'd stayed well and had been able to come to the carol service at school and the end of term play. I didn't have a main part but it had been great to see her smiling from the audience and waving at me. As a little girl, I'd been oblivious to Mum's illness. My memories, before I knew, had always been the warmth of her smiles and her wishing me a beautiful day before I ran into the classroom, full of excitement and full of anticipation. I'd had lots to tell Mum when she picked me up from school. All good things, positive things that made her smile even more. The painting is of a happy time before the insecurities set in: growing up, having to deal with life's challenges, not knowing what I wanted for my future, making my own decisions, making friends, worrying about Mum, hoping that I wasn't like Mum in some ways but wishing I were in others. I screw my eyes up to squeeze those insecurities out of my mind. The music playing from the kitchen blends into my thoughts and the good feelings come flowing back. I raise my arms above my head to stretch my upper body, my fingers interlaced like a tall arch, and I hear pops and creaks like a symphony in my neck.

Anton taps on the open studio door when his work is done, when all the discs from my new CD have played and we've thrown in some vocal jazz from Mum's collection. Unashamedly, Anton has been singing and scatting from the kitchen all day. I've been singing too but not so loud that he'd hear me.

He's looking at his phone as he comes in, white cement dust on his forearm.

'You off?' I ask.

'Yes, I'm exhausted. You can use the sink with no problem about getting the tiles wet. It's practically dry but watch out because I've painted one wall.'

'Will do. Thanks, Anton.'

'All part of the service.'

'I mean, for my present and for being good company. I was feeling a bit … you know … before you came over, but I've had a great day and that music is brilliant.'

He's looking at my work in progress with a serious expression.

'You have had a good day.'

'It's almost done.'

'Is that your Mum?'

I nod.

'She'll love it.'

'I hope so.'

When Anton leaves, I play the album all over again, make myself some dinner and tap my fork as I chew and listen. I realise I've hardly thought of Reef and I refuse to wallow. Instead, I grab a pad and a pen, click on my laptop and I begin to plan Christmas dinner. Despite how much it smarts to do so, I can't help smiling.

28

The Frim Fram Sauce

In Cat's painting, I've tried to capture her in her early twenties, after she'd returned from her travels and announced she was in love and moving to Australia for good. The part about moving to Australia she had kept close to her chest, telling me later that the last thing she wanted to do was send Mum spiralling with worry, although she herself had been worried senseless about leaving the country and permanently being so far from Mum. She wanted to be sure that I could cope on my own. Neither of us had left home lightly. But Cat had always had a sense of adventure, her determination to travel and see the world conflicting with the responsibility she felt towards Mum. But the wanderlust was overwhelming and she'd become a monster to live with. In the end, Mum had told her to pack a bag and go somewhere, she would be absolutely fine and the last thing she wanted was to hold either of us back. After all, Mum herself had travelled here from the other side of the world. I was at university when Cat made her announcement about leaving the country for a man. It had been a wrench for me to move out, too, but I was close by and checked in on Mum with so much regularity you'd think I was still living at home.

Cat needn't have worried about the impact her decision to move to Australia would have on Mum. She had been overjoyed for her. She was happy her daughter was in love and couldn't believe that Cat would be moving not far from the place she'd grown up. So it had been a happy Christmas. One of celebration, joy and relief. It had been a Christmas of storytelling. Mum telling us all about her childhood in Australia in a way we'd never heard it before. We almost couldn't believe what a daring and exciting life Mum had led and, just like Cat, it was a man who'd convinced her of wanting to travel less and settle down. Cat had told us all the stories of daring and discovery she'd made in New Zealand and how on arriving in Australia, she and the country just seemed to fit.

The kitchen had been strewn with treasure and trinkets from Cat's Antipodean journey. Rocks, shells, native artwork and jewellery had been laid on the old table. One of the presents she'd brought back for me was a necklace she'd made with a pendant filled with sand from a beach in Bali. Then there were the photographs, hundreds of them. We'd sat in the kitchen until it had grown dim and even the light bulb seemed to fade from tiredness. Of course, I'd painted dozens of pictures from the stills. My paintings were nothing like the photos which were also nothing compared to the scenery I discovered on my first and only trip to Australia to visit Cat in her new home.

I've tried to capture some of the excitement of that Christmas in this painting and the look on Cat's face when she said she was in love with the most boring man in Australia but that she knew they would always be happy. In the picture, Cat is in bright colours that light up our kitchen and she is surrounded by some of the treasures she'd brought back on that trip.

The paintings and the other Christmas presents I bought are on their way to Mum and Cat and should reach them in good time. My face is back to its normal size and shape, and the kitchen is shiny and new. I can't get over the transformation and what great work Anton has done. Anton and I have seen each other in the mornings but he's usually gone by the time I get home from work. We've been leaving each other messages. Mostly Anton has been recommending albums I just have to listen to and I've been adding them to a list. A few of them I've already treated myself to for Christmas. I've heard from Reef practically every day. He has sent photos of Noé, who appears to be having the time of his life, bless him. I notice that Reef never takes any with Natalia in. Except the one where her arm appears while hugging Noé. The media has gone to town about her pulling out of *Dancing On Ice Down Under – Celebrity Special* and how her replacement, a morning breakfast presenter, wasn't able to take part as she had broken an ankle on a skiing holiday. A ripple of a sensation was caused when it was reported that Reef and Natalia were back together again because a picture was leaked to the press of the three of them out Christmas shopping. I didn't see the picture, but Amira from work had told me. What followed was a statement from the soon-to-be Birmingham City manager who denied any truth in the rumour. Reef had spoken to me about the pictures and insisted that he was living in a hotel close to Natalia's family home and only came to visit Noé. They would both be back for Christmas.

'The three of us could have a festive pizza,' he'd joked.

'Actually, I've made plans to have people over and I was hoping you'd both be able to join us. Noé knows them all so he should be fine. But I'll understand if you both want to be in Spain for the day. Noé will be with family and he might feel happier there. I could see Noé when he's spent New Year with Natalia.'

'There you go,' he'd said, 'putting everyone's feelings before yours. I want to see you at Christmas. I want to spend it with you. Believe it or not, I'm missing you like mad.'

'You'll be back to start your manager's job on the twenty-seventh. I can wait until then,' I'd said, but it sounded half-hearted because, admittedly, I was missing him like mad, too.

'I can't wait. And without the risk of sounding like The Terminator, I'll be back.' Thankfully he didn't do the voice. We'd ended the call with laughter. Reef had revealed he'd bought my Christmas present but that it was a surprise. Though I'd bought a present for Noé, I hadn't decided what I'd get for Reef or what I'd buy for the ladies from the Monday Afternoon Knitters Circle. Christmas is twelve days away.

At four thirty, when the sky is almost indigo and the wind chill factor is such that I can't feel my fingers from the second I step out of the practice, I make my way to the knitting circle. The townspeople are hurrying to keep warm and in no mood for pleasantries like nodding or stopping for chats. My scarf swaddles my neck. I pull it up over my nose and I hurry along until I reach Rhiannon's Eatery.

'Annie,' Rhiannon bellows as I enter the coffee shop. 'Come in and warm up, you poor thing. Hard day at work?'

She wants to help me off with my coat but I'm seriously stiff with cold and I want to stay wrapped up. My sense of touch comes back gradually in tingles as I adjust to the warmth inside, hugging myself on the comfy chair while Judith and Bea click away and look over their glasses at me.

263

'You young people.' Judith tuts as she watches me trying to stop my teeth chattering. 'What you would have done when there was no such thing as central heating, I don't know.'

'Oh leave her alone,' says Bea, winking at me. 'As if you've ever had to grow up without heating.'

'Well, I didn't have central heating,' says Judith about to take another suck of her lemon.

'But heat all the same,' Bea interrupts. 'Don't worry, Annie, lover boy will be back and he'll keep you warm.' She begins to giggle in her usual youthful and uncontrollable way, hinting at a sex life that eludes me. I won't dispel the fantasy – she'd never believe me if I told her that all Reef and I had done was share a few passionate kisses. I'm still waiting for a night alone with Reef but I've been trying not to build it up in my head.

Rhiannon hands me a mug of hot chocolate. I hold it with gloved hands and feel damp heat coming to my fingers. After taking a mouthful or two of the cream on the top of my drink, I'm ready to come out of my pink coat cocoon and Rhiannon is quick to assist. I give her a gentle hug.

'What's that for?' She smiles on her way to hang up my things.

'Nothing, just a hug for always being so kind. Well, all of you are.'

'It's not a hard job, my pet,' Rhiannon says, going behind the counter for a plate of digestive biscuits. 'You're a treasure, Annie. Now eat up before you perish from starvation. We need to finalise dinner arrangements.'

I nod and bite into a biscuit and the others put their knitting down.

'I suggested to the others,' says Judith, 'that we split the cost of everything. You've already spent a fortune on getting the house done, the heating fixed, new windows, a fitted kitchen.'

'How's it all going?' Rhiannon interrupts and claps her chubby fingers together.

'Great,' I say, thinking about the kitchen, all shiny and new. It may have lost the look and feel of my past but it isn't without personality. Brightness streams through the modern windows, framing the scenery outside in a fresh new way. Warmth circulates within the walls from the loving care Anton puts into restoring it and the laughter he has created in it. My favourite colours and the music I've heard for the first time creates a new atmosphere that flows through the room. I can begin new memories in this kitchen with the extended family that grows around me and grows closer to me every day. This new family is going to be influential in the life I continue to write for myself. In this life I see Judith, Bea and Rhiannon coming over more often. I see Jade popping round when she finally moves back. Music plays and we all laugh and I let go of my anxieties, gradually. One by one.

'But I invited you,' I say. 'I should really be paying.'

'We've already decided,' says Rhiannon, 'and there's no arguing with it. Also, pressies. We're none of us to spend more than a fiver for each.'

'And don't be obliged to buy anything for Bertie,' Bea says, blushing slightly in a way I've never seen before. 'He's my guest for the day and I've already splashed out a sizeable sum on his present.'

'Well, okay,' I say. 'But just so you know, I've extended the invite so we may have an extra two for dinner.'

'So tell us who they are,' Judith says. 'I'll need to think about extra presents.'

'They definitely won't accept presents. I … er … I invited Dez and Phoenix.' I wait for the fallout.

'A dog and a homeless person!' Judith's face pinches so far in I'm sure she'll never get it straight again.

'It's fine.' I shake my head amicably so they don't panic. 'Dez isn't really into four walls so he might just stop off for a quick bite to eat. A doggy bag for him and Phoenix and they'll probably be off.'

'Please tell me this will be the end if it, Annie.' Judith sighs heavily and fiddles with her circular knitting needles. 'You've got to put a stop to all this night walking and you really shouldn't be mixing with someone like that.'

'He's a really good guy,' I say, looking into the mug on my knees where rings of dry chocolate paint the inside. 'He's had an unfortunate life but he's not bitter and he's not horrible. He might not have a home but I like him and he also looks out for me. I'd like all the people who care about me with me at Christmas.'

'And he's very welcome,' says Rhiannon. 'And I'm sure he wouldn't mind having a shower before we sat down to eat.'

'I'm sure he'd love one. Also,' I say, 'Reef and Noé will be joining us. It's confirmed. I just want us all to enjoy ourselves.'

'Okay,' says Rhiannon. 'And enjoy ourselves we will. Regardless of numbers, hygiene levels and plus ones, we're going to have an amazing time.' She fiddles in her bag. 'It's all in the details of course. Here's my suggestion.'

She hands me a laminated menu. A choice of starter, a main meal of turkey with all the trimmings and three choices for dessert.

'Wow,' I say, amazed. There are even holly and ivy graphics to separate the courses. 'I thought tonight was supposed to be the discussion to finalise things.'

'Well, I've had plenty of time to think about it since the invite, my lovely. Hope you don't mind. If you'd like to change anything…'

'No, no,' I say, noticing that both Bea and Judith's lips are quivering and creasing at the corners as they try not to laugh. 'Should I do the food shopping?'

'You've got to get the timing right when shopping for a big meal,' Rhiannon says, whisking the menu away and putting it into her bag between the pages of an A4 wallet folder. 'I've already got the turkey ordered, my homemade stuffing already made, pigs in blankets are in the freezer because they always go fast at the supermarket. I couldn't leave them to the last minute, could I? Bought a few condiments and some Christmas crackers, oh and Christmas pud. I had to because time was passing and you don't have a big freezer but I do, see?'

'That's true. But the rest, we three could make a list, split it up. What do you think, Rhi?'

'I've already taken the liberty,' Rhiannon says, pulling out three pink shopping lists with each of our names on it. All the items are written beautifully by hand in ink, and I want to ask Rhiannon when she had time to study calligraphy just as the other two burst out laughing.

'You have no idea what you've unleashed,' says Bea almost choking. 'She's in her absolute element, you realise. I don't know why you're not a wedding planner or something, bless you Rhi. Oh and before I forget, Bertie is taking care of all the booze.'

'Blimey,' I say. 'You guys have been in planning mode.'

'Just one more thing,' says Judith.

'Don't tell me. You've organised a vodka luge.'

'No dear, nice idea but, no.' Judith places a delicate and well-manicured hand on her chest. 'It's about the name of our knitting club. I thought it would be a very good idea to give Spool and the Gang a shot. It might encourage a younger membership. People have been asking to join and so why not a new name for a new kind of knitting group?'

'I'm happy with that,' I say, giving a sideways glance to Bea who winks at me. 'It would be nice to increase the gang. Especially if you promise to recruit people who are worse knitters than me.'

More laughter rings out in the coffee shop and a glow of warmth surrounds us for the next hour until it's time to pack away.

I'm giddy with excitement when I leave the knitting circle in the early evening. Once again, I haven't managed to knit a single stitch. But who's counting?

29

The Christmas Song

Rhiannon and a very sleepy-looking William arrive at 7.30 on Christmas morning. Rhiannon is carrying full shopping bags whose handles pinch into her skin while in her arms there's a large cardboard box, so full I can only just see her face above the small fake Christmas tree at the top.

'Grab the tree and the small bag of decorations in my right hand and get cracking. I knew you didn't have one and we'll need somewhere to put presents.'

She pushes past me on the way to the kitchen, the tree and decorations whizzing by as if on a conveyor belt, and I grab them without upsetting the other contents of the box. I'm still in my pyjamas because Rhiannon specifically said she'd be here at 9.00 a.m not 7.30. When they'd knocked on the door, I'd woken from a dream in which I had to kill my own turkey. I'd chased the bird around the living room, but in the end, it managed to slip out the back door and hotfoot it into the forest beyond my garden. I'd had no sleep at all until about five in the morning, so I feel battered and groggy.

'William!'

Rhiannon's vocal cords have stretched so that the sound is high-pitched and full volume. Both William and I shudder. From the kitchen, she shouts, 'Hurry up and bring everything in from the car and then get the coffee brewing.'

William moves slowly past me towards the kitchen, carrying a trifle on a cake stand. I follow him in.

'Trifle?' I ask Rhiannon, still holding the fake tree and the bag of decorations. 'That wasn't on the menu.'

'Oh, you know me, petal. I get antsy and I have to cook or bake something. And who knows how much the homeless chap will eat when he gets here.'

'*If* he gets here,' I say under my breath. Although I'd only allowed myself to got out walking late into the night once this week, I hadn't seen anything of Dez and Phoenix since I'd invited them for Christmas and I was more than a little concerned. The temperatures have been perishing. Well into the minus figures some nights. I'd looked all around the town centre, my eyes trained on every shadow, every little movement or anything that resembled a man and his dog bundled up and huddled against the wind. They weren't in the mall, by the library, under the market square building. Or anywhere. I'd had a terrible feeling about them both which is why I'd specifically ventured out. But when the cold got so bad, I'd had to take myself home again. I ran most of the way. Well, the best I could in so many layers. The small roads in town were pitch black; the path through the graveyard cracked under my feet as if there'd been a sheet of ice across it. Perhaps there was – I could barely see two feet in front of me. Dez had always told me it was dangerous to be outdoors in the dark under any circumstances, so what the hell was I thinking, running on slippery surfaces when I had no idea where I was landing my feet?

I'd stood just inside the front door when I'd finally got home, shaking. I needed to bring life back into my body. To wake up every cell within me, to thaw it out and feel the blood rushing though to revitalise all the parts that had set in ice. I'd made a cup of tea while still wearing all my outdoor clothes, a dull pain in my head and a sinking feeling in my stomach about Dez and Phoenix.

I try to push my concerns to the back of my mind, brushing my teeth, taking a shower and putting on a pair of old jeans and a chunky sweater. The tiny tree won't decorate itself. William hands me a mug of freshly brewed coffee and I sip it gratefully.

'Want a hand with that?' he asks, nodding towards the tree. I've set it next to the window in the living room. It's so tiny it won't be seen from outside.

'You could hand me the decorations. Has Rhiannon booted you out of the kitchen?'

He doesn't need to answer, his face says it all. He holds out a silver bauble. The two of us spend the next half hour making small talk about the weather, his grandchildren, his garden, which he has spent so much time working on since he retired. If he's not in the garden, he's reading a book.

'I get so bored,' he says. 'I wonder why I didn't keep on working.'

'Did you ever think about working alongside Rhiannon in the eatery?'

'I couldn't stand being ordered around all day.' He grunts and hands me a little silver bell. 'She hired someone quickly enough when she first opened the shop and didn't ask me. Besides, I've been in the military, the last thing I'd want was to enter it again at my stage of life.'

We both laugh and give a cautious look over our shoulders. Rhiannon is a sweet and gentle creature, but something I've now learnt is that she's a whirling dervish when it comes to organising in the kitchen.

'And she gets on really well with the new girl she hired. They're a perfect fit. Tyler. Know her, do you?'

'Not that well.'

'Lovely lass. Perhaps on the slow side if you catch my drift.' He taps the side of his head. 'She thinks a *cul de sac* is a fashionable French handbag.'

I turn to William and burst out laughing. He's the last person I'd imagine would make a joke like that. His laugh is infectious and neither of us can stop.

'What on earth is going on in here?' Rhiannon puts her chubby face around the door. It's quite pink from all the activity I could hear going on in the kitchen.

'Your husband cracks me up,' I say, trying to catch my breath.

'Well, less mirth and more movement,' says Rhiannon. 'William, I'll need you on potato peeling just now.' She leaves us to it and I look at my watch. It's just coming up for 9.00 a.m. I thank goodness I'm not doing all the cooking today after all. I didn't realise it could be so involved.

When the tree is done, I go upstairs to put on a deep red dress with tiny, white flowers printed on it. I spray on some perfume and put on some lipstick and take my hair down so that it's wild and wavy around my shoulders. Then I hunt down some fairy lights I have in a box in one of the bedrooms. I drape them over the tree, and because the tree is so little, there are enough left over for me to put a halo of lights around the window behind it. Earlier, I'd spoken to Mum and my family in Australia. They'd had their Christmas dinner already. Cat's children had wreaked havoc and their tree had come down in the process. Their dad had marched them to the bottom of the garden where they'd had to sit cross-legged repeating times tables as a punishment.

272

'We would have laughed at a fallen down tree,' Mum had said. 'Laughed and danced around it.'

Mum and Cat absolutely loved the presents I'd sent them. Cat had raved on and on about making my artwork a full time venture, especially with the exhibit at the gallery in town coming up. Having not seen any of my paintings or sketches in such a long time, she'd remarked on how much more accomplished I'd become.

'They're both so amazing, Annie,' Cat had said amidst the squeals and play stabbings of her children in the background. 'You've been an artist since you could hold a pencil.' She'd smiled at me proudly, as if the racket behind her wasn't happening. 'Look at us. I never wanted to be tied to anywhere and all I wanted was adventure. Now I'm married with kids. And you, well, you ended up as a physiotherapist of all things when really, you're an artist, Annie. A bloody good one.'

Looking up at the fairy lights, I notice a car pulling up that I don't recognise. Bea steps out of the passenger side of a long silver Bentley in her high heels, gold capri pants and an enormous faux fur jacket and matching hat. She takes a box out of the back seat of the car and chats to Bertie who is dragging an even larger container out of the boot. I go to open the door to them. They cry out their greetings and Rhiannon calls for them to stop letting the cold in.

'She's been working away like a wizard in the kitchen,' I say, taking the box from Bea who reaches up to kiss me. 'We're in for some great food and lots of added extras by the looks of things.'

Bea whispers. 'Has she let you into the kitchen at all?'

'Twice. Once to get some breakfast, the other time was to tell me I'm not allowed in.'

'That sounds about right.'

Bea introduces everyone to Bertie who puts a large crate of booze of all descriptions onto the kitchen floor.

'We have champers but we need to get in the fridge,' he announces.

The house begins to buzz with excitement. Lively chatter and belts of laughter ring in the living room, broken momentarily by a knock on the door. In the corridor, the air is filled with a heady mix of food baking, expensive perfume, bucks fizz and snowballs.

'Look who I have,' says Judith as I open the front door. She steps inside to hug me, adding her flowery perfume to the cocktail of scents. Behind her stands Reef and Noé who is jigging uncontrollably, waiting for his turn to hug me. Dependably, he burrows his head of large, looping curls into my middle and grips on tight. I've missed these hugs so much. Above him, Reef leans in and touches his lips to mine.

'Merry Christmas. I said we'd be here.'

'And here you are.' I breathe him in and find I don't recognise his smell. He always has a delicious, signature scent, but today there is something different or new about him that I can't put my finger on.

'Come on, buddy,' Reef says to his son. 'Let Annie breathe and let's close this door.'

Gradually, Noé releases me and I instantly miss the shape of him. I shiver as the door closes and hold their hands as I guide Reef and Noé into the living room and then the kitchen to announce them.

By midday, everyone has arrived. Everyone except Dez and Phoenix. Noé hasn't left my side and I can't stop looking out of the window for my friend and his lovely dog.

Despite the warm, clammy contact of Noé's hand in mine, I'm preoccupied by Dez and Phoenix's absence. I feel as if I'm outside the hubbub of festivity, the clinking of glasses from Bea and Bertie, the tipsy trill of Rhiannon's voice and the low rumble of laughter from William as he and Reef talk football and the impending World Cup.

Judith nudges me.

'Are you okay, my dear?'

'Er, yes, yes I'm fine.' Both of us are sat on dining chairs in the living room with our backs to the window. Noé is wriggling on my lap while looking at a picture book, a present from Rhiannon. I've looked out of the window countless times. The day is grey and white. We weren't hit by the predicted snow storms, in fact there is just a light flurry of white on the cars which is quickly becoming icy. Not enough to make snowmen or to throw snowballs. I picture the snow landing on Phoenix's coat and Dez brushing it away with his fingerless gloves. I wish they would show up.

'You're worried about Dez,' Judith says. I nod my head. 'He's been living on the street a long time, Annie. He knows how to stay safe and warm. Perhaps it's not convenient for him to come today. Or maybe he doesn't care for Christmas and all its tradition and formalities anymore, and he might turn up another day. Tomorrow.'

'Maybe. I hope so.'

'I think you're overthinking things,' says Judith. 'Don't worry, there'll be a perfectly good explanation if he doesn't show up today.'

'I know you're right.'

'I am and look, you're missing something.' She signals with her eyes to the loving embrace Bertie is giving Bea.

'I see what you mean,' I whisper to her. 'Husband number five?'

'It's been a while since I've seen her this close with anyone. It's not just another of her flings. I have a feeling this could be the one that sticks.'

Rhiannon beckons me with the crook of her finger from the living room door. I pop Noé onto my chair but he gets up and follows me to the kitchen anyway. William has already set up a square folding table which adjoins my little one. Between two tablecloths, trays of cutlery and a pile of crockery and glasses, the three of us lay the table.

'This is going to be a fine dinner,' Rhiannon sighs. Her round cheeks swell with heat and pride. I light candles and Noé declares at the front room door that dinner is "swerved", which leads to several chuckles and the tousling of his hair as each makes their way to the kitchen.

The first Christmas memory in the new kitchen is being made and I'm loving every minute of it. I finally relax about Dez. He does know how to look after himself and, as Judith says, he's equipped for this weather – he has lived through many Christmases under the stars. I tell myself he'll be fine as I raise a glass and tap it against Reef's.

'Happy Christmas,' he says and blows a kiss in my direction. Somehow, the kiss doesn't quite reach my heart.

30

My Foolish Heart

I surprise myself and sleep for four hours straight. The first time in years. Bertie kept the drinks coming and Bea kept us entertained until well past midnight. We were all having such a good time that everyone was reluctant to leave and I hadn't wanted them to. Reef and Noé were the first to go. Noé fell asleep with his head in my lap and denied having done so when Reef woke him, holding his coat and saying, 'It's time to go, big man.'

'But it's Christmas,' he kept saying all the way to the car. I'd walked out with them carrying Noé's presents in a couple of carrier bags. We'd said the price per present was limited to £5 each, but we didn't say how many presents or how large. The boy had done well and I could imagine how many presents he'd have waiting for him when he got to London to be with his mum for New Year.

It's still dark and my phone says 6.30 a.m. I'm dreading a knock on the door from Rhiannon who said she'd be back to help me with the rest of the clearing up today. I'd tried desperately hard to put her off – she'd already done so much wiping down of surfaces and packing up of plates that I could easily finish the rest and have all the pots, pans and utensils back to her by Boxing Day afternoon, but she wouldn't hear of it.

I roll onto my side and look at the shapes of trees making themselves known in the stillness of pre-dawn. I'd been too tired to draw the curtains and remember the constellation of stars far in the distance, like silver paint splashed onto a canvas painted black. I remember that either the stars blinked in slow motion or that I was having trouble keeping my eyes open trying to remember their names. Close by, an owl hoots and I yawn deeply. I'm sure that, apart from me, and possibly Rhiannon, everyone who was here yesterday is still asleep.

I wonder, now, about Dez and Phoenix. Judith convinced me yesterday that they would be just fine, but a feeling I have about them stirs something in my stomach and the worry returns. I have a similar feeling about Reef since seeing him yesterday. Something no longer feels right. Every time I looked at him and every touch he laid on my skin, either when he kissed me or held my hand, had brought on a flutter of awkwardness in my body. I didn't swoon or heat up or become liquid. My lips didn't magnetise themselves to his beautiful skin and I'd felt no inclination to run a hand through his immaculate hair. He'd hugged me straight after I'd unwrapped the present he'd bought me. I'd opened a long jewellery box and taken out a gold rope chain with a ruby pendant that had made me gasp because of its beauty. He couldn't have chosen anything more lovely and everyone had remarked on how well it suited me. It was uncanny that it even matched the dress I was wearing.

'Thank you,' I'd said, spinning around to face Reef who had fastened it for me. I'd reached up to wrap my arms around his neck and he'd grabbed around my waist with a tight, strong embrace that left me breathless and made me feel so loved. A tear had come to my eye. Reef had blushed, proud about his excellent choice. But I hadn't been tearful because I was so touched by his thoughtfulness, and it is a beautiful gift, I was tearful because I knew something had been lost between us. I'd thought that perhaps, during the time he'd been in Spain, I'd worked so hard to not allow myself to miss him and to prepare myself that rumours of him reuniting with Natalia might actually be true, that I'd trained my mind to believe I'd lost him. Perhaps. But Reef had made it clear on his return that he feels deeply for me, and now I feel sick with guilt because I know I no longer feel the same.

I roll onto my back again but keep my eyes on the sky. A little light is trickling into view, the shape of the trees beginning to materialise before my eyes. I hear a dog bark. I wonder if it's Phoenix. Maybe he and Dez are on their way now. I have a bag for them already prepared. No one comes.

The view from outside keeps fading into view from black as I doze on and off in various stages of panic and worry, hoping for Dez and his dog to arrive, hoping no one comes before I'm fully awake. I have jumbled dreams and foresee problematic confrontations, and then – someone knocks on the door. I drag my body out of the warm bed and into the chilly corridor.

'Come through. I'll put on a pot of coffee. Or would you prefer tea?' I direct Jade towards the kitchen where everything is not as shiny and pristine as the time she'd visited. Things are a little topsy-turvy with bowls and plates and boxes stacked and in the way, but it is clean.

'Coffee would be great, thanks.' Jade opens the fridge and smiles. 'Anton said you'd be throwing a dinner party. Looks like you've got enough here to have another one.' She closes the door and flops onto a chair next to the table where space is limited but there is an opened packet of chocolate cookies. She helps herself to one and I'm delighted that she feels so at home here.

'How was your day?' I ask her, joining her at the table with a carafe of coffee and two mugs.

'It was just lovely. To see Mum's face so lit up having her two children with her for a change. She said it was like the old days, when we were kids.'

'How is she doing?'

'At the moment she's doing really well. She had a lot of energy yesterday. Not so much today but she insisted that the two of us clear out and give her some peace. She said she's sick of us fussing over her. She was even telling me that I shouldn't give up my place in London to move back, that between the carer and Anton, she's all set.'

'What will you do?'

'Oh, I'm not listening to her. I'm definitely coming home. I'll stay with Mum in Much Marcle but I'll find somewhere to rent soon after. Something small. I hadn't realised how much I missed living here, the pace of life. Don't get me wrong, I love London, but this is my home and you were smart to stay. What's funny?'

I've been gently chuckling but I stop and shake my head.

'It's just, I've admired and envied all of you guys. Moving to London, having great careers. Having all that fun.'

'All what fun?'

'All the things I see Becs and Zarina doing on their Insta accounts.'

'Annie.' She tuts and smiles. 'Anyone can stage a photo so it looks like they're having the time of their life. But you don't have to be in London for that to happen. What does it matter how many people follow you on Instagram? The people around you, the ones who love and care for you are the ones who really count. If you bought a new car or a new pair of shoes, do you really need the approval of eight hundred followers, or wouldn't it be nicer if you could help a neighbour by giving them a lift in your new car or for your best mate to say, *Hey, nice shoes. Where did you get them*? And forgive the cliché, but life really is what you make it.'

'I get it. I shouldn't be looking at everyone having a great life on Instagram, I should be out here getting on with one of my own.'

'Exactly.'

'So, are you going to close your Instagram account?'

'No way!'

'Me neither.'

We burst out laughing and I pour more coffee before diving towards the packet of chocolate cookies.

'Anyway, says Jade, wiping a crumb from her mouth. 'Why would you trade posing in nightclubs with Becs and Zarina with all the wonderful work you've produced in your studio?' She points her thumb at the door.

I contemplate my life situation right now, the number of times I'd felt as though I was missing out on everything. But I'd seen Becs and Zarina only recently and nothing about them spoke of good times or better times than I am having. I have a lovely house that I get to do up and make my own. My paintings are going to be in an exhibition. I know it's not a big deal, just a local place for art and crafts that may only be seen by a few people, but that's a major achievement for me. I have good friends. Work. All my own teeth. I have allowed myself to become envious of so many things and not been grateful for all the things right in front of me. I've let myself worry so much about what I couldn't do, what I might or might not become, that the stress of it has made me a strung-out insomniac. Have I really been too filled with longing to be someone, something or somewhere else that it prevents me from having a good night's sleep? It all seems so ridiculous. I stare into the shallow pool of dark coffee, the overhead light making it shimmer.

'Are you still with us?' Jade waves her fingers in front of my face.

'Sorry, no, yes I am. I was just thinking about something my sister, Cat, said about trying to sell my paintings. I never would have thought I'd get the chance, so I'll always be thankful to you for giving me this opportunity, Jade.'

'I didn't give you this opportunity, it's your work that opened that door. It's what you deserve. And tomorrow I'll come over with Anton's van. He said we could use it and Lorraine is expecting us in the morning to deliver the paintings. Today, the local market square gallery – next stop, the Louvre.'

'Hardly. I don't think it's the start of a bright career. I love to lose myself in the studio but I do love physiotherapy. I've always wanted to care for people. Maybe it has something to do with how much care Mum needed. But you probably knew from school that Mum has a mental illness.'

'Actually, I had no idea.'

'Really? The girl whose mum dressed her daughter in oversized clothes. Cooked way too much food and who sang jazz standards until she was hoarse. Who sat staring at a wall for days at a time, gliding around the house in a butterfly housecoat as if she were invisible to her children?'

'I didn't know, Annie. How could I?'

'I thought everyone knew. I assumed that Becs and Zarina told everyone. You know, that's the reason Becs and Zarina let me tag along with them. They pitied me. After meeting Mum. Probably thought they were doing me a big favour. Mum needed help and plenty of it. I couldn't help her in that way, though I always wished I could. But I could care for people physically, so that's what I did. It made sense to me. Maybe I was never meant to do big and amazing things. I'm not a big and amazing person.'

'I think you are amazing to the people around you, though. Maybe you don't see it.'

I lean forward on my elbows because one person springs to mind when she says this.

'You mean like Anton? Has he said anything?'

'Only that he has dialled his feelings back and that you and he have become good friends because of jazz music.' She rolls her eyes and dismisses my interest in her brother. 'I guess it's better he stays as a friend. How can I tell him that no woman in her right mind would choose my brother over Reef Mayer. Poor deluded fool.' Jade casually gets up to brew a second jug of coffee and I lean back in my chair as she talks about how much stuff she has accumulated in her one-bedroom flat in Hammersmith.

While she chatters away, my heart beats an uncomfortable pattern. It started when I discovered Anton has lost interest in me, doesn't "fancy" me anymore.

In minutes, the house fills with more voices, more movement, when Rhiannon and Judith arrive to help with the rest of the clearing away. Jade puts on the CD player and stays to help, and everything is playing out around me as if it's a film on the television that I'm not really watching. All I'm thinking about is losing Reef as a boyfriend and gaining Anton as just a friend.

31

Good Morning Heartache

I watch Reef as I eat a bagel. A bagel with lashings of butter on it, melted in so deep it seeps through the glazed outer layer. Ordinarily, I don't stuff my face so full of food in front of anyone, though Reef isn't just anyone, is he? He looks cool, smooth, assured, the way he usually does, and he has had his hair cut shorter so there isn't enough length for a man bun. Maybe because he's so determined about going forward with his career, he thinks a man bun will make him look frivolous and he won't be taken seriously by the team. The bust-up with the photographer is a thing of the past now. Reef wears a dark suit and a thin blue tie which he has touched twice in the time he has been speaking and I've been watching him for about four minutes. He's smiling a lot, looks happy, I would say pleased with himself but not cocky. He's dreamy-eyed and sexy which makes it hard for me to say I want to break up with him. Reef's interview with the BBC comes to a close and another news item flicks onto my television screen.

Bea had sent a text earlier saying that she'd just seen Reef on the television and he looks smashing. I'd put the television on and waited until they repeated the item he was in. Reef hadn't told me about the interview for the local news, I only knew that he took over as manager for Birmingham City this morning and he'd asked if we could meet later for supper. Of course I'd said yes. My lips quivered, but I'd tried to stop the shake in my voice so I wouldn't give anything away. My intention, if I could stick to it, was to tell Reef that I didn't feel the same as I did before for him and perhaps this wasn't working out.

I stand by the sink, looking out onto a grey day. Christmas is over and people are gearing up for New Year's Eve celebrations. I'm supposed to spend it with Reef, though that isn't likely to happen now unless I back out of breaking up with him until January. I'm in such a mess about the whole situation. I keep telling myself that I really haven't given our relationship long enough. It has only been a matter of weeks since I met him. Nine weeks and I already want to break up. He'll be shocked, I expect. I have a feeling no one has ever broken up with him, apart from Natalia who probably didn't want to be walked out on by Reef. Their break-up had been on the cards, the acrimony present years later. I don't think Reef will be like that with me. I want us to stay friends – I'd still like to be able to see Noé and I'm pretty sure he'll ask after me from time to time. He sees me as his dad's girlfriend – will he understand that I'm not anymore? I'm not sure I really considered myself to be, anyway. Right now, Noé is in London with his mother, so when I break up with Reef, he will be all on his own. I'm a terrible person. I turn on the hot tap to wash up my breakfast things. I squeeze washing up liquid onto the sponge. No, I'm not a terrible person, I'm honest. *Ow!* The water is scolding hot so I run the cold into the mix. Surely it's better to be up front and tell the truth. I switch off the taps and rest my hands on the edge of the sink. My eyes are closed as I remember the time I almost kissed Anton, standing right here. You idiot. Now you won't have either of them. I dry my hands and send a text out to the Monday Afternoon Knitters for an emergency meeting. Our usual Monday meet up is suspended until the new year and the practice is closed for the holidays. I have too much time on my hands and I won't be able to sit still until my supper with Reef later. Rhiannon says the eatery is deathly so she could do with the company and what on earth is the matter, my lovely? I text back: *I'll tell you all when I see you x*

There's someone else in the window seat at Rhiannon's Eatery. Two women, one in a thick polo neck sweater and a long grey plait down her back who faces a woman in a navy beret. Asleep and parked across her feet is a fat chocolate Labrador. Rhiannon waves from a table at the back and I join the ladies who are all sipping tea. There's a plate of assorted biscuits in the centre of the table.

'You look pale,' Rhiannon says as she pours tea into the cup that's been sitting waiting for me. I put my hands around it and sit quietly before Rhiannon drops a quick splash of milk into the tea. I feel like a sparrow with a broken wing that she is trying to nurse better before she can let it free into the sky. The last thing I'm able to do is fly and the others can see that.

Judith, who sits in the chair beside mine, puts an arm around me. She isn't usually tactile so it feels comforting to have her cuddle me. She places a hand on mine when she allows me to sit up straight.

'Is this anything to do with that Reef person?'

'Why are you calling him "that Reef person"?' Bea asks, indignant. 'He's a very nice man. He wouldn't do anything horrible. You've met him, you know.'

'I didn't say he did anything horrible, I just asked if Annie is sad about him. Not necessarily because of something he did. Maybe something happened to him.'

'Like what?' Bea is still bristling.

'Like anything. We don't know until Annie tells us.'

'Well, why don't you just wait until she says what it is before pointing one of your accusing fingers already?'

'Ladies.' Rhiannon sounds the way I feel. Exasperated and wishing I'd just stayed home. I wish I could have put myself into a deep freeze until my supper date with Reef so I wouldn't have to feel the anguish and have it overwhelm me. 'Annie needs our help and we can't help her if we don't let her speak. You go on, my lovely.'

'Well,' I sniff, though I'm not crying. I just needed a pause to gather myself so I wouldn't cry. 'It does have to do with Reef, actually. But he didn't do anything wrong. In fact he's been doing everything right.'

Bea shifts in her chair and leans her elbows on the table. 'I bet he has.' She winks at me. 'Eh?'

'No,' I say, shaking my head and trying to focus. 'I mean, yes. He's been great. Kind. Sticking up for me with that paparazzi guy. Taking me out. Being really keen on me and everything. He so wants to make a go of it and it's not that I'm not thrilled. I mean, I guess I am. But maybe that's all I am.'

'You don't like him anymore?' says Rhiannon.

'You're breaking up with Reef Mayer?' Bea gasps. 'Have you gone *completely* mad? What I wouldn't give to have had a Reef Mayer in my life in my day. I'd cling on to him and never let go. You realise what you're giving up?'

'There's more to life than glamour, Bea.' Judith sucks a lemon. 'If your heart isn't in it, then that's fair enough.'

'It's not that he's not great,' I say. 'He is. He's fun to be with, good-looking, charming, sexy as hell.'

'I *know*,' says Bea, as if she is going to cry.

'But I don't feel the things I should when I'm with him. I don't think we have anything in common.'

'You grow to love each other's ways, Annie. Do you really think you've given it a good go?' Bea is insistent.

'It's just that, when I've looked at him recently, when I talk to him or he kisses me, there isn't anything there. No sparks. Not anything. I wish there were. I just thought it would be best not to keep him hanging on for something I really don't think I can give.'

'The young are such quitters.' Bea huffs, goes to pour some more tea but finds the pot almost empty. She huffs again.

'Oh Bea,' says Rhiannon. 'Stop carrying on and hear the girl out, would you? Go on, my pet. When are you going to tell him?'

'Tonight. We've got a date. I really wish it wasn't a date but I just think I have to do this soon. He started his new job. He'll be full of excitement and everything. Maybe I should wait. Do you think I should wait?'

'Well,' says Bea, 'you can hardly have him take you out, spend a fortune and then turn around and break up with him.'

'And you'd know all about that, wouldn't you?' Judith tuts.

'You could,' says Rhiannon, 'send him a message to say he should come straight to yours after training and to cancel the date.'

'Then he'd rush straight over to hers expecting to see red petals leading up to her bedroom,' says Bea. 'But instead, he gets a kick in the teeth. And he has such wonderful teeth.' Bea looks wistful.

'I'll get another brew on,' says Rhiannon as she heaves her full curves up from the chair.

'Thanks,' says Bea. 'A girl could die of dehydration in this place.'

'Behave yourself,' Rhiannon calls.

'You could do that,' says Judith. 'Just a message to ask if you could give the date a miss. You're not up for it but you'd like to have a chat.'

'That doesn't sound too bad,' I say. I lean back in my chair. 'Yes, I could cook something nice and–'

'No.' Bea waves a hand. 'No one goes through the trouble of cooking a three course meal if all they're going to do is end things. If you *really* have to do this, then rip off the plaster. Quick. Clean.'

'You make it sound so clinical.' I'm on the verge of tears but I don't want to break down. Rhiannon will force-feed me cake and my tummy is already in knots. She comes back with a fresh pot of tea after serving her only customers who leave with their Labrador and let in a cold gush of air. I'm reminded of Dez and Phoenix, though they haven't exactly been far from my mind.

'Here you go, ladies.' Rhiannon sits opposite and stares deep into my eyes. 'You know what you've got to do?'

I nod.

'And you know what you'll say?'

I shake my head. 'Something will come to me. Thanks ladies. I needed someone to talk it through with.'

'Darling, you're most welcome,' says Bea. 'You know you're speaking to the break-up queen. I could jot down a few notes for you.'

289

'She'll do just fine,' says Judith and pats my hand.

'I know she will,' Bea says. Then she snaps her fingers and her eyes light up. 'I suppose there is always the builder.'

'What?' I ask, about to reach for a biscuit.

'Well, you know, I was trying to get you two fixed up before prince charming came along.'

'I had my suspicions.'

'You say there's nothing there when you look at Reef,' Bea says. 'Anything happen when you look at Anton?'

I am lost for words.

'My oh my.' Rhiannon draws the words out as if we were in a film and the playback has been slowed down. They all stare at me, reading what's behind my silence. And let's face it, they can read me like a book. The hot face, the averted gaze and the need to eat two biscuits in a row without drawing a breath is also a dead giveaway.

'My oh my, indeed.' Bea's glee level is once again replenished. She claps her hands together, then closes them against her cheeks as she leans her elbows on the table. Coquettishly, she blinks. 'You're dumping the rich guy for the hunky builder. I must say, I do approve of that. How did this happen?'

'Well, nothing happened, as such. It did and it didn't, but there's absolutely nothing happening now. We're friends and that's it.'

'Well, it clearly isn't "it",' says Judith. 'But you just deal with one romance at a time. Not everyone has Bea's stamina for break-ups and falling in love again a second later.'

Bea rolls her eyes.

'You don't have to rush into anything, Annie,' Rhiannon says. 'If it's going to happen, it'll happen. You give yourself time to get over Reef, pet. More tea? Some more biscuits?

I've got a nice strawberry shortcake I can box up and you can take with you for later.'

Judith and Bea begin to chat about New Year's Eve celebrations. Bea has been invited to the party at Bertie's golf club and Judith will be joining them. They hadn't asked me as they'd assumed I'd be with Reef. The conversation sags and I make my excuses to leave. Rhiannon rushes to the counter to box up the large cake for me.

'Mind how you go, pet.'

Outside, the wind blows the cake box in its flimsy plastic bag against my leg. I do a long loop around Ross looking for Dez and Phoenix, and there is no sign of them anywhere. If Dez has moved back to Bristol, I'm sad he hasn't said goodbye. I just wish I knew for sure so I could stop worrying.

I turn a corner. The wind picks up and stings my cheeks, so I dip my head down and hurry towards home and towards a situation I really wish I didn't have to face.

The hours have ticked away in the space of seconds. I've tried to work out how I can get the conversation round to the break-up and try to calm my nerves. At the time I know Reef is due to arrive, he snaps the letterbox and I jump. Walking tentatively into the corridor, I step onto a rushing wave that throws me off balance and I reach for the walls, only to find the wave has slapped me into the front door before I'm ready to open it. I crease my face into a smile so as not to give anything away just yet.

'Reef, hi. Come in.' He's brought a winter bouquet with him that he must have picked up in a Marks and Spencer between here and Birmingham. He wasn't too disappointed to not be taking me out and suggested we could order something in. Despite what Bea said, I was going to cook for him, but it felt a little Last Supper so I changed my mind.

'These are lovely. I'll put them in water.' I take the flowers and turn towards the kitchen, but Reef pulls me back by the wrist.

'Is that it? No kiss Hello, no "Hey Reef, how's the new job?"'

'I'm sorry. Of course.' I throw my arms around his neck like a scene in a film where the heroine is saying farewell to the hero she may never see again, and that's it. My cover is blown.

Reef slowly pulls my arms from his shoulders and holds my elbows so that the bouquet forms a soft barrier between us.

'What is it?' His face is dark with anticipation. I never was a good actress. My wanting to break up with him must be written all over my face. A face I don't know what to do with and a pair of eyes that don't know where to look. I focus on the small, white carnations in the centre of the bouquet and Reef drops his hands.

'Why didn't you want to go out for the meal, Annie? Something is wrong, I can tell.'

'Could we go into the living room?'

He follows behind, sighing a loud puff of air. I place the flowers on the coffee table and turn to Reef whose eyes are like arrows directed straight to my heart. I blink several times.

'I knew something had changed,' he says, stepping backwards as if he wants to run out of the door. 'Just admit it.'

'Please, Reef, don't be angry with me.'

'I'm not angry. I just don't understand what went wrong between that meal when everything seemed great until Christmas Day. Was it something I did? Something I didn't? Was it because I went away?'

'I'm sorry. I don't know what happened. The thing is, it's just … you and I happened really fast and I felt a bit swept away by it. By you. By everything.'

'You mean all that media stuff? I can do a better job of keeping you out of it, Annie. I know you don't like the spotlight on you.'

'There's that but there's more to it.'

'You just don't like me.'

'I do. Of course I like you. How can you say that?' I put my head down. 'I just don't think I like you in the way you do me.'

'I more than like you, Annie. I'm crazy about you. You know that.'

'I know. I did feel that way but now … and I don't think I'll get there.'

'Because of the media attention?' He walks towards me, arms open and my strength fails me, I can hardly stand. The warmth of his body draws close and I want to respond. I feel the magnetic force weakening my intention as I step towards Reef. He sighs and takes me in his arms. I close my eyes. Tightly. I see Anton. Just as Reef lowers his head, probably to kiss me, I step away.

'No, Reef. No. I'm so sorry.'

He huffs and slaps his hand on his forehead. I read the disbelief in his expression and he turns his back on me for a fraction of a second.

'And that's it, then?'

I nod slowly.

'And don't say that thing about you hope we can be friends.'

'Because you don't want me as a friend?'

'Because I want you for more and I'm greedy like that. If I can't have you, then that really is that.' He heads for the front door, I follow. He turns the latch, thinks better of it and turns back, cheeks blazing. 'I'm sorry, Annie. I'm a bad loser. And yes, we can be friends. Who else would bring Noé over when he's visiting?'

'You mean I can still see him?'

'Of course you can. Even though it won't be easy.' He softly runs his knuckles down my cheek.

'Are you just going to go?' I ask.

'What do you expect me to do?' Then he unlatches the door and stands on the outside mat, the icy outside colliding with the warmth from the corridor and winning. I wrap my arms around my body.

'Talk to you soon.' I really don't know what else I should say.

'Happy New Year, Annie. Let's hope the next one looks up, yeah? For both of us.'

'Um, yes. Me too. And Happy New…' The words fade as I watch Reef's broad back in his dark overcoat retreat along the path.

I close the door gently and exhale for so long my next breath comes in a gasp and the one that follows comes with tears and snotty sobs. I call Mum to tell her what happened.

'Oh Annie, I'm so sorry. But if you don't love him, you did the right thing.' Mum has just walked in after a yoga class looking flushed, a cardigan over a sleeveless top as she sits on the bottom step of her stairwell.

294

'I just feel so rotten, so mean. I don't know. But he'll get over it, right?'

'He will but I hope you do, too. That you won't punish yourself and stay indoors and become gloomy.'

'Gloomy?'

'You know what I mean. Don't put his feelings first, the way you always do mine. The way you do for everyone. Be selfish and put yourself first. Stop worrying about others, they can look after themselves. Promise me that, Annie. Don't think I didn't notice how much you were there for me when you could have been having a full life, you put my well-being first and it's taken its toll. Do more, Annie and please don't be afraid anymore.'

'What do you mean?'

'Catalina told me you've been worried you could get … that you might end up with my problems. My issues. I want you to get that out of your head because it isn't true. I'm me and you're you. So just be yourself and just get on and live your life.'

'Yes, Mum. I am trying. I promise you. And Cat wasn't supposed to say anything.'

'I'm glad she did. Take risks, Annie. Give yourself permission to be happy, my beautiful, kind and talented daughter.'

I begin to cry with joy, and Mum says, 'That's it, let it all go.'

In the wee small hours I have the whole strawberry shortcake on a plate on my lap as I sit on the floor in my pyjamas with my back against the sofa. Holding a spoon, I probe the strawberries and cream. Loading it up, I direct it to my mouth in regular intervals as I stare at the winter flower arrangement I made earlier. I'm grieving, saying goodbye to

Reef, but gradually and finally I allow Mum's words to overtake that grief.

32

'Round Midnight

It's New Year's Eve morning. I stare out into the dark sky wondering what went wrong in the planning stages. I had a boyfriend, a gorgeous one who I let go. Reef had suspected that something had changed in me and he'd been right. Though, as I lie here, I'm not sure the change has anything to do with Reef himself. Before I'd met him, I'd already concocted him on lonely nights when my dreams ran wild. He was the drop-dead gorgeous hunk of a boyfriend who made heads turn and made women wish they were me. In the dreaming stages, I'd been in love with the gorgeous guy. I'm not in love with Reef. Love was the fantasy, it just hadn't translated to real life.

My septuagenarian friends are all busy this evening. What I wouldn't give for a knitting circle and a bottle of champagne with those three tonight. Jade is in London. She'd been persuaded to return for tonight by her friends. The party to end all parties, they'd said. Who could resist? She'd been shocked to hear I'd split up with Reef and wondered how I fancied going down to London with her. I didn't like the idea of hauling my pathetic self to a party in someone's house when I'd only know one person. At least here, it was familiar. At least here, I had the food hamper that Rhiannon had dropped off when she knew I'd be all alone.

Close to midnight I have the television on in the living room and the speakers rattle with *Jools' Annual Hootenanny*. I'm trying to create a party atmosphere on my own. I keep edging up the volume to block out the laughter and music of the party going on at my neighbour's house. Fee Milligan had invited me, with a bit of apprehension, as she knows I'm not one of Rosie's favourite humans, but I wasn't so keen on being hissed and growled at by a bad tempered feline all night, so I'd pretended I had big plans.

I've spent the day working my way through my food hamper and feeling a bit queasy on oily sausage rolls and mini chocolate éclairs. There was a bottle of Prosecco in the hamper which I'd kept chilling in the fridge to be ready for midnight, but it's 11.30 p.m. and I can't see the point in waiting. While Coldplay perform a medley of their greatest hits, I pop open the bottle, giggle to no one and fill a tumbler with sparkly Prosecco. Sipping, rather rapidly, I watch an interview with an ageing rock star whose name I can't remember for the life of me. I give up trying to guess his name and start chugging from the tumbler, stopping only to hiccup and belch.

I wake with a woozy feeling and hear the sound of Big Ben. A crowd of people in the cold and dark are gathered by the Thames singing *Auld Lang Syne*. I'm feeling shaky and can't remember where I am. I sit up and see a knocked-over tumbler that smells of Prosecco. I realise I've passed out from an overdose of simple carbohydrates.

I stumble to my feet and turn the television down because the fireworks on there start to whizz and bang and begin to annoy me. Eventually, I mute the TV because the firework shenanigans won't shut up. I look out of the window, puzzled, and see there's a real firework display happening

298

next door. Lights and colour fizz in the sky and disperse into tiny, white sparks. Fee Milligan's party has taken to the sky. I reach for my boots, my coat, my hat and my scarf. I'm not about to gatecrash, I just need to get out. To walk off the food I've eaten and to clear my head of the drink. Perhaps Dez is back from wherever he has been with Phoenix and I can wish them a Happy New Year.

My body feels warm after an evening of indulgence and the temperature outside doesn't hit me until I see the Christmas lights on the main road and see a group of people walking away from the market square, laughing and holding each other up. Inside the Market House, a stack of my paintings have already been installed for the exhibition that starts in two days right through until the end of the month. I smile to myself and wish I could talk to someone about it, someone I haven't already talked endlessly about it to. Mum and Cat congratulated me again about the exhibition when they'd called to wish me a Happy New Year.

I set about trying to find Dez. More than once I circle the usual places Dez and Phoenix settle for the night but there's no sign. I decide to widen the search. They may have been asked to move on for all I know. I have nothing to rush home for, just hours of sleeplessness, loneliness and an empty bottle of Prosecco, so I keep on walking. Soon my feet are hurting in boots that are usually comfortable. My warm food glow wore off ages ago and my toes and fingers feel as if they are being stabbed by icy nails. I turn towards the church so that I can take the quick path through the cemetery. As I approach, I hear voices, all male. They are laughing but they sound sinister and I can't tell if it's anyone I know. I hover at the steps leading up to the graves and I see a group of at least five figures looking like blobs of ink with ragged edges that move unsteadily by the headstones. It's so dark their faces are hidden. I'm sure I don't know these people. I'm standing under a streetlamp, frozen to the spot. Though the light is dim, if they turned around, they'd see me, and my pulse races at a danger my wild imagination starts to create. In seconds the voices of everyone who has told me to stop my nighttime walking crashes into my mind and my head pounds. *You know you shouldn't be out here. I hate to think of you out in the dark on your own. Another sleepless night, Annie? This has to stop. It's far too dangerous, Annie. In the wee small hours of the morning when the whole wide world is fast asleep.* I step back, turning quickly towards the river. This will take me out of my way but I don't have time to think it through. I can't seem to think. Cold, fear and tiredness are conspiring against me and my response is to run. I pass the Phoenix Theatre and follow the bend to The Royal on the corner. Stupidly, I continue down the quiet St Mary's Road in the opposite direction to home. I can get back on track but I've landed on the fast-moving Wilton Road which is a main thoroughfare between Ross and Hereford. There is no pavement and it's not meant for pedestrians. But it's a quiet night, no cars. I can cross to the other side and turn back towards town, do the loop again. Suddenly, I see the headlamps of a car and I freeze. The car slows, passes me and I hear its brakes screech. Someone leaps out and is stomping towards me. I feel as if I've leapt from a massive frying pan into the arms of an abductor. I have to go. It doesn't matter where because the dark figure is speeding up.

'Annie!'

I know the voice and I stop just as another driver flies past me and toots their car horn so loudly I instinctively begin to race away.

'Annie, stop! What are you doing?'

I turn around slowly and Anton is right behind me. Though I know it's him and though I know I'm safe now, I shrink at his touch.

'Jesus. Come here.' His voice is softer now. 'You're freezing. I need to move my car before someone smacks into it.'

I let him lead me like a lifeless rag doll to the passenger side and I flop into the seat. Anton jumps in the driver's side. The engine is running and the warmth makes me slump further into the comfort of the seat. Soft music is playing, jazz. Anton looks over his shoulder, not at me, before pulling off.

'I didn't know you had a car as well as a van,' I whisper.

'Is that all you have to say? Annie, what are you doing out here on your own? What were you thinking? Have you been drinking?'

'I'm sorry. I don't know. Yes I have, but I wasn't drunk.'

'You sure? You got your seatbelt on?'

I haven't so I fasten it. We're already a few feet from my house.

'Where were you going?' I ask.

'On my way home. I just dropped someone off after a party.'

'Any good?'

Anton doesn't answer. He just turns off the engine and shakes his head.

'I know it's crazy,' I say. 'I'm sorry I scared you but there was someone in the graveyard and I panicked.'

'Too right you panicked. You shouldn't be walking around the streets like that. Why would you…? Are you trying to…? Oh, I give up. Look, you're home now. You'd better get in. I'll wait until you're at the door.'

'Oh, this is a quiet road,' I begin, but I see a flash of anger in Anton's eyes. I know he's concerned and I am grateful, but right now, I feel like an idiot under his gaze. 'Would you like to come in?' I'm hoping he'll soften and not drive away this mad at me. He nods a brief yes and follows me indoors where we strip off our outer layers and drape them over the bannister. I lead Anton to the living room. The lamps are still on.

'Looks like you had a little party of your own.' He raises his eyebrows.

'It wasn't a very good party. You didn't say what yours was like.'

'Nothing special.'

'Let's go to the kitchen. I'll make us some tea and you can tell me about it.'

I fill the kettle and set out two cups. I lean against the counter while it boils.

'Didn't you want to spend New Year's with your boyfriend?' Anton is by the music player, selecting a radio station but changes his mind and puts on the vocal jazz album I'd been listening to earlier, and the voice of Lena Horne singing *More Than You Know* spreads a calm feeling over us and tension begins to leave my body.

'We broke up.'

'Really?' Anton makes no attempt to hide his pleasure. 'When?'

'After Christmas?'

'Wow. I'm sorry, that must have been a blow.'

302

'I broke up with him, you know?' I say, looking at him sideways as I pour the water.

'I see.'

Holding the cups, I lead the way back to the living room where I do my best to clear away the evidence of the party of one.

'He can't have gone into his new job feeling all that good about himself,' Anton says, reaching for one of the cups and leaning back into the sofa.

'Well, say it as if you actually care.' I sit beside him and smile. Then a loud yawn escapes my lips.

'You're tired. And you're right, I don't care that you've broken up with him. I'm glad you have.'

'Really? Why?' I yawn again, my hand over my mouth as I shake my head in apology.

'Because I really like you, Annie.'

'I did wonder,' I say quietly, not looking directly at Anton. 'I thought at one point there was something. That almost kiss in the kitchen, but then you found out about him and I thought you stopped … liking me.'

'You're joking, right?'

'Jade said you wanted to be friends and that was all.' Another long yawn I can't suppress.

'Well, despite what goes on in my sister's imagination, she isn't the boss of me. Why would I want to be only friends with you? I thought I was being obvious.'

I want to yawn and smile at the same time. My body has reached exhaustion point but it also craves the warmth of Anton's arms. He gets up and offers me a hand which I take and he pulls me off the sofa.

'Come on,' he says, effortlessly lifting me off my feet so I'm cradled into his arms, my face as close to his as the day we almost kissed. I've thought about the kiss that might have been so many times and wish he will kiss me now, but he doesn't. He carries me up the stairs, carefully angling my body so I don't bump into anything. I feel as if I'm gliding. My chest rises dramatically high, and when it sinks, my body feels drained of all energy. Anton pushes my bedroom door open with his foot and lays me on the bed before switching on the side lamp. I sit up and ease towards him, but as he softly strokes my hair, all I want to do is yawn even more. Damn my tiredness.

'You look as if you could do with a good night's sleep.'

'I haven't had one of those in years.'

He rests my head back onto the pillow and pulls the duvet out from under me so that he can cover me. He sits on the edge of the bed and takes off his shoes, then he tucks himself in beside me. I lay my head against his chest and listen to the slow thrum of his heart and bend into the rhythmic wave of his torso as his breath deepens. My body relaxes further. I listen to the rallentando of our breathing until a soft, delicious cloud embraces me and I fall…

*

It must be late. We hadn't thought to close the curtains and winter sun seeps into the room. The heating is on so the contrast of a frosty morning outside doesn't correspond with the heat my body generates beneath the duvet. I go to fan the covers but I don't want to wake Anton. I turn to him, but all I see is a puffed duvet beside me like a barrier and no one lying on the other side of it. I lean on my elbows wondering if Anton had actually been there at all. Had I just had a series of wild dreams and terrifying nightmares. Sadness floods over me even though the part where I fell asleep in Anton's arms was wonderful. Then I hear something that lets me know right away that I hadn't dreamt it. The voice of Nina Simone floats upstairs from the kitchen with warm contralto tones as she sings one of Mum's all-time favourite songs. One she used to play straight after one of her silent episodes.

I check the time. It's what I do most mornings before getting up to start my day, whether that's from the sofa or my bed. I want to calculate how many hours I've been asleep. It's 9.30 a.m. which means I've slept for over eight hours. *Eight.* I should be celebrating, I should get up and do a dance, something.

In the kitchen, Anton stands with his back to me, the smell of bacon in the air, mingling with toast and coffee. He's scrambling eggs when I lean over his shoulder.

'You're up,' he says. 'I wanted to serve you breakfast in bed.'

I wrap my arms over his shoulders and he turns to hold me.

'This is amazing, thank you.'

'Well, don't thank me until you taste it.'

I pull away slightly and look into his eyes. 'I mean, it's amazing that I've slept right through for so many hours. Thank you.'

'I didn't do anything. All I did was be there.'

'And it worked.'

'Well, if I really have to get into bed with you every night so that you can sleep, I'm more than happy to oblige. Can't guarantee that all we'll do is sleep but...'

There's a badly timed knock on the door and reluctantly I go to see who it is. As close to New Year's as they could get, the Monday Afternoon Knitters are here to wish me a Happy New Year and they've brought breakfast.

'Oh!' Rhiannon exclaims as she kisses my cheek and sniffs the air. 'Oh,' she says again when she sees that someone is already here trying to feed me. 'Oh,' she says once more as she turns to me when I walk into the kitchen.

'Rhiannon, Judith, this is Anton.'

'The builder?' Judith's eyes widen but there is no lemon sucking. In fact she has a slight grin.

'The handsome builder,' says Bea, waving at Anton who greets them all with a "good morning, ladies".

'Are you staying for breakfast?' he asks.

'Not at all,' declares Bea as she ushers the women towards the front door. 'Wouldn't want to get in the way.'

'Here, my pet,' says Rhiannon. 'Take this.' She hands me a stack of Tupperware boxes. They weigh me down. 'You might develop an appetite later, if you know what I mean.'

'We all know what you mean.' Judith sucks a lemon and is the first to step outside. 'Should we have a talk later?' she asks gravely.

'What about? The birds and the bees?' Bea shrieks. 'It's too late for that by the looks of things. We'll see you at the art exhibition tomorrow. And look.' She shows me a large diamond stone on a platinum ring. 'Dear Bertie proposed last night and I want you to be chief bridesmaid. Come on, ladies. All back to mine so you can ogle my ring again.'

When I close the door, Anton is at the threshold to the kitchen extending a hand that says breakfast is served.

33

Feeling Good

It's the last day of the art exhibition, late afternoon, and Anton and I have popped in on our way to his place so that I can thank Lorraine once more. A whole month has flown by and I still can't believe this has happened to me. Not many people attend the gallery in January, but all the same, I've sold five paintings and only one went to someone I knew. Bertie couldn't resist one of them but I'd made Bea, Judith, Rhiannon, Jade and Anton swear a blood oath that they would not buy a painting just so I could feel good about myself. They could only have my paintings as gifts and I was very final about that.

Lorraine is keen to do another exhibition later in the year when there's time to publicise it. She's very interested in my portraits and the charcoal and chalk images of the local area. She has also given me phone numbers of galleries and art shops where I could potentially get further sales, but I haven't contacted anyone yet. But I feel like a real artist now.

'I'll come tomorrow to pick up the remaining paintings,' I say to Lorraine.

'I'll be here until five, so any time before that is fine.'

I wave goodbye and gesture to Anton for us to leave. The two of us have been enjoying a day off together before I'm back at the practice tomorrow afternoon and he is back to redecorating the house.

'Annie Swynnerton.' A familiar voice shocks me and I turn to see Dez, a crooked grin on his face, standing a few feet away. He's wearing clothes I don't recognise. A sweater, black jeans, a warm winter jacket and ankle boots.

'Dez! You're back.' I go to hug him but he comes across as embarrassed and shy, ducking away so that all I can do is pat his upper arms. 'How are you? Where's Phoenix? Where have you both been? What name did you just call me?'

'Annie Swynnerton. She was a famous British painter from Manchester.' Dez casts a quick eye over the paintings. 'But you're Annie Lambert, aren't you? Famous painter from right here in Ross-on-Wye.' He steps closer to one of the night scenes and can see himself and a curled up Phoenix in the background fast asleep. I stand beside him.

'Hardly famous,' I say. 'But Dez, how have you been? Where have you been? I've been so worried about you. I missed you, both of you.' I touch his shoulder to make him face me.

'I'm sorry, Annie Lambert. I meant to come and say goodbye. That is, I did come by. Christmas Day. After you left that night, when I told you about my son, I couldn't stop thinking about what you said. God it made me think.' He tuts and I see his eyes are watery. 'I'd shut out everything, you see? Everything that wasn't to do with me and Phoenix in the here and now. Obliterated memories of back then. It was easy to do as time went by, but after hearing you speak, a space opened up, in here.' He taps his heart. 'And all I wanted was to have my son back in my life. Like he should have been. But anyway, like I say, I did come Christmas Day but I bottled it and thought I'd better leave you to it.'

308

'I wish you'd knocked on the door. You wouldn't have had to come in or anything. And how on earth did you know I was here today?'

'I didn't until I got to Ross. I had a letter I was going to drop over to your house but I wanted one more look around the old town and I saw a poster by the door. Your name. Not the ones I give you.' He grins. 'Had to come in, didn't I? And there you were.'

'Thank goodness you remembered my real name.' We both laugh. I look up and down at Dez's clothes, finding it hard to take in the change in his appearance. He looks healthier, bigger and I see joy glinting in his eyes. 'How has it been?'

'It's a big adjustment for me. Going back to a life with regular people in it. Really hard but I'm trying.'

'But your son must be thrilled to have you back.'

'Well, I moved in like he wanted. It's strange getting to know each other. He's trying to get his head around all the wasted years and how I did what I did. We'll both get there, I suppose.'

'Dez, where is Phoenix?'

'That fella? He's fine. He's got a new home not far from my boy's place and a family who love him. Just like you said. That was an adjustment, too, not having my dog by my side all the time. My son paid for vet bills and you wouldn't recognise Phoenix now.'

'I'd love to see him again.'

'Any time, Annie girl.' He dips a hand into his jacket pocket and pulls out an envelope with "Annie" written on the outside. 'I've got to go, only my son is waiting in the car. My address and telephone are on there. Now there's something I never thought I'd hear myself say.'

I hug Dez despite his awkwardness and he hugs me back, breathing the words "Thank you so much, Annie" by my ear. He pulls away.

'You mind you look after yourself and stay home at night. Got me?'

I salute and watch his tall frame exiting the gallery.

Anton and I step outside, underneath the red-bricked building of Market House just before dusk, and walk hand in hand to his car. Anton drives back to his place while I take in the familiar roads. I know the tiny, hidden alleyways and know where they lead. I know the parks, the routes to the river, all the coffee shops and charity shops, too. But I don't miss walking by them on my own at night. I have a grin on my face because the circle is complete – I finally found out what happened to Dez and Phoenix and I can relax completely. About everything.

The house is getting close to being completely decorated. Any delay has come from spending so much downtime with Anton that he can't get anything done. He sings to me in the kitchen when we're cooking, we sit on the sofa talking into the night about our respective days. The house is looking lovely all the same.

I lie in Anton's bed. It's very late. The meal he cooked was enormous and makes me feel sleepy, but we carry on chatting, our voices slurring from fatigue. I find sleep comes easier these nights, and though I don't always get the recommended eight hours a night, it's rare to wake up feeling anxious with a mind crowded with chatter and confusion. If I do, I can usually relax again and drift off. The music player is on, as low as a whisper. A slow and mesmerising version of *Lullaby of Birdland* swirls around the room. I close my eyes and once again I fall ... into a deep and calming sleep.

END

Thank you for choosing

The Wee Small Hours

I really hope you enjoyed it. Your thoughts mean the world to me, and I'd love to hear what you think. If you have a moment, please consider leaving a review—it makes such a difference in helping new readers discover the book. You can share your review on Amazon or your preferred retailer.

I also love connecting with readers on social media, so please do follow my journey and say hello on @RosaTempleAuthor

Thanks so much for your support!

Connect: Hop onto my *website* for links & info!

And: Join my *mailing list* and be the first to know about the next publication, grab a preview copy and be ahead of all my news and updates!

For more books by Rosa Temple please visit
www.rosatemple.co.uk

Appendix: *Annie's Jazz Playlist*

A musical companion to the chapters in The Wee Small Hours

Each chapter title in this book is drawn from a jazz standard —songs that echo Annie's quiet nights, tender memories, and hopeful beginnings. Below is a curated list of these songs, including their original release dates, credited writers, and the first notable jazz recording. May they bring you comfort, joy, and a little swing in your step.

In the Wee Small Hours of the Morning
Written: 1955 — David Mann, Bob Hilliard
First Jazz Recording: Frank Sinatra (1955)

Someone to Watch Over Me
Written: 1926 — George Gershwin, Ira Gershwin
First Jazz Recording: Gertrude Lawrence (1926); Ella Fitzgerald (1950)

Stardust
Written: 1927 — Hoagy Carmichael, Mitchell Parish
First Jazz Recording: Louis Armstrong (1931)

In the Still of the Night
Written: 1937 — Cole Porter
First Jazz Recording: Tommy Dorsey Orchestra (1937)

You Go to My Head
Written: 1938 — J. Fred Coots, Haven Gillespie
First Jazz Recording: Larry Clinton Orchestra (1938); Billie Holiday (1938)

The Good Life
Written: 1962 — Sacha Distel, Jack Reardon
First Jazz Recording: Tony Bennett (1963)

Softly, As in a Morning Sunrise
Written: 1928 — Sigmund Romberg, Oscar Hammerstein II
First Jazz Recording: Artie Shaw (1938); John Coltrane
(1958)

God Bless the Child
Written: 1941 — Billie Holiday, Arthur Herzog Jr.
First Jazz Recording: Billie Holiday (1941)

Bewitched, Bothered and Bewildered
Written: 1940 — Richard Rodgers, Lorenz Hart
First Jazz Recording: Doris Day (1949); Ella Fitzgerald
(1956)

Ain't Misbehavin'
Written: 1929 — Fats Waller, Harry Brooks, Andy Razaf
First Jazz Recording: Fats Waller (1929)

You Can Depend on Me
Written: 1931 — Charles Carpenter, Louis Dunlap, Earl
Hines
First Jazz Recording: Louis Armstrong (1931)

Me and My Shadow
Written: 1927 — Al Jolson, Billy Rose, Dave Dreyer
First Jazz Recording: Al Jolson (1927); Frank Sinatra (1955)

Taking a Chance on Love
Written: 1940 — Vernon Duke, John Latouche, Ted Fetter
First Jazz Recording: Benny Goodman (1940); Ella
Fitzgerald (1943)

I've Got You Under My Skin
Written: 1936 — Cole Porter
First Jazz Recording: Virginia Bruce (1936); Frank Sinatra (1946)

Prelude to a Kiss
Written: 1938 — Duke Ellington, Irving Mills, Mack Gordon
First Jazz Recording: Duke Ellington (1938)

Night and Day
Written: 1932 — Cole Porter
First Jazz Recording: Fred Astaire (1932); Artie Shaw (1937)

Smoke Gets in Your Eyes
Written: 1933 — Jerome Kern, Otto Harbach
First Jazz Recording: Paul Whiteman Orchestra (1933); Nat King Cole (1958)

Desafinado
Written: 1959 — Antônio Carlos Jobim, Newton Mendonça
First Jazz Recording: João Gilberto (1959); Stan Getz & Charlie Byrd (1962)

Can't We Be Friends
Written: 1929 — Kay Swift, Paul James
First Jazz Recording: Libby Holman (1929); Red Nichols (1929)

The Way You Look Tonight
Written: 1936 — Jerome Kern, Dorothy Fields
First Jazz Recording: Fred Astaire (1936); Billie Holiday (1936)

A Fine Romance
Written: 1936 — Jerome Kern, Dorothy Fields

First Jazz Recording: Fred Astaire (1936); Billie Holiday (1936)

Sophisticated Lady
Written: 1932 — Duke Ellington, Irving Mills, Mitchell Parish
First Jazz Recording: Duke Ellington (1933)

How Long Has This Been Going On
Written: 1927 — George Gershwin, Ira Gershwin
First Jazz Recording: Bobbe Arnst (1928); Ella Fitzgerald (1959)

Song for My Father
Written: 1964 — Horace Silver
First Jazz Recording: Horace Silver Quintet (1964)

My Baby Just Cares for Me
Written: 1930 — Walter Donaldson, Gus Kahn
First Jazz Recording: Eddie Cantor (1930); Nina Simone (1957)

Do Nothing Until You Hear from Me
Written: 1944 — Duke Ellington, Bob Russell
First Jazz Recording: Duke Ellington (1944)

The Best Is Yet to Come
Written: 1959 — Cy Coleman, Carolyn Leigh
First Jazz Recording: Jesse Belvin (1960); Frank Sinatra (1964)

The Frim Fram Sauce
Written: 1945 — Redd Evans, Joe Ricardel
First Jazz Recording: Nat King Cole Trio (1945)

The Christmas Song
Written: 1945 — Mel Tormé, Robert Wells
First Jazz Recording: Nat King Cole Trio (1946)

My Foolish Heart
Written: 1949 — Victor Young, Ned Washington
First Jazz Recording: Gordon Jenkins (1949); Billy Eckstine (1950)

Good Morning Heartache
Written: 1946 — Irene Higginbotham, Ervin Drake, Dan Fisher
First Jazz Recording: Billie Holiday (1946)

Round Midnight
Written: 1943 — Thelonious Monk, Bernie Hanighen, Cootie Williams
First Jazz Recording: Cootie Williams (1944); Thelonious Monk (1947)

Feeling Good
Written: 1964 — Anthony Newley, Leslie Bricusse
First Jazz Recording: Cy Grant (1964); Nina Simone (1965)

These songs kept me company during my own wee small hours. I hope they bring you comfort, joy, and maybe a little swing in your step.
—Rosa Temple

About the author

Rosa Temple is the pseudonym of published author, Fran Clark.

A mother of two and married to a musician, she recently moved from London to Herefordshire where she leads a community choir, teaches vocals and performs the occasional gig, singing, soul, jazz and Latin tunes.

She writes every day while drinking herbal tea and eating chocolate biscuits and tries, almost every day, to improve her piano and guitar skills.

Printed in Dunstable, United Kingdom

70956911R00184